The Soldier Boy; or, Tom Somers in the Army

Oliver Optic

THE SOLDIER BOY

OR

TOM SOMERS IN THE ARMY

A Story of the Great Rebellion

BY

OLIVER OPTIC

AUTHOR OF "RICH AND HUMBLE, " "ALL ABOARD, " "LITTLE BY LITTLE, " ETC., ETC.

TO

William Lee, Esq.

THIS BOOK

IS RESPECTFULLY DEDICATED

BY HIS FRIEND

WILLIAM T. ADAMS.

PREFACE.

This volume is not altogether a military romance, though it contains the adventures of one of those noble-hearted and patriotic young men who went forth from homes of plenty and happiness to fight the battles of our imperilled country. The incidents of the story may be stirring and exciting; yet they are not only within the bounds of probability, but have been more than paralleled in the experience of hundreds of the gallant soldiers of the loyal army.

The work is not intended to approach the dignity of a history, though the writer has carefully consulted the "authorities, " both loyal and rebel, and has taken down the living words of enthusiastic participants in the stirring scenes described in this volume. He has not attempted to give a full picture of any battle, or other army operation, but simply of those movements in which the hero took a part. The book is a narrative of personal adventure, delineating the birth and growth of a pure patriotism in the soul of the hero, and describing the perils and privations, the battles and marches which he shared with thousands of brave men in the army of the Potomac.

The author has endeavored to paint a picture of the true soldier, one who loves his country, and fights for her because he loves her; but, at the same time, one who is true to himself and his God, while he is faithful to his patriotic impulses.

The work has been a pleasure to me in its preparation, and I hope it will not disappoint the reasonable expectation of those partial friends whose smile is my joy, whose frown is my grief. But, more than all, I trust this humble volume will have some small influence in kindling and cherishing that genuine patriotism which must ever be the salvation of our land, the foundation of our national prosperity and happiness.

WILLIAM T. ADAMS.

DORCHESTER, Feb. 22, 1864.

CONTENTS.

CHAPTER

I. The Battle of Pinchbrook

II. The Somers Family

III. Taming a Traitor

IV. The Committee come out, and Tom goes in

V. The Attic Chamber

VI. The Way is Prepared

VII. A Midnight Adventure

VIII. Signing the Papers

IX. The Departure

X. Company K

XI. In Washington

XII. On to Richmond

XIII. The Battle of Bull Run

XIV. After the Battle

XV. Tom a Prisoner

XVI. A Perplexing Question

XVII. Dinner and Danger

XVIII. The Rebel Soldier

XIX. Through the Gap

XX. Down the Shenandoah

XXI. The Problem of Rations

XXII. The Picket Guard

XXIII. The End of the Voyage

XXIV. Budd's Ferry

XXV. In the Hospital

XXVI. Tom is Sentimental

XXVII. The Confederate Deserter

XXVIII. On the Peninsula

XXIX. The Battle of Williamsburg

XXX. More of the Battle

XXXI. Glory and Victory

XXXII. "Honorable Mention"

XXXIII. Lieutenant Somers and Others

The Soldier Boy; or, Tom Somers in the Army

CHAPTER I.

THE BATTLE OF PINCHBROOK.

"Fort Sumter has surrendered, mother!" shouted Thomas Somers, as he rushed into the room where his mother was quietly reading her Bible.

It was Sunday, and the exciting news had been circulated about the usually quiet village of Pinchbrook Harbor. Men's lips were compressed, and their teeth shut tight together. They were indignant, for traitors had fired upon the flag of the United States. Men, women, and children were roused by the indignity offered to the national emblem. The cannon balls that struck the walls of Sumter seemed at the same time to strike the souls of the whole population of the North, and never was there such a great awakening since the Pilgrim Fathers first planted their feet upon the rock of Plymouth.

"Fort Sumter has surrendered!" shouted the indignant young patriot again, as his mother looked up from the blessed volume.

"You don't say so!" exclaimed Mrs. Somers, as she closed the Bible, and removed her spectacles.

"Yes, mother. The infernal rebels hammered away at the fort for two days, and at last we had to give in."

"There'll be terrible times afore long," replied the old lady, shaking her head with prophetic earnestness.

"The President has called for seventy-five thousand volunteers, and I tell you there'll be music before long!" continued the youth, so excited that he paced the room with rapid strides.

"What's the matter, Thomas?" asked a feeble old gentleman, entering the room at this moment.

"Fort Sumter has surrendered, gran'ther," repeated Thomas, at the top of his lungs, for the aged man was quite deaf; "and the President has called for seventy-five thousand men to go down and fight the traitors."

The Soldier Boy; or, Tom Somers in the Army

"Sho!" exclaimed the old man, halting, and gazing with earnestness into the face of the boy.

"It's a fact, gran'ther."

"Well, I'm too old to go," muttered gran'ther Greene; "but I wa'n't older'n you are when I shouldered my firelock in 1812. I'm too old and stiff to go now."

"How old were you, gran'ther, when you went to the war?" asked Thomas, with more moderation than he had exhibited before.

"Only sixteen, Thomas; but I was as tall as I am now," replied the patriarch, dropping slowly and cautiously into the old-fashioned high-back chair, by the side of the cooking stove.

"Well, I'm sixteen, and I mean to go."

"You, Thomas! You are crazy! You shan't do any thing of the kind," interposed Mrs. Somers. "There's men enough to go to the war, without such boys as you are."

"You ain't quite stout enough to make a soldier, Thomas. You ain't so big as I was, when I went off to York state," added gran'ther Greene.

"I should like to go any how," said Thomas, as he seated himself in a corner of the room, and began to think thoughts big enough for a full-grown man.

"Fort Sumter has surrendered," shouted John Somers, rushing into the house as much excited as his brother had been.

"We've heard all about it, John," replied his mother.

"The President has called for seventy-five thousand men, and in my opinion the rebels will get an awful licking before they are a fortnight older. I should like to go and help do it."

The exciting news was discussed among the members of the Somers family, as it was in thousands of other families, on that eventful Sunday. Thomas and John could think of nothing, speak of nothing, but Fort Sumter, and the terrible castigation which the rebels would receive from the insulted and outraged North. They were loyal even to enthusiasm; and when they retired to their chamber at night, they ventured to express to each other their desire to join the great army which was to avenge the insult offered to the flag of the Union.

They were twin brothers, sixteen years of age; but they both thought they were old enough and strong enough to be soldiers. Their mother, however, had promptly disapproved of such suggestions, and they had not deemed it prudent to discuss the idea in her presence.

On Monday, the excitement instead of subsiding, was fanned to a fever heat; Pinchbrook Harbor was in a glow of patriotism. Men neglected their usual occupations, and talked of the affairs of the nation. Every person who could procure a flag hung it out at his window, or hoisted it in his yard, or on his house. The governor had called out a portion of the state militia, and already the tramp of armed men was heard in the neighboring city of Boston.

Thomas Somers was employed in a store in the village, and during the forenoon he mechanically performed the duties of his position; but he could think of nothing but the exciting topic of the day. His blood was boiling with indignation against those who had trailed our hallowed flag in the dust. He wanted to do something to redeem the honor of his country—something to wipe out the traitors who had dared to conspire against her peace. On his way home to dinner, he met Fred Pemberton, who lived only a short distance from his own house.

"What do you think now, Fred?" said Thomas.

"What do I think? I think just as I always did—the North is wrong, and the South is right," replied Fred.

"Who fired upon Fort Sumter? That's the question," said Thomas, his eyes flashing with indignation.

"Why didn't they give up the fort, then?"

"Give up the fort! Shall the United States cave in before the little State of South Carolina. Not by a two chalks!"

"I think the North has been teasing and vexing the South till the Southerns can't stand it any longer. There'll be war now."

"I hope there will! By gracious, I hope so!"

"I hope the South will beat!"

"Do you? Do you, Fred Pemberton?" demanded Tom, so excited he could not stand still.

"Yes, I do. The South has the rights of it. If we had let their niggers alone, there wouldn't have been any trouble."

"You are as blind as a bat, Fred. Don't you see this isn't a quarrel between the North and the South, but between the government and the rebels?"

"I don't see it. If the North had let the South alone, there wouldn't have been any fuss. I hope the North will get whipped, and I know she will."

"Fred, you are a traitor to your country!"

"No, I'm not!"

"Yes, you are; and if I had my way, I'd ride you on a rail out of town."

"No, you wouldn't."

"Yes, I would. I always thought you were a decent fellow; but you are a dirty, low-lived traitor."

"Better be careful what you say, Tom Somers!" retorted the young secessionist, angrily.

"A fellow that won't stand by his country ain't fit to live. You are an out-and-out traitor."

"Don't call me that again, Tom Somers," replied Fred, doubling up his fist.

"I say you are a traitor."

"Take that, then."

Tom did take it, and it was a pretty hard blow on the side of his head. Perhaps it was fortunate for our young patriot that an opportunity was thus afforded him to evaporate some of his enthusiasm in the cause of his country, for there is no knowing what might have been the consequence if it had remained longer pent up in his soul. Of course, he struck back; and a contest, on a small scale, between the loyalty of the North and the treason of the South commenced. How long it might have continued, or what might have been the result, cannot now be considered; for the approach of a chaise interrupted the battle, and the forces of secession were reënforced by a full-grown man.

The gentleman stepped out of his chaise with his whip in his hand, and proceeded to lay it about the legs and body of the representative of the Union side. This was more than Tom Somers could stand, and he retreated in good order from the spot, till he had placed himself out of the reach of the whip.

"What do you mean, you young scoundrel?" demanded the gentleman who had interfered.

Tom looked at him, and discovered that it was Squire Pemberton, the father of his late opponent.

"He hit me first," said Tom.

"He called me a traitor," added Fred. "I won't be called a traitor by him, or any other fellow."

"What do you mean by calling my son a traitor, you villain?"

"I meant just what I said. He is a traitor. He said he hoped the South would beat."

"Suppose he did. I hope so too," added Squire Pemberton.

The squire thought, evidently, that this ought to settle the question. If he hoped so, that was enough.

"Then you are a traitor, too. That's all I've got to say," replied Tom, boldly.

The Soldier Boy; or, Tom Somers in the Army

"You scoundrel! How dare you use such a word to me! " roared the squire, as he moved towards the blunt-spoken little patriot.

For strategic reasons, Tom deemed it prudent to fall back; but as he did so, he picked up a couple of good-sized stones.

"I said you were a traitor, and I say so again, " said Tom.

"Two can play at that game, " added Fred, as he picked up a stone and threw it at Tom.

The Union force returned the fire with the most determined energy, until one of the missiles struck the horse attached to the chaise. The animal, evidently having no sympathy with either party in this miniature contest, and without considering how much damage he might do the rebel cause, started off at a furious pace when the stone struck him. He dashed down the hill at a fearful rate, and bounded away over the plain that led to the Harbor.

Squire Pemberton and his son had more interest in the fate of the runaway horse than they had in the issue of the contest, and both started at the top of their speed in pursuit. But they might as well have chased a flash of lightning, or a locomotive going at the rate of fifty miles an hour.

Tom Somers came down from the bank which he had ascended to secure a good position. He had done rather more than he intended to do; but on the whole he did not much regret it. He watched the course of the spirited animal, as he dashed madly on to destruction. The career of the horse was short; for in the act of turning a corner, half a mile from the spot where Tom stood, he upset the chaise, and was himself thrown down, and, being entangled in the harness, was unable to rise before a stout man had him by the head.

"I wish that chaise had been the southern confederacy, " said Tom to himself, philosophically, when he saw the catastrophe in the distance. "Well, it served you right, old Secesh; and I'll bet there ain't many folks in Pinchbrook Harbor that will be willing to comfort the mourners. "

With this consoling assurance, Tom continued on his way home. At dinner, he gave the family a faithful account of the transaction.

"You didn't do right, Thomas, " said his mother.

"He hit me first. "

"You called him a traitor. "

"He is a traitor, and so is his father. "

"I declare, the boys are as full of fight as an egg is of meat, " added gran'ther Greene.

"You haven't seen the last of it yet, Thomas, " said the prudent mother.

"No matter, Tom; I'll stand by you, " added John.

After dinner, the two boys walked down to the Harbor together.

CHAPTER II.

THE SOMERS FAMILY.

The town of Pinchbrook is not a great distance from Boston, with which it is connected by railroad. If any of our young readers are of a geographical turn of mind, and are disposed to ascertain the exact locality of the place, we will save them any unnecessary trouble, for it is not laid down on any map with which we are familiar. We live in times of war, and probably our young friends have already learned the meaning of "military necessity. " Our story is essentially a military story, and there are certain military secrets connected with it which might be traced out if we should inform our inquisitive readers exactly where Pinchbrook is situated.

Squire Pemberton, we doubt not, is very anxious to find out certain persons connected with some irregular proceedings in and around his house on the evening of Monday, April 16th. Fidelity to the truth of history compels us to narrate these proceedings in our humble volume; but we should exceedingly regret thereby to get any of our friends into a scrape by informing the squire that they were active participants in the scenes of that eventful night, or to say any thing which would enable him, a lawyer, to trace out the authors of the mischief through these pages. Therefore we cannot say where Pinchbrook is, or even give a hint which would enable our readers to fix definitely its locality.

Pinchbrook is a town of about three thousand inhabitants, engaged, as the school books would say, in agriculture, manufactures, commerce, and the fisheries, which, rendered into still plainer English, means that some of the people are farmers; that wooden pails, mackerel kegs, boots and shoes, are made; that the inhabitants buy groceries, and sell fish, kegs, pails, and similar wares; and that there are about twenty vessels owned in the place, the principal part of which are fishermen.

We have not the agricultural and commercial statistics of the place at hand; but the larger territorial part of the town was devoted to the farming interest, and was rather sparsely populated, while the principal village, called Pinchbrook Harbor, was more densely peopled, contained two stores, four churches, one wharf, a blacksmith shop, and several shoe and bucket manufactories.

We are willing to acknowledge that Pinchbrook is rather a singular name. The antiquarians have not yet had an opportunity to determine its origin; but our private opinion is that the word is a corruption of *Punch*-brook. Perhaps, at some remote period in the history of the town, before the Sons of Temperance obtained a foothold in the place, a villainous mixture, known to topers under the general appellation of "punch, " may have been largely consumed by the Pinchbrookers. Though not a very aged person ourself, we have heard allusions to festive occasions where, metaphorically, the punch was said to "flow in streams. " Possibly, from "streams" came "brooks, " — hence, "Punchbrook, " — which, under the strange mutations of time, has become "Pinchbrook. " But we are not learned in these matters, and we hope that nothing we have said will bias the minds of antiquarians, and prevent them from devoting that attention to the origin of the word which its importance demands.

The Somers family, which we have already partially introduced, occupied a small cottage not quite a mile from Pinchbrook Harbor. Captain Somers, the head of the family, had been, and was still, for aught his wife and children knew, master of the schooner Gazelle. To purchase this vessel, he had heavily mortgaged his house and lands in Pinchbrook to Squire Pemberton. But his voyages had not been uniformly successful, though the captain believed that his earthly possessions, after discharging all his liabilities, would amount to about five thousand dollars.

The mortgage note would become due in June, and Captain Somers had been making a strong effort to realize upon his property, so as to enable him to pay off the obligation at maturity. Captain Somers had a brother who was familiarly known in the family as uncle Wyman. He had spent his life, from the age of eighteen, in the South, and at the time of which we write, he was a merchant in Norfolk.

Captain Somers and his brother had been interested together in certain mercantile transactions, and uncle Wyman being the business man, had the proceeds of these ventures in his own hands.

On the 10th of April, only two days before the bombardment of Fort Sumter, Captain Somers had sailed in the Gazelle, with an assorted cargo, for Norfolk. Before leaving home he had assured his wife that he should not return without effecting a settlement with Wyman, who had postponed it so many times, that the honest sailor began to fear his brother did not mean to deal justly with him. Nothing had been heard of the Gazelle since her departure from Boston.

Uncle Wyman was known to be a northern man with southern principles, while his brother, though not in the habit of saying much about politics, was fully committed on the side of the government, and was willing to sustain the President in the use of all the coercion that might be necessary to enforce obedience to the laws. The threatening aspect of affairs at the South had made Captain Somers more than ever anxious to have his accounts adjusted, as all his earthly possessions, except the schooner, were in the hands of his brother; and the fact that uncle Wyman was so strong an advocate of Southern rights, had caused him to make the declaration that he would not return without a settlement.

The financial affairs of the Somers family, therefore, were not in a very prosperous condition, and the solvency of the house depended entirely upon the adjustment with uncle Wyman. The mortgage note which Squire Pemberton held would be due in June, and as the creditor was not an indulgent man, there was a prospect that even the little cottage and the little farm might be wrested from them.

The family at home consisted of Mrs. Somers and three children. The two oldest daughters were married to two honest, hard-working fishermen at the Harbor. Thomas and John were twins, sixteen years of age. The former had a place in one of the stores at the village, and the latter occasionally went a fishing trip with his brothers-in-law. Both of the boys had been brought up to work, and there was need enough now that they should contribute what they could to the support of the family. The youngest child, Jane, was but eleven years of age, and went to school. Mrs. Somers's brother, a feeble old man, a soldier in the war of 1812, and a pensioner of the government, had been a member of the family for twenty years; and was familiarly known in town as "Gran'ther Green."

Having thus made our readers acquainted with Pinchbrook and the Somers family, we are prepared to continue our story.

Thomas and John walked down to the Harbor together after dinner. The latter had listened with interest and approbation to his brother's account of the "Battle of Pinchbrook," as he facetiously called it; and perhaps he thought Thomas might need his assistance before he reached the store, for Fred and his father would not probably be willing to let the matter rest where they had left it.

We are sorry not to be able to approve all the acts of the hero of this volume; but John, without asking our opinion, fully indorsed the action of his brother.

"Fred is a traitor, and so is his father, " said he, as they passed out at the front gate of the little cottage.

"That's so, Jack; and it made my blood boil to hear them talk, " replied Thomas. "And I couldn't help calling things by their right names. "

"Bully for you, Tom! " added John, as he turned round, and glanced at the house to assure himself they were out of the hearing of their mother. "Between you and me, Tom, there will be music in Pinchbrook to-night. "

He lowered his voice, and spoke in tones big with mystery and heavy with importance.

"What do you mean? " asked Thomas, his interest excited by the words and manner of his brother.

"There is fun ahead. "

"Tell me what it's all about. "

"You won't say a word—will you? "

"Of course I won't. "

"Not to mother, I mean, most of all. "

"Certainly not. "

"Squire Pemberton has been talking too loud for his own good. "

"I know that; he was in the store this forenoon, and Jeff Davis himself is no bigger traitor than he is. "

"Some of the people are going to make him a call to-night. "

"What for?"

"What do you suppose? Can't you see through a millstone, Tom, when there is a hole in it?"

"I don't know what you mean."

"You can come with us if you like, and then you will know all about it," added John, mysteriously.

"But what are you going to do?"

"We are going to make him hoist the American flag on his house, or hang it out of his window."

"Well, suppose he won't."

"Then we'll hang him where the flag ought to be. We'll pull the house down over his head."

"I'm with you, Jack," replied Thomas, with enthusiasm.

"We won't have a traitor in Pinchbrook. If we can't cure him, we'll ride him on a rail out of the town."

"I don't know as you and I ought to get into this scrape," added Thomas, thoughtfully.

"Why not?"

"You know the squire has a mortgage on our house, and he may get ugly."

"Let him, if he likes. I'm not going to tolerate a traitor because he has a mortgage on my father's house. Besides, that is a fair business transaction; the squire gets his interest."

"Mother is afraid of him, as she is of the evil spirit."

"Women are always timid," said John, sagely.

"By George! there comes the very man himself!" exclaimed Thomas, as he discovered a horse and chaise slowly approaching.

"So it is; that old chaise looks rather the worse for the wear. It looks as though it had been through the wars."

The vehicle did bear very evident marks of hard usage. One of the shafts was broken, the dasher wrenched off, and the top stove in. The horse was covered with mud, and limped badly from the effects of his fall. The broken shaft and the harness were now plentifully adorned with ropes and old straps. In fact, the catastrophe had utterly ruined all claim which the chaise ever might have had to be considered a "hahnsome kerridge."

"There'll be fun nearer home, I reckon," said John, as he obtained his first view of the sour visage of the squire.

"Can't help it," added Thomas.

"Keep a stiff upper lip, Tom."

"I intend to do so."

"Don't say a word about to-night, Tom."

"Of course not."

When the chaise had approached near enough to enable the squire to recognize the author of his misfortunes, he stopped the horse, and got out of the vehicle, with the whip in his hand.

"Now, you young scoundrel, I will teach you to insult me and my son, and destroy my property. Stay in the chaise, Fred, and hold the horse," he added to his son.

But there was not much need of holding the horse now, for he was too lame to run fast or far. Thomas and John came to a halt; and if the squire had been a prudent man, he might have seen by the flash of their eyes, that he was about to engage in an unsafe operation.

"I am going to horsewhip you within an inch of your life, you villain, you!" roared the squire, brandishing the whip.

"No, you are not," replied Thomas, coolly.

"If you drop the weight of that lash on my brother, I'll smash your head," added John.

The squire paused, and glanced at the wiry form of the young sailor. Better thoughts, or at least wiser ones, came to his aid.

"I can bring you to your senses in another way," said he, dropping his whip, and getting into the chaise again. "You will hear from me before the week is out."

"Let him go; don't say a word, Tom," added John.

"He will prosecute me, I suppose he means by that."

"Let him prosecute and be hanged! I'll bet by to-morrow morning he will think better of it. At any rate, he will find out what the people of Pinchbrook think of him."

The boys resumed their walk, and soon reached the store, where they found the group of idlers, that always frequent shops in the country, busily engaged in discussing the affair in which Thomas had been the principal actor. As the boys entered, the hero of the Pinchbrook Battle was saluted with a volley of applause, and his conduct fully approved and commended, for a copperhead in that day was an abomination to the people.

CHAPTER III.

TAMING A TRAITOR.

With the exception of Squire Pemberton, Pinchbrook was a thoroughly loyal town; and the people felt that it was a scandal and a disgrace to have even a single traitor within its border. The squire took no pains to conceal his treasonable sentiments, though the whole town was in a blaze of patriotic excitement. On the contrary, he had gone out of his way, and taken a great deal of pains, to condemn the government and the people of the North.

Squire Pemberton was a wealthy man, and he had always been a person of great influence in the place. He had occupied all the principal official positions in town and county. He had come to regard himself, as his townsmen were for the most part willing to regard him, as the social and political oracle of the place. What he thought in town meeting was generally the sense of his fellow-citizens, and when he expressed himself in words, his word was law.

When, on Sunday morning, with Fort Sumter in ruins, with the national flag trodden under the feet of traitors, with the government insulted and threatened, Squire Pemberton ventured to speak in tones of condemnation of the free North, the people of Pinchbrook listened coldly, at first, to the sayings of their oracle; and when he began to abuse the loyal spirit of the North, some ventured to dissent from him. The oracle was not in the habit of having men dissent, and it made him angry. His treason became more treasonable, his condemnation more bitter. Plain, honest men, to whatever party they might have belonged, were disgusted with the great man of Pinchbrook; and some of them ventured to express their disapprobation of his course in very decided terms. Some were disposed to be indulgent because the Squire had a sister in Georgia who had married a planter. But there was not found a single person, outside of his own family, who was mean enough to uphold him in his treacherous denunciation of the government.

The squire was too self-sufficient and opinionated to be influenced by the advice of friends or the warning of those who had suddenly become his enemies. He had so often carried the town to his own views, that, perhaps, he expected to manufacture a public sentiment in Pinchbrook that would place the town on the side of the rebels.

All day Sunday, and all day Monday, he rode about the Harbor preaching treason. He tried to convince the people that the South had all the right, and the North all the wrong; but he had never found them so obstinate and incredulous before.

Towards night one of the ministers ventured to suggest to him that he was sowing the wind, and would reap the whirlwind. The good man even hinted that he had roused a storm of indignation in the town which he might find it difficult to allay.

The squire laughed at the minister, and told him he was not afraid of any thing. He intended to speak his honest sentiments, as every citizen had a right to do; and he would like to see any man, or any body of men, who would dare to meddle with him.

"I am afraid you will see them, Squire Pemberton, " added the minister.

"Let them come where they please and when they please. "

"What will you do? What is your single arm against scores of strong men? "

"Nothing, perhaps, but I don't fear them. I am true to my convictions; why need I fear? "

"I think your convictions, as you call them, are deluding you. Do you think Benedict Arnold's convictions, if he had any, would have saved his neck from the halter? "

"Do you mean to compare me to Benedict Arnold, sir? "

"I came to you, as a friend, to warn you of impending danger; and, as your friend, I am compelled to say that I don't see much difference between your position and that of Benedict Arnold. "

"Do you mean to insult me? "

"Not at all, sir. I was only expressing my honest conviction. Instead of placing yourself on the side of your government, on the side of law and order, you are going about Pinchbrook Harbor denouncing the legitimate government of your country, and pleading the cause of rebels and traitors. "

The Soldier Boy; or, Tom Somers in the Army

"Am I not at liberty to say what I please of the government? "

"In ordinary times, you are. Just now, the country is in a state of war, and he who is not for the flag is against it. You may criticize the government as its friend, but not as its foe. When armed men conspire against the peace of the land, he who pleads their cause is a traitor—nay, sir, don't be angry; these are my convictions. "

"Political parsons have been the ruin of the country, " sneered the squire. "That is my conviction. "

"Squire Pemberton, I beg you not to be rash. If you must cherish these pernicious views, I entreat you, keep them to yourself. You may think what you please, but the utterance of treason makes a traitor. "

"I shall proclaim my views from the housetop, " replied the squire, angrily, as he abruptly turned away from the minister.

The squire continued obdurate to the last. Neither the persuasions of his friends nor the threats of his enemies had any effect in silencing his tongue; and as late as sundown on that day of the Great Awakening he was pouring treachery and treason into the ears of a neighbor who happened to pass his house. Half an hour later in the day, there was a great gathering of men and boys at the bridge on the outskirts of the village. They were singing Hail Columbia and the Star-spangled Banner. Thomas and John Somers were there.

Presently the assemblage began to move up the road which led to Squire Pemberton's house, singing patriotic songs as they marched. It was a multitude of persons for Pinchbrook; and no doubt the obnoxious oracle thought so when he saw the sea of heads that surrounded his dwelling. If this was a mob, it was certainly a very orderly mob, for the crowd thus far had done nothing worse than to sing the national airs.

The arrangements had all been made before the multitude started from the place of rendezvous. Three gentlemen, the principal of whom was Captain Barney, had been appointed a committee to wait upon the squire, and politely request him to display the American flag on his premises.

In the road, in front of the house, a large fire had been kindled, which threw a broad, bright glare on the house and the surrounding grounds. It was as light as day in the vicinity when the committee walked up to the front door of the house and rang the bell. The squire answered the summons himself.

"Squire Pemberton, " said Captain Barney, "your fellow-citizens, about two hundred in number, have called upon you with a simple and reasonable request. "

"What is it? " demanded the squire.

"That you hoist the Stars and Stripes on your house. "

"I won't do it! " roared the victim, as he slammed the door in the faces of the committee.

"That is insolence, " said Captain Barney, quietly. "We will go in. "

The captain led the way; but the door had been locked upon them. The shoulders of three stout men pressed against it, and the bolt yielded.

"What do you mean, you villains? " thundered the squire, as he confronted the committee in the entry.

"You were so impolite as to close the door in our faces before we had finished our story, " replied the immovable old sea captain.

"How dare you break in my door? " growled the squire.

"We shall do worse than that, squire, if you don't treat us respectfully. "

"A man's house is his castle, " added the squire, a little more moderately.

"That's very good law, but there isn't a house in Pinchbrook that is big enough or strong enough to shield a traitor from the indignation of his fellow-citizens. We do not purpose to harm you or your property, if you behave like a reasonable man. "

"You shall suffer for this outrage," gasped the squire, whose rage was increased by the cool and civil manner of Captain Barney.

"When you closed the door in my face, I had intimated that your fellow-citizens wish you to display the national flag."

"I refuse to do it, sir."

"Consider, squire, what you say. The people have made up their minds not to tolerate a traitor within the corporate limits of the town of Pinchbrook."

"I am no traitor."

"That is precisely what we wish you to demonstrate to your fellow-citizens assembled outside to witness an exhibition of your patriotism."

"I will not do it on compulsion."

"Then, sir, we shall be obliged to resort to disagreeable measures."

"What do you mean by that, sir?" asked the squire, who was evidently alarmed by the threat. "Do you mean to proceed to violence?"

"We do, Squire Pemberton," answered Captain Barney, decidedly.

"O my country!" sighed the victim, "has it come to this? The laws will no longer protect her citizens."

"That's very fine, sir. Do you expect the laws to protect you while you are aiding and abetting those who are trying to destroy them? Is there any law to protect a traitor in his treason? But we waste time, Squire Pemberton. Will you display the American flag?"

"Suppose I refuse?"

"We will pull your house down over your head. We will give you a coat of tar and feathers, and remove you beyond the limits of the town. If you ever come back, we will hang you to the nearest tree."

"Good Heaven! Is it possible that my fellow-citizens are assassins—incendiaries! "

"Your answer, squire. "

"For mercy's sake, husband, do what they ask, " interposed his wife, who had been an anxious listener in the adjoining room.

"I must do it, " groaned the squire, speaking the truth almost for the first time in forty-eight hours. "Alas! where is our boasted liberty of speech! "

"Fudge! squire, " replied Captain Barney, contemptuously. "If your friend Jeff Davis should come to Massachusetts to-morrow, to preach a crusade against the North, and to raise an army to destroy the free institutions of the country, I suppose you think it would be an outrage upon free speech to put him down. We don't think so. Up with the flag, squire. "

"Fred, you may hang the flag out at the front window up stairs, " said the squire to his son.

"All right, squire. Now a few words more, and we bid you good night. You may *think* what you please, but if you utter another word of treason in Pinchbrook during the term of your natural life, the party outside will carry out the rest of the programme. "

By this time Fred Pemberton had fastened the flag to one of his mother's clothes poles, and suspended it out of the window over the porch. It was hailed with three tremendous cheers by the multitude who were in waiting to discipline the squire, and exorcise the evil spirit of treason and secession.

The work of the evening was finished, not wholly to the satisfaction, perhaps, of a portion of the younger members of the assemblage, who would gladly have joined in the work of pillage and destruction, but much to the gratification of the older and steadier portion of the crowd, who were averse to violent proceedings.

CHAPTER IV.

THE COMMITTEE COME OUT, AND TOM GOES IN.

While the committee which the loyal citizens of Pinchbrook had appointed to conduct their case with Squire Pemberton were in the house, engaged in bringing the traitor to terms, the younger members of the assemblage were very impatient to know how matters were progressing. Thomas Somers was particularly anxious to have the affair brought to a crisis. In vain he and a few other of the young loyalists attempted to obtain a view of the interior of the house, where the exciting interview was in progress.

Captain Barney, on shore as well as at sea, was a thorough disciplinarian. Of course, he was aware that his proceedings were technically illegal; that in forcing himself into the house of the squire he was breaking the law of the land; but it seemed to him to be one of those cases where prompt action was necessary, and the law was too tardy to be of any service. He was, however, determined that the business should be done with as little violence as possible, and he had instructed the citizens at the bridge to do no needless injury to the property or the feelings of the squire or his family.

When he entered the house, he had stationed three men at the door to prevent any of the people from following him. He had also directed them not to enter the yard or grounds of the house until he gave the signal. These directions proved a great hardship to the boys in the crowd, and they were completely disgusted when they saw the flag thrown loose from the front window.

The mansion of Squire Pemberton was an old-fashioned dwelling, about a hundred feet from the road. In front of it was a green lawn, adorned with several large buttonwood trees. There was no fence to enclose what was called the front yard. The crowd was assembled on this lawn, and agreeably to the directions of the leader, or chairman of the committee, none of them passed into the yard in the rear and at the end of the house, which was separated from the lawn by a picket fence.

Boys are instinctively curious to know what is going on, and the "living room" of the squire, in which the exciting conversation was taking place, was in the rear of the house. The windows on the front were dark and uncommunicative. The boys were restless and impatient; if there was to be any fun, they wanted to see it. Thomas was as impatient as his fellows, and being more enterprising than the others, he determined, while obeying the instructions of Captain Barney in the spirit, to disobey them in the letter.

He had been a sufferer to the extent of two great wales on the calves of his legs by the treason of the squire, and no doubt he thought he ought to be regarded as an exception to those who were called on to observe the instructions of the chairman of the committee. Leaving the group of inquiring minds near the front door of the house, he walked down the driveway till he came to a rail fence, through which he crawled, and entered the field adjoining the garden of the squire. His fellow-citizens, men and boys, were too intently watching the house to heed him, and no one noticed his enterprising movement.

From the field, he entered the garden, and made his way to the rear of the house. But even here, he was doomed to disappointment, for Mrs. Pemberton had drawn her curtains. Our hero was not, however, to be utterly defeated, and as the curtains had not been fitted by an accomplished upholsterer, there were openings on either side, through which he might command a full view of the interior of the room.

Thomas proceeded slowly and cautiously to obtain a position which would enable him to gratify his curiosity, and witness the humiliation of the haughty squire. Beneath the window which, he had chosen to look through, there was a cellar door, from which a pile of seaweed, placed upon it to keep the frost out of the cellar, had just been removed. The adventurous inquirer crept up the slippery boards, and gained the coveted position. He could not only see the committee and the squire, but he could hear all they said. He was perfectly delighted with the manner in which the captain put the question to the squire; and when the latter ordered Fred to hang out the flag, he was a little disposed to imitate the masculine occupants of the hen-house, a short distance from his perch; but Tom, as we have before intimated, had a very tolerable idea of the principles of strategy, and had the self-possession to hold his tongue, and permit the triumphant scene within to pass without a crow or a cheer.

The battle had been fought and the victory won; and though Tom felt that he was one of the victors, he deemed it prudent, for strategical reasons, to commence a retreat. The cellar doors, as we have before hinted, were very slippery, having been thoroughly soaked with moisture while covered with the seaweed. When the hero of this unauthorized reconnoissance wheeled about to commence his retreat, his feet incontinently slipped up upon the inclined surface of the doors, and he came down heavily upon the rotten boards. This, in itself, would have been but an inconsiderable disaster, and he might still have withdrawn from the inconvenient locality, if circumstances had not conspired against him, as circumstances sometimes will, when they ought to be conciliatory and accommodating. The force with which Tom fell upon the decayed boards was too much for them, and the unlucky adventurer became another victim to the treachery of rotten wood, which has hurled so many thousands from time into eternity.

But Tom was not hurled so far as that on the present occasion, though for all practical purposes, for the succeeding half hour, he might as well have been a hundred fathoms under water, or beneath the wreck of a twenty-ton locomotive at the bottom of the river. That cellar door was a bad place to fall through, which may be accounted for on the supposition that it was not made to fall through. In his downward progress, Tom had unluckily struck his head against the side of the house; and when he landed at the bottom of the stairs, he was utterly oblivious to all distinctions between treason and loyalty. Tom was not killed, I need not inform the ingenious reader, or this would otherwise have been the last chapter of the story; but the poor fellow did not know whether he was dead or alive.

In fact, he had not sense enough left to consider the question at all; for there he lay, in the gloom of the traitor's dark cellar, silent and motionless—a solemn warning to all our young readers of the folly and wickedness of indulging an illegal and sinful curiosity. It may seem cruel and inhuman in us to forsake poor Tom in this sad plight; but we must, nevertheless, go up stairs, in order that the sufferer may be duly and properly relieved in due and proper season.

When the committee of three, appointed by the indignant loyalists of Pinchbrook, had completed their mission in the house of the squire, like sensible men they proposed to leave; and they so expressed themselves, through their spokesman, to the unwilling host. They put their hats on, and moved into the front entry, whither they were followed by the discomfited traitor. They had scarcely left the room before a tremendous crash greeted the ears of that portion of the family which remained in the apartment. This was the precise moment at which poor Tom Somers found himself on the bottom of the cellar; or, to be entirely accurate, when he lost himself on the bottom of the cellar.

Mrs. Pemberton heard the crash, and she very naturally concluded that the hour of retribution had actually come; that the terrible mob had commenced the work of destruction. To her "fear-amazed" mind it seemed as though the whole side of the house had fallen in, and, for a moment, she confidently expected the chimneys would presently go by the board, and the roof come thundering down upon the devoted heads of her outraged family. Perhaps, at that terrible moment, she wished her husband had been like other women's husbands, a true and loyal man, cheering the old flag, and hurling harmless anathemas at the graceless rebels.

But the chimney did not go by the board, nor the roof come thundering down upon her head. There was not even a sound of destruction to be heard, and the sides of the house seemed to be firm and decided in their intention to maintain their perpendicular position. A few minutes later, when the committee announced to the multitude the success of their undertaking, and Fred had displayed the flag from the window, peal upon peal of stunning huzzas saluted her ears, and the awful peril of the preceding moments appeared to be averted. The squire, having closed and barricaded the broken door as well as he could, returned to the room, with curses deep and bitter upon his lips. He was not in the habit of swearing, but the magnitude of the occasion seemed to justify the innovation, and he swore hugely, roundly, awfully. He paced the room, ground his teeth, and stamped upon the floor.

"Father, did you hear that terrible racket just now? " asked Mrs. Pemberton. "I thought the side of the house had fallen in. "

"What racket? " demanded the squire, pausing in his excited walk.

"I am sure they have broken something. "

"It sounded as though it was down cellar, " added Susan, the daughter.

"What was it? " asked the father.

"I don't know. It sounded like breaking boards. Do go down cellar, and find out what it was. "

"The scoundrels! " roared the squire, as he rushed up and down the room again with the fury of a madman. "I'll teach them to break into my house! "

"Be calm, father, " interposed Mrs. Pemberton, who, like most New England mothers, called her husband by the title which belonged exclusively to the children.

"Calm? How can I be calm? Don't you hear the ruffians shout and yell? "

"They are only cheering the flag. "

The squire muttered a malediction upon the flag, which would probably have procured for him a coat of tar and feathers, if the mob had heard it. Mrs. Pemberton was silent, for she had never seen her husband so moved before. She permitted him to pace the room in his frenzy till his anger had, in some measure, subsided.

"I wish you would go down cellar and find out what that noise was," said Mrs. Pemberton, as soon as she dared to speak again. "Perhaps some of them are down there now. Who knows but they will set the house afire. "

Squire Pemberton was startled by this suggestion, and, seizing the lamp, he rushed down cellar to prevent so dire a calamity.

CHAPTER V.

THE ATTIC CHAMBER.

Squire Pemberton rushed down cellar. He was very much excited, and forgot that he had been troubled with the rheumatism during the preceding winter. When he opened the cellar door, he was considerably relieved to find that no brilliant light saluted his expectant gaze. It was as cold and dark in the cellar as it had been when he sorted over the last of his Warren Russets, a few days before.

It was certain, therefore, that the house was not on fire; and, invigorated by this thought, he descended the stairs. A strong current of fresh, cold air extinguished the light he carried. As this was contrary to his usual experience when he went down cellar in the evening after an apple or a mug of cider, it assured him that there was a screw loose somewhere. Returning to the room above, he procured a lantern, and proceeded to the cellar again to renew his investigations.

The squire felt the cold blast of the April air, and immediately made his way to the cellar door, holding the lantern up as high as his head, to ascertain the nature of the mischief which the fanatical abolitionists had perpetrated. He saw that the cellar door was broken through. The rotten boards lay upon the steps, and with another malediction upon the mob, he placed the lantern upon a barrel, and proceeded to repair the damage. As he stepped forward, he stumbled against the body of the enterprising hero of this volume, who lay as calm and still as a sleeping child.

The squire started back, not a little alarmed at the sight of the motionless body. He felt as though a terrible retribution had fallen upon somebody, who had been killed in the act of attempting to destroy his property. Seizing his lantern, he retreated to the cellar stairs by which he had descended, and stood there for a moment, his tongue paralyzed, and his knees smiting each other, in the agony of terror.

We do not know what he was afraid of, but we suppose that instinctive dread which some people manifest in the presence of death, had completely overcome him. Certainly there was nothing to be afraid of, for a dead man is not half so likely to do a person an injury as a living one. But in a few minutes Squire Pemberton in some measure recovered his self-possession.

"There is a dead man down here! " he called up the staircase, in quaking tones.

"Mercy on us! " exclaimed Mrs. Pemberton. "Who is he? "

"I don't know, " replied the squire.

"Look and see who it is, father, " added Mrs. Pemberton. "Perhaps he isn't dead. "

"Stone dead, " persisted the squire. "He fell into the cellar and broke his neck. "

"Go and see who it is—will you? "

"Well, you come down and hold the light, " said the squire, who was not quite willing to say that he was scared out of his wits.

Mrs. Pemberton descended the stairs, followed by Susan and Fred, who had just returned from the front window, where he had exhibited the flag, which the crowd outside were still cheering.

"Who can it be? " continued the old lady, as she slowly and cautiously walked forward to the scene of the catastrophe.

"I don't know, " replied the squire, in whom the presence of his family had spurred up a semblance of courage; for if a man ever is brave, it is in the presence of his wife and children. "If it is one of the ruffians who came here to destroy my house, I am glad he has lost his life in the attempt. It is a righteous retribution upon him for his wickedness. "

Mrs. Pemberton took the lantern, and the squire, still excited and terrified, bent over the prostrate form of the young marauder. The victim lay upon his face, and the squire had to turn him over to obtain a view of his countenance.

"I declare it is one of the Somers boys! " exclaimed Mrs. Pemberton, as her husband brought the face of Thomas to her view.

The Soldier Boy; or, Tom Somers in the Army

"The young villain! " ejaculated the squire. "It is lucky he was killed, or the house would have been in flames before this time. He is a desperate young scoundrel. "

"But he isn't dead, father! " said Mrs. Pemberton, as she knelt upon the cold ground, and felt the pulse of the insensible boy. "He is only stunned. "

"I am sorry for it. If it had killed him, it would have served him right, " added the squire, who had suddenly become as bold as a lion—as bold as two lions.

"Come, father, let's carry him up stairs, and put him to bed. "

"Do you think I am going to do anything for this young scoundrel! " exclaimed the squire, indignantly. "Why, he stoned Fred and me to-day, and stoned the horse, and made him run away and break the chaise all to pieces. "

"But we mustn't leave him here in this situation. He may die. "

"Let him die. "

"But what will folks say? "

The more humane wife evidently understood the weak point of the squire, for nothing but slavery and the Southern Confederacy could have induced him to set at defiance the public sentiment of Pinchbrook.

"Well, carry him up stairs then; but he never will get out of my house till he has been severely punished for his crimes. "

The squire and Fred took hold of the senseless form of poor Tom, and carried it up stairs, where it was placed upon the sofa in the sitting room. Mrs. Pemberton had the reputation of being "an excellent hand in sickness, " and she immediately applied herself to the duty of restoring the sufferer to consciousness.

"Don't you think you had better go after the doctor, father? " asked the good woman. "Some of his bones may be broken, or he may be injured inwardly. "

"I shall not go for any doctor, " snarled the squire. "Do you think I will trust myself out doors while that howling mob is hanging round the house? "

"Fred can go, " suggested Susan.

"He can, but he shall not, " growled the squire, throwing himself into his arm chair in the corner, with an appearance of indifference and unconcern, which were far from representing the actual state of his mind.

Mrs. Pemberton said no more, but she and Susan went to work upon the sufferer with camphor and hartshorn in good earnest, and in a short time they had the satisfaction of seeing him open his eyes. They continued the treatment for some time longer, with the most satisfactory result, till Tom astonished them by jumping off the sofa, and standing up in the middle of the room. He rubbed his forehead, hunched up his left shoulder, and felt of his shins.

"Are you hurt, Thomas? " asked Mrs. Pemberton, with more of tenderness in her tones than the squire deemed proper for the occasion.

"No, marm, I guess not, " replied Tom. "My shoulder feels a little stiff, and I think I barked one of my shins; but I shall be as good as new by to-morrow. "

But there was an ugly bump on the side of his head, which he had not yet discovered, but which Susan pointed out to him. He acknowledged the bump, but declared it was only a little sore and would be all right by the next day.

"I feel pretty well, " continued Tom, "and I guess I'll go home now. "

"I think you won't, young man, " interposed Squire Pemberton.

Tom looked at him, and for the first time since he had come to himself, he remembered in what manner he had received his injuries. He immediately came to the conclusion that he had got into a bad scrape. He was in the house of, and in the presence of, his great enemy. The events of the day passed in rapid succession through his mind, and he could not help thinking that he was destined to be the first victim in Pinchbrook to the war spirit which had just been awakened all over the country.

The squire thought he would not go home, which was as much as to say he would not let him go home. Tom's wits were a little confused, after the hard knock he had received upon the head, and all he could do was to stand and look at the oracle of Pinchbrook, and wait for further developments.

"Young man, " said the squire, sternly, and in tones that were intended to make a deep impression upon the mind of the young man, "your time has come. "

The squire paused, and looked at the culprit to ascertain the effect of the startling announcement; but Tom seemed to be perfectly cool, and was not annihilated by the suggestive remark of the great man of Pinchbrook.

"You have become a midnight marauder, " added the squire, poetically.

"It isn't seven o'clock yet, " said Tom pointing to the great wooden clock in the corner of the room.

"You joined a mob to pillage and destroy the property of a peaceable citizen. You broke in—"

"No, sir; the cellar door broke in, " interposed the culprit.

"You broke into my house to set it afire! " continued the squire, in a rage.

"No, sir, I did not. I only went round there to see the fun, " replied Tom, pointing to the rear of the house; "and the cellar door broke down and let me in. I did not mean to do you or your house any harm; and I didn't do any, except breaking the cellar door, and I will have that mended. "

"Don't tell me, you young villain! You meant to burn my house. "

"No, I didn't mean any thing of the kind, " replied Tom, stoutly. "I was going off when the door broke down. The boards were rotten, and I should think a man like you ought to have better cellar doors than those are."

The squire didn't relish this criticism, especially from the source whence it came. There was a want of humility on the part of the culprit which the magnate of Pinchbrook thought would be exceedingly becoming in a young man in his situation. The absence of it made him more angry than before. He stormed and hurled denunciations at the offender; he rehearsed the mischief he had done during the day, and alluded in strong terms to that which he intended to perpetrate in the "dead watches of the night"—which was the poetical rendering of half-past six in the evening; for the squire was fond of effective phrases.

Tom ventured to hint that a man who would not stand by his country when her flag was insulted and "trailed in the dust"—Tom had read the daily papers—ought to be brought to his senses by such expedients as his fellow-citizens might suggest. Of course this remark only increased the squire's wrath, and he proceeded to pronounce sentence upon the unlucky youth, which was that he should be taken to the finished room in the attic, and confined there under bolts and bars till the inquisitor should further declare and execute his intentions.

Mrs. Pemberton and Susan remonstrated against this sentence, prudently suggesting the consequences which might result from detaining the boy. But the squire declared he should not go till he had at least horsewhipped him; and if there was any justice left in the land, he would send him to the county jail in the morning.

Tom wanted to resist the execution of his sentence, but he was still weak from the effects of his fall, and he could not expect to vanquish both the squire and his son; so, with an earnest protest, he permitted himself to be led to the attic chamber. The squire thrust him into the room, and after carefully securing the door, left our hero to meditate upon the reverse of fortune which had overtaken him.

CHAPTER VI.

THE WAY IS PREPARED.

"Where do you suppose Thomas is? " said Mrs. Somers, as she glanced at the clock, which indicated half-past nine.

"I don't know, " replied John. "He can't be a great ways off. I saw him in front of the squire's house when the committee went in. "

"The boy's gone down to the Harbor again with the rest of the folks, talking about the war, " added gran'ther Greene, as he rose from his chair, and hobbled into his chamber adjoining the kitchen.

At ten o'clock, the mother began to be a little uneasy; and at eleven, even John had some fears that all was not well with his brother. Neither of them was able to suggest anything that could possibly have happened to the absentee. There had been no battle fought, and so nobody could have been killed. There had been no violence used in the transactions of the evening further than breaking in the front door of Squire Pemberton, so that it was not easy to believe that any accident had happened to him.

John had given a glowing account of the proceedings at the house of the squire and the family had been much interested and excited by the stirring narrative. His mother was perfectly satisfied, as no one had been injured, and hoped the great man of Pinchbrook would be brought to his senses. All these topics had been fully discussed during the evening. John had informed his mother that Captain Benson, who had formerly commanded the Pinchbrook Riflemen, intended to raise a company for the war. He mentioned the names of half a dozen young men who had expressed their desire to join. The family had suggested that this and that man would go, and thus the long evening passed away.

"I don't see what has become of Thomas, " said Mrs. Somers, when the clock struck eleven, as she rose from her chair and looked out of the window.

"Well, I don't see, either, " replied John. "I don't believe there is anything going on at this time of night. "

"I hope nothing has happened to him," continued the anxious mother, as she went to the door and looked out, hoping, perhaps, to discover him in the gloom of the night, or to hear his familiar step.

"What could have happened to him?" asked John, who did not believe his brother was fool enough to fall overboard, or permit any serious accident to happen to him.

"I don't know. I can't see what has got the boy. He always comes home before nine o'clock. Have you heard him say anything that will give you an idea where he is?"

"He hasn't said anything to me."

"Try, and see if you can't think of something," persisted the anxious mother.

"He hasn't talked of anything but the war since yesterday morning."

"What did he say?"

"I don't know, now," answered John, musing. "He said he should like to join the army, and go down and fight the rebels."

Mrs. Somers had heard as much from him, but she had given no particular attention to his remarks on this subject, for they seemed wild and visionary. John's words, under the present circumstances, appeared to be full of importance; and taking her stocking, she seated herself before the stove, and resumed her knitting. She was silent now, for her heart was heavy with the premonitions of impending trouble.

"I will take a walk down to the Harbor, mother, and see if I can find anything of him. There may be something going on there that I don't know about. He may be at the store, talking about the war with Captain Barney and the rest of the folks."

Mrs. Somers offered no objection to this plan, and John put on his cap, and left the house. The poor mother brooded upon her trouble for another hour, and with every new moment, the trouble seemed more real. The clock struck twelve before John returned; and more than once during his absence, as she plied her needles, she had wiped away a tear that hung among the furrows of her care-worn cheek. She had been thinking of her husband, as well as of her son. He was, or soon would be, in the midst of the traitors, and she trembled for him. Uncle Wyman was a secessionist; and, beyond this, she had not much confidence in his integrity, and if Captain Somers came home at all, his property would all be swept away, and he would be a beggar.

The events of that day were not calculated to conciliate Squire Pemberton towards them, and the farm and the cottage would pass away from them. All these things had been considered and reconsidered by the devoted mother. Poverty and want seemed to stare her in the face; and to add to all these troubles, Thomas did not come home, and, as fond mothers will, she anticipated the worst.

John entered the kitchen, and carelessly flung his cap upon the table. Mrs. Somers looked at him, and waited patiently to hear any intelligence he might bring. But John threw himself into a chair, looking more gloomy than before he left the house. He did not speak, and therefore he had no good news to tell.

"You didn't see anything of him—did you?" asked Mrs. Somers; but it was a useless question, for she had already interpreted the meaning of his downcast looks.

"No, mother; there isn't a man, woman, or child stirring in the village; and I didn't see a light in a single house."

"What do you suppose can have become of him?"

"I'm sure I don't know. Tom is old enough and smart enough to take care of himself."

"It's very strange."

"So it is. I haven't any idea what has become of him."

"Did you look around Squire Pemberton's house, where he was seen last?"

"I looked about on both sides of the road, going and coming from the Harbor. I whistled all the way, and if he had been any where round, he would have whistled back, as he always does."

"What do you *suppose* has become of him? " demanded the poor mother, worried beyond expression at the mysterious disappearance of her son.

"I can't tell, mother. "

"Don't you think we had better call up the neighbors, and have something done about it? "

"I don't know, " replied John, hardly less anxious than his mother.

"I don't suppose they would be able to find him if we did, " added Mrs. Somers, wiping away the tears from her face.

"I can't think anything has happened to him, mother. If he had been on the water, or anything of that kind, I should feel worse about it. "

"If I only knew where he was, I shouldn't feel so bad about it, " said she; and her position, certainly, was a reasonable one.

"What's the matter, sister? " called gran'ther Greene, from his chamber. "Hasn't that boy got home yet? "

"No, he hasn't come yet, and I am worried to death about him, " replied Mrs. Somers, opening the door of her brother's room.

"What o'clock is it? "

"After twelve. Thomas never stayed out so late in his life before. What do you suppose has become of him? "

"Law sake! I haven't the leastest idea, " answered the old man. "Thomas is a smart boy, and knows enough to keep out of trouble. "

"That's what I say, " added John, who had unlimited confidence in his brother's ability to take care of himself.

"I'll tell you what *I* think, John, " said Mrs. Somers, throwing herself into her chair with an air of desperation.

But she did not tell John what she thought: on the contrary, she sat rocking herself in silence, as though her thought was too big and too momentous for utterance.

"Well, what do you think, mother?" asked John, when he had waited a reasonable time for her to express her opinion on the exciting topic.

Mrs. Somers rocked herself more violently than before, and made no reply.

"What were you going to say?"

"I think the boy has gone off to Boston, and gone into the army," replied she, desperately, as though she had fully made up her mind to commit herself to this belief.

"Do you think so, mother?"

"I feel almost sure of it."

"I don't think so, mother. Tom wouldn't have gone off without saying something to me about it."

"If he wouldn't say it to me, he wouldn't be likely to say it to you, John. It don't look a bit like Thomas to go off and leave his mother in this way," moaned the poor woman, wiping away a deluge of tears that now poured from her eyes.

"I don't believe he has done any such thing, mother," protested John.

"I feel almost certain about it, now. If the boy wanted to go, and couldn't stay at home, he ought to have told me so."

"He did say he wanted to go."

"I didn't think he really meant it. I want my boys to love their country, and be ready to fight for it. Much as I should hate to part with them, if they are needed, they may go; but I don't like to have them run away and leave me in this mean way. I shouldn't feel half so bad if I knew Thomas was in the army now, as I do to think he ran away from home, just as though he had done some mean thing. I am willing he should go, and he wouldn't be a son of mine if he wasn't ready to go and fight for his country, and die for her too, if there was any need of it. I didn't think Thomas would serve me in this way."

"I don't believe he has."

"I know he's gone. I like his spunk, but if he had only come to me and said he *must* go, I wouldn't have said a word; but to go off without bidding us good by—it's too bad, and I didn't think Thomas would do such a thing."

Mrs. Somers rose from her chair, and paced the room in the highest state of agitation and excitement. The rockers were not adequate to the duty required of them, and nothing less than the whole floor of the kitchen was sufficient for the proper venting of her emotion.

"Do you mean to say, mother, that you would have given him leave to go, even if he had teased you for a month?" asked John.

"Certainly I should," replied his mother, stopping short in the middle of the floor. "I'm ready and willing to have my boys fight for their country, but I don't want them to sneak off as though they had been robbing a hen-roost, and without even saying good by to me."

"If Tom were here, do you mean to say you would let him go?" demanded John, earnestly.

"Certainly I do; I mean so. But I don't think there is any need of boys like him going, when there are men enough to do the fighting."

"You told Tom he shouldn't go."

"Well, I didn't think he really meant it. If he had—What's that, John?" asked she, suddenly, as a noise at the window attracted her attention.

"Only the cat, mother."

"If Thomas or you had asked me in earnest, and there was need of your going, I wouldn't have kept either of you at home. I would go to the poorhouse first. My father and my brother both fought for their country, and my sons shall when their country wants them."

"Then you are willing Tom should go?"

"I am, but not to have him sneak off like a sheep-stealer."

"Three cheers for you, mother!" shouted Thomas, as he threw up the window at which he had been standing for some ten minutes listening to this interesting conversation.

"Where have you been, Thomas?" exclaimed the delighted mother.

"Open the door, Jack, and let me in, and I will tell you all about it," replied the absentee.

"Come in; the door isn't locked," said John.

He came in; and what he had to tell will interest the reader as well as his mother and his brother.

CHAPTER VII.

A MIDNIGHT ADVENTURE.

Tom Somers was an enterprising young man, as our readers have already discovered; and when the door of the finished room in the attic of Squire Pemberton's house was fastened upon him, he was not at all disposed to submit to the fate which appeared to be in store for him. The idea of becoming a victim to the squire's malice was not to be entertained, and he threw himself upon the bed to devise some means by which he might make his escape.

The prospect was not encouraging, for there was only one window in the chamber, and the distance to the ground was suggestive of broken limbs, if not of a broken neck. Tom had read the Life of Baron Trenck, and of Stephen Burroughs, but the experience of neither of these worthies seemed to be available on the present occasion.

As the family had not yet retired, it would not be safe to commence operations for some hours. The stale, commonplace method of tying the sheets and blankets together, and thus forming a rope by which he could descend to the ground, occurred to him; but he had not much confidence in the project. He lay quietly on the bed till he heard the clocks on the churches at the Harbor strike twelve. It was time then, if ever, for the family to be asleep, and he decided to attempt an escape by another means which had been suggested to him. If it failed, he could then resort to the old-fashioned way of going down on the rope made of sheets and blankets.

The apartment in which Tom was confined was not what people in the country call an "upright chamber. " The sides of the room were about four feet in height; and a section of the apartment would have formed one half of an irregular octagon. In each side of the chamber there was a small door, opening into the space near the eaves of the house, which was used to store old trunks, old boxes, the disused spinning-wheel, and other lumber of this description. Tom had been in the attic before, and he remembered these doors, through one of which he now proposed to make his escape.

When the clock struck twelve, he cautiously rose from the bed, and pulled off his boots, which a proper respect for his host or the bed had not prompted him to do before. The house was old, and the floors had a tendency to creak beneath his tread. With the utmost care, he crawled on his hands and knees to one of the doors of the lumber hole, which he succeeded in opening without much noise.

Making his way in among the old boxes, trunks, and spinning-wheels, he was fully embarked in his difficult venture. The dust which he stirred up in his progress produced an almost irresistible desire to sneeze, which Lord Dundreary might have been happy to indulge, but which might have been fatal to the execution of Tom Somers's purpose. He rubbed his nose, and held his handkerchief over the intractable member, and succeeded in overcoming its dangerous tendency. His movements were necessarily very slow, for he was in constant dread lest some antiquated relic of the past should tumble over, and thus disturb the slumbers of the family who occupied the chambers below.

But in spite of the perils and difficulties that environed his path, there was something exciting and exhilarating in the undertaking. It was a real adventure, and, as such, Tom enjoyed it. As he worked his way through the labyrinth of antiquities, he could not but picture to himself the surprise and chagrin of Squire Pemberton, when he should come up to the attic chamber to wreak his vengeance upon him. He could see the magnate of Pinchbrook start, compress his lips and clinch his fists, when he found the bird had flown.

"Better not crow till I get out of the woods, " said he to himself, while his imagination was still busy upon the agreeable picture.

After a series of trials and difficulties which our space does not permit us to describe in full, Tom emerged from the repository of antiquities, and stood in the open space in front of the finished chamber. With one boot in each hand, he felt his way to the stairs, and descended to the entry over the front door. All obstacles now seemed to be overcome, for he had nothing to do but go down stairs and walk out.

It often happens, amid the uncertainties of this unstable world, that we encounter the greatest trials and difficulties precisely where we expect to find none. As Tom walked along the entry, with one hand on the rail that protected the staircase to guide him, he struck his foot against the pole upon which Fred Pemberton had suspended the flag out of the window. It was very careless of the squire, when he took the flag in, to leave the stick in that unsafe position, for one of his own family might have stumbled against it, and broken a leg or an arm, or possibly a neck; and if it might have been a "cause of offence" to one of the Pembertons, it certainly laid a grievous burden upon the shoulders of poor Tom Somers.

When the pole fell, it made a tremendous racket, as all poles will when they fall just at the moment when they ought to stand up, and be decent and orderly. This catastrophe had the effect to quicken the steps of the young man. He reached the stairs, and had commenced a rapid descent, when the door of the squire's room, which was on the lower floor, opened, and Tom found himself flanked in that direction.

"Who's there? What's that? " demanded the squire, in hurried, nervous tones.

Tom was so impolite as to make no reply to these pressing interrogatories, but quickly retreated in the direction from which he had come.

"Wife, light the lamp, quick, " said the squire, in the hall below.

Just then a door opened on the other side of the entry where Tom stood, and he caught a faint glimpse of a figure robed in white. Though it was the solemn hour of midnight, and Tom, I am sorry to say, had read the Three Spaniards, and Mysteries of Udolpho, he rejected the suggestion that the "sheeted form" might be a ghost.

"Who's there? " called the squire again.

A romantic little scream from the figure in white assured Tom that Miss Susan was the enemy immediately on his front. Then he caught the glimmer of the light below, which Mrs. Pemberton had procured, and the race seemed to be up. Concealment was no longer practicable, and he seized upon the happy suggestion that the window opening upon the portico over the front door was available as a means of egress.

Springing to the window, he raised it with a prompt and vigorous hand, and before the squire could ascend the stairs, he was upon the roof of the portico. Throwing his boots down, he grasped the gutter, and "hung off. " He was now on *terra firma*, and all his trials appeared to have reached a happy termination; but here again he was doomed to disappointment.

"Bow, wow, wow-er, woo, row!" barked and growled the squire's big bull dog, when he came to realize that some unusual occurrences were transpiring.

The animal was a savage brute, and was kept chained in the barn during the day, and turned loose when the squire made his last visit to the cattle about nine in the evening. Tom was thoroughly alarmed when this new enemy confronted him; but fortunately he had the self-possession to stand his ground, and not attempt to run away, otherwise the dog would probably have torn him in pieces.

"Come here, Tige! Poor fellow! Come here! He's a good fellow! Don't you know me, Tige?" said Tom, whose only hope seemed to be in conciliation and compromise.

If Tige knew him, he appeared to be very unwilling to acknowledge the acquaintance under the present suspicious circumstances, and at this unseemly hour. The brute barked, snarled, howled, and growled, and manifested as strong an indisposition to compromise as a South Carolina fire-eater. He placed himself in front of the hero of the night's adventure, as resolute and as intractable as though he had known all the facts in the case, and intended to carry out to the letter the wishes of his master.

Tom slowly retreated towards the garden fence, the dog still following him up. He had tried coaxing and conciliation, and they had failed. As he cautiously backed from the house, his feet struck against a heavy cart stake, which seemed to suggest his next resort. He was well aware that any quick movement on his part would cause the dog to spring upon him. Placing his toe under the stake, he raised it with his foot, till he could reach it with his hand, keeping his gaze fixed upon the eyes of the dog, which glared like fiery orbs in the gloom of the hour.

Tige saw the stick, and he appeared to have a wholesome respect for it—a sentiment inspired by sundry beatings, intended to cure a love of mutton on the hoof, or beef on the shelf. The brute retreated a few paces; but at this moment Squire Pemberton appeared at the front door, with a lantern in his hand. He understood the "situation" at a glance.

The Soldier Boy; or, Tom Somers in the Army

"Take him, Tige! Stu' boy! " shouted the squire.

The dog snarled an encouraging reply to this suggestion, and moved up towards the fugitive. Tom's courage was equal to the occasion, and he levelled a blow at the head of the bull dog, which, if it had hit him fairly, must have smashed in his skull. As it was, the blow was a heavy one, and Tige retreated; but the shouts of the squire rallied him, and he rushed forward to the onslaught again.

Tom, as we have before had occasion to suggest, was a master of strategy, and instead of another stroke at the head of his savage foe, with only one chance in ten of hitting the mark he commenced swinging it vigorously to the right and left, as a mower does his scythe. His object was to hit the legs of the dog — a plan which was not entirely original with him, for he had seen it adopted with signal success by a fisherman at the Harbor. The consequence of this change of tactics was soon apparent, for Tige got a rap on the fore leg, which caused him to yelp with pain, and retire from the field. While the dog moved off in good order in one direction, Tom effected an equally admirable retreat in the other direction.

On reaching the road, he pulled on his boots, which he had picked up after the discomfiture of his canine antagonist. Squire Pemberton still stood at the door trying to bring Tige to a sense of his duty in the trying emergency; but the brute had more regard for his own shins than he had for the mandate of his master, and the victor was permitted to bear away his laurels without further opposition.

When he reached his father's house, supposing the front door was locked, he went to the kitchen window, where he had heard the patriotic remarks of his mother. Tom told his story in substance as we have related it.

"Do you mean what you have said, mother? " inquired he, when he had finished his narrative.

Mrs. Somers bit her lip in silence for a moment.

"Certainly I do, Thomas, " said she, desperately.

It was half-past one when the boys retired, but it was another hour before Tom's excited brain would permit him to sleep. His head was full of a big thought.

CHAPTER VIII.

SIGNING THE PAPERS.

Thomas went to sleep at last, and, worn out by the fatigue and excitement of the day, he slept long and soundly. His mother did not call him till eight o'clock, and it was nine before he reached the store of his employer, where the recital of the adventure of the preceding night proved to be a sufficient excuse for his non-appearance at the usual hour.

In the course of the week Captain Benson had procured the necessary authority to raise a company for three years or for the war. When he exhibited his papers, he found twenty persons ready to put down their names. A recruiting office was opened at the store, and every day added to the list of brave and self-denying men who were ready to go forward and fight the battles of liberty and union. The excitement in Pinchbrook was fanned by the news which each day brought of the zeal and madness of the traitors.

Thomas had made up his mind, even before his mother had been surprised into giving her consent, that he should go to the war. At the first opportunity, therefore, he wrote his name upon the paper, very much to the astonishment of Captain Benson and his employer.

"How old are you, Tom?" asked the captain.

"I'm in my seventeenth year," replied the soldier boy.

"You are not old enough."

"I'm three months older than Sam Thompson; and you didn't even ask him how old he was."

"He is larger and heavier than you are!"

"I can't help that. I'm older than he is, and I think I can do as much in the way of fighting as he can."

"I don't doubt that," added the captain, laughing. "Your affair with Squire Pemberton shows that you have pluck enough for anything. I should be very glad to have you go; but what does your father say?"

"He hasn't said anything. He isn't at home. He went away before Sumter was fired upon by the rebels."

"True—I remember. What does your mother say?"

"O, she is willing."

"Are you sure, Tom?"

"Of course, I am. Suppose you write something by which she can give her consent, and she will sign it."

Captain Benson drew up the document, and when Tom went home to dinner, he presented it to his mother for her signature.

"I hope you won't back out, mother," said he, as she put on her spectacles, and proceeded to ascertain the contents of the document.

"Back out of what, Thomas?"

"I've signed the muster roll, and I belong to Captain Benson's company now."

"You!" exclaimed Mrs. Somers, lowering the paper, and gazing earnestly into the face of the young man, to discover whether he was in earnest.

"Yes, mother; you said you were willing, and I have signed the papers; but Captain Benson wants your consent in writing, so that there shall be no mistake about it."

The mother read the paper in silence and sadness, for the thought of having her noble boy exposed to the perils of the camp and the march, the skirmish and the battle, was terrible, and nothing but the most exalted patriotism could induce a mother to give a son to his country.

"I don't want to sign this paper, Thomas," said she, when she had finished reading it.

"Have you forgot what you said the other night, mother?"

"No, I haven't forgot it, and I feel now just as I did then. If there is any real need of your going, I am willing you should go."

"Need? Of course there is need of soldiers. The President wasn't joking when he called for seventy-five thousand men."

"But there are enough to go without you."

"That's just what everybody might say, and then there wouldn't be anybody to go."

"But you are young, and not very strong."

"I'm old enough, and strong enough. When I can get a day to myself, I don't think it's any great hardship to carry father's heavy fowling-piece from sunrise to sunset; and I guess I can stand it to carry a musket as long as any of them."

"You are only a boy."

"I shall be a man soon enough."

"When you have gone, John will want to go too."

"No, mother, I don't want to go into the army," said John, with a sly wink at his brother. "I shall never be a soldier if I can help it."

"What am I going to do, if you all go off and leave me?" added Mrs. Somers, trying hard to keep down a tear which was struggling for birth in her fountain of sorrows.

"I don't think you will want for anything, mother. I'm sure I wouldn't leave you, if I thought you would. I don't get but two dollars and a half a week in the store, and I shall have eleven dollars a month in the army, and it won't cost me any thing for board or clothes. I will send every dollar I get home to you."

"You are a good boy, Thomas," replied Mrs. Somers, unable any longer to restrain the tear.

"I know you and John both will do every thing you can for me. If your father was only at home, I should feel different about it."

"He would believe in my fighting for my country, if he were here."

"I know he would," said Mrs. Somers, as she took the pen which Thomas handed her, and seated herself at the table. "If you are determined to go, I suppose you will go, whether I am willing or not."

"No, mother, I will not," added Thomas, decidedly. "I shouldn't have signed the muster roll if you hadn't said you were willing. And if you say now that you won't consent, I will take my name off the paper."

"But you want to go—don't you?"

"I do; there's no mistake about that: but I won't go if you are not willing."

Mrs. Somers wrote her name upon the paper. It was a slow and difficult operation to her, and during the time she was thus occupied, the rest of the family watched her in silent anxiety. Perhaps, if she had not committed herself on the eventful night when she fully believed that Thomas had run away and joined the army, she might have offered more and stronger objections than she now urged. But there was a vein of patriotism in her nature, which she had inherited from her father, who had fought at Bunker Hill, Brandywine, and Germantown, and which had been exemplified in the life of her brother; and this, more than any other consideration, induced her to sign the paper.

Thousands of loving and devoted mothers have given their sons to their country in the same holy enthusiasm that inspired her. She was not a solitary instance of this noble sacrifice, and if both her sons had been men, instead of boys, she would not have interposed a single objection to their departure upon a mission so glorious as that to which Thomas had now devoted himself.

"There's my name, Thomas," said his mother, as she took off her spectacles. "I've done it, and you have my free consent. You've always been a good boy, and I hope you will always be a good soldier."

"I shall always try to do my duty, mother; and if ever I turn my back to a rebel, I hope you'll disown me."

"Good, Tom!" exclaimed John, who had been deeply interested in the event of the hour.

"Well, Thomas, I'd rather face two rebels than that bull dog you fit with t'other night," added gran'ther Greene. "You are as bold as a lion, Thomas."

"Do you think I can stand it, gran'ther?" added Tom, with a smile.

"Stand it? Well, Thomas, it's a hard life to be a soldier, and I know something about it. When we marched from—"

"Dinner's ready," interposed Mrs. Somers, for gran'ther Greene had marched that march so many times that every member of the family knew it by heart.

"There's one good thing about it, Tom," said John: "you have got a first-rate captain."

"I'm thankful you are going with Captain Benson, for if there ever was a Christian in Pinchbrook, he is the man," added Mrs. Somers.

"And all the company will be your own friends and neighbors," said gran'ther Greene; "and that's something, I can tell you. I know something about this business. When we marched from—"

"Have some more beans, brother?" asked Mrs. Somers. "You will be among your friends, Thomas, as gran'ther says."

"That's a great thing, I can tell you," added the veteran. "Soldiers should stick together like brothers, and feel that they are fighting for each other, as well as for the country. Then, when you're sick, you want friends. When we marched from Sackett's Harbor, there was a young feller—"

"Have some more tea, brother?"

"Part of a cup, Nancy," replied the old man, who never took offence even when the choicest stories of his military experience were nipped in the bud.

After dinner, Thomas hastened back to the store. That day seemed to him like an epoch in his existence, as indeed it was. He felt that he belonged to his country now, and that the honor of that old flag, which had been insulted by traitors, was committed to his keeping. He was taking up the work where his grandfather had left it. He was going forth to fight for his country, and the thought inspired him with a noble and generous enthusiasm, before which all the aspirations of his youth vanished.

As he passed the house of Squire Pemberton, he bestowed a pitying reflection upon the old traitor; but his mind was so full of the great event which was dawning upon him, that he did not even think of the exciting incidents which had occurred there. He had neither seen nor heard any thing of the squire since he had escaped from the attic chamber.

Just beyond the squire's house he met Captain Barney, who was riding up to the town hall.

"What's this I hear of you, Tom? " demanded the captain, as he reined in his horse. "They say you have joined the company. "

"Yes, sir. I have. "

"Bravo! my boy. Good on your head! You ought to go out as a brigadier general. What does your mother say? "

"I have her written consent in my pocket. "

"All right. God bless you, my boy! " said the old salt, as he started his horse.

"Thank you, sir. There's only one thing that troubles me. "

"Eh? What's that, my boy? " demanded Captain Barney as he reined up the horse again.

"I suppose you have heard of my scrape at Squire Pemberton's the other night. "

"Yes; and shiver my timbers if I didn't want to keelhaul the old traitor when I heard of it. "

"I don't care anything about the scrape, sir; only I'm afraid the squire will bother my mother when I'm gone, " said Thomas, with some diffidence.

"If he does, he'll settle the matter with Jack Barney, " replied the captain, decidedly.

"My father may never come back, you know, and if he does he will be a beggar. He owes the squire a note, which will be due in June. "

"I'll pay it myself! " roared Captain Barney. "Go and fight for your country, Tom, like a man. I'll call and see your mother once a week, or every day in the week, if you say so. She shall not want for any thing as long as I have a shot in the locker. "

"Thank you, Captain Barney; thank you, sir. "

"I'll take care of your mother, my lad, and I'll take care of the squire. He shall not foreclose that mortgage, Tom. Don't bother your head about any of those things. You're a good boy, Tom, and I'll keep every thing all right at home. "

"Thank you, sir, " repeated the soldier boy, as Captain Barney started his horse again.

The captain was a retired shipmaster, of ample means, and Tom knew that he was not only able, but willing, to do all he had promised. His heart was lighter; a load had been removed from his mind.

CHAPTER IX.

THE DEPARTURE.

At the time of which we write, recruiting officers were not very particular in regard to the age of those whom they received into the volunteer army. If the young man seemed to have the requisite physical qualifications, it was of little consequence what his age was; and Tom Somers was tall enough and stout enough to make a very good soldier.

Captain Benson examined the certificate brought to him by the young recruit, not, however, because it was deemed a necessary legal form, but because he was acquainted with his father and mother, and would not willingly have done any thing to displease them. The matter, therefore, was disposed of to the satisfaction of all the parties concerned, and Tom actually commenced his career as a soldier boy. He immediately resigned his situation in the store, for the company now numbered forty men, not half a dozen of whom had any knowledge whatever of military drill.

As the volunteers of the Pinchbrook company could ill afford to lose the time devoted to drill before they should be mustered into the service of the United States, the town voted to pay each man fifteen dollars a month for three months. This generous and patriotic action of the town rejoiced the heart of Tom Somers, for his mother actually needed the pittance he had earned at the store. Mrs. Somers had heard nothing from her husband; but the destruction of the Gosport Navy Yard, and the seizure of several northern vessels in the harbor of Norfolk, left her little to hope for in that direction. Suddenly an impregnable wall seemed to rise up between the North and the South, and she not only feared that Captain Somers had lost all his worldly possessions, but that he would hardly be able to escape himself from the fiery furnace of secession and treason.

To her, therefore, the future looked dark and forbidding. She foresaw that she and her family would be subjected to the pressure of want, or at least be dependent upon the kindness of friends for support. She had freely stated her fears to her children, and fully exhibited the insufficiency of the family resources. The vote of the town was a perfect godsend to Tom, and a fat legacy from a rich relative would not have kindled a stronger feeling of gratitude in his soul.

For the next five weeks, Tom was employed forenoon, afternoon, and evening, in the drill, and he soon made himself proficient. The company was recruited nearly up to its maximum number, and was then attached to the —th regiment, which had just been formed and ordered to Fort Warren.

On the 27th day of May, the company, escorted by the patriotic citizens of Pinchbrook, marched to Boston, and Tom took a sorrowful farewell of his mother, his brother and sisters, and a score of anxious friends.

"Now don't let the rebels hit you in the backbone, Thomas, " said gran'ther Green, as he shook the hand of the soldier boy.

"No, gran'ther; if I can't fight, I won't run away, " replied Tom.

"You've got good blood in your veins, my boy: don't disgrace it. I don't know as you'll ever see me again, but God bless you, Thomas;" and the old man turned away to hide the tears which began to course down his wrinkled cheek.

"Be a good boy, Thomas, " added his mother.

"I will, mother. "

"And remember what I've been telling you. I'm not half so much afraid of your being killed by a bullet, as I am of your being ruined by bad men. "

"You needn't fear any thing of that kind, mother. "

"I shall pray that you may be saved from your friends as well as from your enemies. We shall see you again before you go off, I hope."

"Yes, mother; we shall not be sent south yet. "

"Don't forget to read your Testament, Thomas, " said Mrs. Somers.

"I won't, mother, " replied the soldier boy, as he again shook hands with all the members of the family, kissed his mother and his sisters, and hitching up his knapsack, took his place in the ranks.

His heart seemed to be clear up in his throat. During the tender scene he had just passed through, he had manfully resisted his inclination to weep, but he could no longer restrain the tears. Suddenly they came like a flood bursting the gates that confined it, and he choked and sobbed like a little girl. He leaned upon his musket, covering his face with his arm.

"It's a hard case, " said private Hapgood, who stood next to him in the ranks.

"I didn't think it would take me down like this, " sobbed Tom.

"Don't blubber, Tom. Let's go off game, " added Ben Lethbridge, who stood on the other side of him.

"I can't help it, Ben. "

"Yes, you can—dry up! Soldiers don't cry, Tom. "

"Yes, they do, my boy, " said Hapgood, who was a little old man, nearly ten years beyond the period of exemption from military duty. "I don't blame Tom for crying, and, in my opinion, he'll fight all the better for it. "

"Perhaps he will, old un; but I don't think much of a soldier that blubbers like a baby. I hope he won't run away when he sees the rebels coming, " sneered Ben.

"If he does, he'll have a chance to see how thick the heels of your boots are, " answered the old man.

"What do you mean by that, old un? " demanded Ben.

"Attention—company! Shoulder—arms! Forward—march! " said the captain; and the discussion was prevented from proceeding any further.

The band, which was at the head of the citizens' column, struck up an inspiring march, and Tom dried his tears. The escort moved off, followed by the company. They passed the little cottage of Captain Somers, and Tom saw the whole family except John, who was in the escort, standing at the front gate. The old soldier swung his hat, Tom's sisters and his mother waved their handkerchiefs; but when they saw the soldier boy, they had to use them for another purpose. Tom felt another upward pressure in the region of the throat; but this time he choked down his rising emotions, and saved himself from the ridicule of his more callous companion on the left.

In violation of military discipline, he turned his head to take one last, fond look at the home he was leaving behind. It might be the last time he should ever gaze on that loved spot, now a thousand times more dear than ever before. Never had he realized the meaning of home; never before had he felt how closely his heart's tendrils were entwined about that hallowed place. Again, in spite of his firmness and fortitude, and in spite of the sneers of Ben Lethbridge, he felt the hot tears sliding down his cheek.

When he reached the brow of the hill which would soon hide the little cottage from his view, perhaps forever, he gazed behind him again, to take his last look at the familiar spot. His mother and sister still stood at the front gate watching the receding column in which the son and the brother was marching away to peril and perhaps death.

"God bless my mother! God bless them all!" were the involuntary ejaculations of the soldier boy, as he turned away from the hallowed scene.

But the memory of that blessed place, sanctified by the presence of those loving and devoted ones, was shrined in the temple of his heart, ever to go with him in camp and march, in the perils of battle and siege, to keep him true to his God, true to himself, and true to those whom he had left behind him. That last look at home and those that make it home, like the last fond gaze we bestow on the loved and the lost, was treasured up in the garner of the heart's choicest memories, to be recalled in the solemn stillness of the midnight vigil, amid the horrors of the battle-field when the angry strife of arms had ceased, and in the gloom of the soldier's sick bed when no mother's hand was near to lave the fevered brow.

The moment when he obtained his last view of the home of his childhood seemed like the most eventful period of his existence. His heart grew big in his bosom, and yet not big enough to contain all he felt. He wept again, and his tears seemed to come from deeper down than his eyes. He did not hear the inspiring strains of the band, or the cheers that greeted the company as they went forth to do and die for their country's imperilled cause.

"Blubbering again, Tom? " sneered Ben Lethbridge. "I thought you was more of a man than that, Tom Somers. "

"I can't help it, Ben, " replied Tom, vainly struggling to subdue his emotions.

"Better go back, then. We don't want a great baby in the ranks. "

"It's nateral, Ben, " said old Hapgood. "He'll get over it when he sees the rebels. "

"Don't believe he will. I didn't think you were such a great calf, Tom."

"Shet up, now, Ben, " interposed Hapgood. "I'll bet my life he'll stand fire as well as you will. I've been about in the world some, and I reckon I've as good an idee of this business as you have. Tom's got a heart under his ribs. "

"I'll bet he runs away at the first fire. "

"I'll bet he won't. "

"I know I won't! " exclaimed Tom, with energy, as he drew his coat sleeve across his eyes.

"It isn't the cock that crows the loudest that will fight the best, " added the old man. "I'll bet Tom will be able to tell you the latest news from the front, where the battle's the hottest. I fit my way up to the city of Mexico long er old Scott, and I've heard boys crow afore today. "

"Look here, old un! If you mean to call me a coward, why don't you say so, right up and down? " growled Ben.

"Time'll tell, my boy. You don't know what gunpowder smells like yet. If you'd been with the fust Pennsylvany, where I was, you'd a-known sunthin about war. Now, shet up, Ben; and don't you worry Tom any more."

But Tom was no longer in a condition to be worried. Though still sad at the thought of the home and friends he had left behind, he had reduced his emotions to proper subjection, and before the column reached Boston, he had even regained his wonted cheerfulness. The procession halted upon the wharf, where the company was to embark on a steamer for Fort Warren. As the boat which was to convey them to the fort had not yet arrived, the men were permitted to mingle with their friends on the wharf, and, of course, Tom immediately sought out his brother. He found him engaged in a spirited conversation with Captain Benson.

"What is it, Jack?" asked the soldier boy.

"I want to join this company, and the captain won't let me," replied John.

"You, Jack!"

"Yes, I."

"Did mother say so?"

"No, but she won't care."

"Did you ask her?"

"No; I didn't think of going till after I started from home."

"Don't think of it, Jack. It would be an awful blow to mother to have both of us go."

For half an hour Tom argued the matter with John; but the military enthusiasm of the latter had been so aroused by the march and its attendant circumstances, that he could not restrain his inclination.

"If I don't join this company, I shall some other," said John.

"I shall have to go home again, if you do; for I won't have mother left alone. We haven't been mustered in yet. Besides, I thought you wanted to go into the navy."

"I do; but I'm bound to go somehow, " replied John.

But what neither Tom nor Captain Benson could do, was accomplished by Captain Barney, who declared John should go home with him if he had to take him by the collar. The ardent young patriot yielded as gracefully as he could to this persuasion.

The steamer having arrived, the soldiers shook hands with their friends again, went on board, and, amid the hearty cheers of the citizens of Pinchbrook, were borne down the bay.

CHAPTER X.

COMPANY K.

Tom Somers felt that he was now a soldier indeed. While the company remained in Pinchbrook, he had slept every night in his own bed, and taken his meals in the kitchen of the little cottage. He fully realized that he had bade a long farewell to all the comforts and luxuries of home. That day, for the first time, he was to partake of soldiers' fare, and that night, for the first time, he was to sleep upon a soldier's bed. These thoughts did not make him repine, for before he signed the muster roll, he had carefully considered, with the best information he could obtain, what hardships and privations he would be called to endure. He had made up his mind to bear all things without a murmur for the blessed land of his birth, which now called upon her sons to defend her from the parricidal blow of the traitor.

Tom had not only made up his mind to bear all these things, but to bear them patiently and cheerfully. He had a little theory of his own, that rather more than half of the discomforts of this mortal life exist only in the imagination. If he only *thought* that every thing was all right, it went a great way towards making it all right—a very comforting and satisfactory philosophy, which reduced the thermometer from ninety down to seventy degrees on a hot day in summer, and raised it from ten to forty degrees on a cold day in winter; which filled his stomach when it was empty, alleviated the toothache or the headache, and changed snarling babies into new-fledged angels. I commend Tom's philosophy to the attention and imitation of all my young friends, assured that nothing will keep them so happy and comfortable as a cheerful and contented disposition.

"Tom Somers, " said a voice near him, cutting short the consoling meditation in which he was engaged.

His name was pronounced in a low and cautious tone, but the voice sounded familiar to him, and he turned to ascertain who had addressed him. He did not discover any person who appeared to be the owner of the voice, and was leaving the position he had taken on the forward deck of the steamer, when his name was repeated, in the same low and cautious tone.

"Who is it? Where are you?" said Tom, looking all about him, among the groups of soldiers who were gathered on various parts of the deck, discussing the present and the future.

"Here, Tom," replied the voice, which sounded more familiar every time he heard it.

He turned his eye in the direction from which the sound proceeded, and there, coiled up behind a heap of barrels and boxes, and concealed by a sail-cloth which had been thrown over the goods to protect them from an expected shower, he discovered Fred Pemberton.

"What in the name of creation are you doing there, Fred?" exclaimed Tom, laughing at the ludicrous attitude of the embryo secessionist.

"Hush! Don't say a word, Tom. Sit down here where I can talk with you," added Fred.

"What are you doing here?"

"I'll tell if you will keep quiet a moment. Is the company full?"

"What company?"

"Captain Benson's, of course."

"No."

"I want to join."

"You!" ejaculated Tom.

"Come, come, Tom, no blackguarding now. You and I used to be good friends."

"I've nothing against you, Fred—that is, if you're not a traitor."

"I want to join the company."

"Is your father willing?"

"Of course he isn't; but that needn't make any difference."

"But you don't believe in our cause, Fred. We don't want a traitor in the ranks."

"Hang the cause! I want to go with the company."

"Hang the cause? Well, I reckon that's a good recommendation."

"I'm all right on that."

"Are you willing to take the oath of allegiance, and swear to sustain the flag of your country?"

"Of course I am. I only followed the old man's lead; but I have got enough of it. Do you think Captain Benson will take me into the company?"

"Perhaps he will."

"Ask him—will you? You needn't say I'm here, you know."

"But what will your father say?"

"I don't care what he says."

Tom thought, if Fred didn't care, he needn't, and going aft, he found the captain, and proposed to him the question.

"Take him—yes. We'll teach him loyalty and patriotism, and before his time is out, we will make him an abolitionist," replied Captain Benson. "What will his father say?"

"His father doesn't know anything about it. Fred ran away, and followed the company into the city."

"Squire Pemberton is a traitor, and I believe the army will be the best school in the world for his son," added the captain. "It will be better for him to be with us than to be at home. If it was the son of any other man in Pinchbrook, I wouldn't take him without the consent of his father; as it is, I feel perfectly justified in accepting him."

Tom hastened to the forward deck to report the success of his mission. The result was, that Fred came out of his hiding-place, and exhibited himself to the astonished members of the Pinchbrook company. When he announced his intention to go to the war, and, with a pardonable flourish, his desire to serve his country, he was saluted with a volley of cheers. Captain Benson soon appeared on the forward deck, and the name of the new recruit was placed on the enlistment paper.

Fred was seventeen years of age, and was taller and stouter than Tom Somers. No questions were asked in regard to his age or his physical ability to endure the hardships of a campaign.

The steamer arrived at Fort Warren, and the company landed. After waiting a short time on the wharf, the color company of the —th regiment, to which they were attached, came down and escorted them to the parade ground within the fort. It was a desolate and gloomy-looking place to Tom, who had always lived among green fields, and the beautiful surroundings of a New England rural district.

If the fort itself looked dreary, how much more so were the casemates in which the company was quartered! But Tom's philosophy was proof against the unpleasant impression, and his joke was as loud and hearty as that of any of his companions. The men were divided off into messes, and they had an abundance of work to do in bringing up the company's luggage, and making their new habitation as comfortable and pleasant as the circumstances would permit.

The next day the Pinchbrook boys were designated as Company K, and placed in the regimental line. The limits of this volume do not permit me to detail the every-day life of the soldier boy while at Fort Warren, however interesting and instructive it might be to our friends. A large portion of the forenoon was devoted to squad and company drill, and of the afternoon to battalion drill. The colonel, though a very diminutive man in stature, was an enthusiast in military matters, and had the reputation of being one of the most thorough and skilful officers in the state. Tom Somers, who, since he joined the company, had felt ashamed of himself because he was no bigger, became quite reconciled to his low corporeal estate when he found that the colonel of the regiment was no taller and no heavier than himself. And when he heard the high praise bestowed upon the colonel's military skill and martial energy, he came to the conclusion that it does not require a big man to make a good soldier. With a feeling of satisfaction he recalled the fact that Napoleon Bonaparte, when he commanded the army of Italy, was scarcely a bigger man than the colonel or himself.

The colonel was a strict disciplinarian, and he soon diffused his energy throughout the regiment. It made rapid progress in its military education. Tom was deeply interested in the details of his new profession, and used his best endeavors to do his duty promptly and faithfully. This was not the case with all the boys in the company from Pinchbrook, and I am sorry to say that some of them, including the brave and chivalric Ben Lethbridge, had to sit upon the stool of repentance in the guard room on several occasions.

Fred Pemberton was clothed in the uniform of the United States volunteers, and we must do him the justice to say that he performed his duty to the entire satisfaction of his officers. Fred was a good fellow, and barring his treason, which he had derived from his father, was highly esteemed by those who knew him. The only stain that had ever rested upon his character was removed, and he and Tom were as good friends as ever they had been. His motive in joining the army, however, could not be applauded. He thought all his friends were going off to the South upon a kind of frolic, spiced with a little of peril and hardship to make it the more exciting, and he did not like the idea of being left behind. To the sentiment of patriotism, as developed in the soul of Tom Somers and many of his companions, he was an entire stranger. He was going to the war to participate in the adventures of the —th regiment, rather than to fight for the flag which had been insulted and dishonored by treason.

Every day the steamers brought crowds of visitors to the fort to see their friends in the regiments quartered there, or to witness the drills and parades which were constantly succeeding each other. Among them came many of the people of Pinchbrook, and Tom was delighted by a visit from his whole family. His mother found him so comfortable and contented that she returned with half the heavy burden on her soul removed.

While the Pinchbrook boys were generally rejoiced to see their friends from home, there was one in the company who was in constant dread lest he should recognize a too familiar face in the crowds which the steamers daily poured into the fort. Fred Pemberton did not wish to see his nearest friends; but after he had been in the company some ten days, just as the boys had been dismissed from the forenoon drill, he discovered at a distance the patriarchal form of his father.

"My pipe's out, Tom, " said Fred, as he rushed into the casemate where a group of his companions were resting from the fatigues of the morning.

"What's the matter now, Fred? "

"The old man has just come into the fort. "

"Has he? "

"Yes—what shall I do? "

"Keep a stiff upper lip, Fred, and we will put you through all right, " said Sergeant Porter.

"What shall I do? " demanded Fred, who, whatever his views in regard to the justice or injustice of coercion, did not wish to be taken from the company.

"Come with me, " said the sergeant, as he led the way into an adjoining casemate. "No; nobody else will come, " added he, motioning back other members of the mess who was disposed to follow.

In the casemate to which Sergeant Porter conducted Fred, there was a pile of boxes, in which the muskets of one of the regiments had been packed. The fugitive from his father's anxious search was directed to get into one of these boxes, from which the sergeant removed the gun rests. He obeyed; his confederate put on the lid so as to permit him to receive a plentiful supply of air, and other boxes were placed upon that containing the runaway.

Squire Pemberton presented himself before Captain Benson, and demanded his son. Fred was sent for, but could not be found. Sergeant Porter kept out of the way, and not another man in the company knew anything about him. The boys were very willing to assist the indignant father in his search, but all their efforts were unavailing. The squire examined every casemate, and every nook and corner upon the island, but without effect.

"I want my son, sir, " said the squire, angrily, to the captain. "I require you to produce him. "

"I don't know where he is, " replied Captain Benson.

"You have concealed him, sir. "

"I have not. "

The squire appealed to the colonel, but obtained no satisfaction, and was obliged to leave without accomplishing his purpose. As soon as he had gone, Fred appeared, and the boys laughed for a week over the affair.

CHAPTER XI.

IN WASHINGTON.

On the 17th of June, the regiment left Port Warren, and after being conveyed by steamer to Boston, marched to Camp Cameron. Here the "little colonel" displayed his energy and military skill to much greater advantage than when within the narrow confines of the fort. The men were not only carefully and persistently drilled, but they were educated, as far as the circumstances would permit, for the arduous duties of a campaign.

Tom Somers had already begun to feel a soldier's pride in his new situation; and though he found that being a soldier boy was not always the easiest and the pleasantest thing in the world, he bore his trials with philosophical patience and fortitude, and made the most of whatever joys the circumstances placed within his reach.

Others grumbled, but he did not. He declared that he had enlisted for the war, and meant to take things as they came. It was not exactly agreeable to stand on guard for two hours, on a cold, rainy night; but grumbling would not make it any the more agreeable, and only made the grumbler discontented and unhappy. It did not look like "the pomp and circumstance of war, " and no doubt most of the boys in the Pinchbrook company would have been better satisfied in their own houses in "the village by the sea. " But most of these men had left their happy homes under the inspiration of the highest and truest motives. They were going forth to fight the battles of their imperilled country, and this reflection filled them with a heroism which the petty trials and discomforts of the camp could not impair.

While the regiment was at Camp Cameron, the state colors and a standard, procured by the liberality of its friends, were presented; and the patriotic speeches delivered on this occasion made a deep impression upon the mind and heart of the soldier boy. To him they were real—perhaps more real than to those who uttered the burning words. He was in a situation to feel the full force of the great sacrifice which the soldier makes for his country. He devoted himself, heart and soul, to the cause; and what was but an idle sentiment in the mind of the flowery speech-makers, was truth and soberness to him who was to meet the foe at the cannon's mouth and at the bayonet's point.

"We are off on the 29th, " said old Hapgood, one evening, as he entered the barrack where Tom was writing a letter to his mother.

"Good! I am glad to hear it. I was just telling my mother that I hoped we should not have to stay much longer in this place, " replied Tom.

"I think we are having an easy time of it here, " added the veteran. "When you find out what hunger and fatigue mean, you will learn to be contented with such a place as this. "

"I'm contented enough; but I want to get into the field, and have something done. "

"Time enough, my boy. I used to feel just so, Tom, when I went to Mexico; but after a while I got so I didn't care what we did or where we went. "

Tom added a postscript to his letter, informing his mother of the time fixed for the departure of the regiment. The intelligence in this instance proved to be correct, for on the appointed day the little colonel marched his command into the city, where it was duly embarked on the cars for New York. It was a day of excitement, for the streets of the city were thronged with people, whose cheers and applause were the benison with which the regiment went forth to do and to die for the nation. Tom was delighted with this warm reception, but more by meeting his mother and his brother and sisters at the station. It was a joyous and yet a sad meeting. Mrs. Somers wept; and what mother would not weep to see her son go forth to encounter the perils of the battle-field, and the greater perils of the camp?

It was a sad parting; and many a mother's heart was torn with anguish on that day, when she pressed her noble boy to her bosom, for the last time, as she gave him to his country. Cold, stern men, who had never wept before, wept then—the flesh that was in their stony hearts yielded its unwilling tribute to nature and affection.

"All aboard! " shouted the officers, when the train was ready to depart.

"God bless you, my boy! " sobbed Mrs. Somers, as she kissed her son. "Be good and true, and don't forget to read your Testament. "

"Good by, mother, " was all that Tom could say, as he grasped his musket, which John had been holding for him, and rushed into the car.

The train moved off amid the cheers of the thousands who had gathered to witness their departure. At this moment, more than ever before, the soldier boy realized what he had done when he entered the service. He listened to the shouts of the multitude, but he was sad and silent. He sank into his seat, and gave himself up to the anguish of the hour. On and on dashed the train, and his thoughts still dwelt upon the home and the mother he had left behind him.

Our readers can better imagine than we can describe the feelings of the soldier boy during that long night. The regiment arrived in New York at half-past ten in the forenoon of the following day, and was escorted up Broadway by the Sons of Massachusetts. At the Park, it was warmly welcomed by the President of the Sons, and as the little colonel was a better soldier than a speech-maker, the response was made by the surgeon. By this time, Tom was able to enter into the spirit of the occasion, and the flattering ovation bestowed upon the regiment was a source of personal pride and satisfaction. The little colonel's command was declared to be the best drilled and most soldierly body of men which had yet departed for the battle-fields of the republic.

The great city was full of wonders to the soldier boy, and during the few hours he remained there, he was in a constant whirl of excitement. If the mission before him had been less grand and sublime, he could have wished to spend a few days in exploring the wonders of the great metropolis; but the stupendous events that loomed up in the future, prophetic even to the inexperienced eye of youth, engrossed all his thoughts. He partook of the bountiful collation in the Park, and was content to march on to scenes more thrilling and exciting than the tumult of the busy city.

The regiment took a steamer, at half-past four for Elizabethport, and thence proceeded by railroad to Washington, by the way of Harrisburg. Some portions of the journey were performed under the most trying circumstances. The men were crowded, like sheep, into unsuitable cars, so that not only were they subjected to many needless discomforts, but their very lives were endangered. On the way, two men were crowded out of a car, and, for a time, were supposed to have been killed.

The Soldier Boy; or, Tom Somers in the Army

On the 2d of July, they arrived at Washington, and Tom had an opportunity to see the "city of magnificent distances, " of which he had heard so much. The regiment marched from the station, through Pennsylvania Avenue, to their camp ground in the rear of the White House. They were received with enthusiasm by the people, but the miserable uniforms with which they had been supplied, now faded and dilapidated, with the finishing touch of destruction given to them by the perilous journey they had made, gave the politicians their first lesson on the worthlessness of "shoddy. "

The regiment entered the grounds of the White House, and as it passed up the avenue, President Lincoln appeared in front of his mansion. The boys greeted him with a volley of stunning cheers, which the President acknowledged by a series of bows, which were not half so ungraceful as one might have expected after reading the descriptions of him contained in the newspapers.

To Tom Somers the President was a great institution, and he could scarcely believe that he was looking upon the chief magistrate of this great nation. He was filled with boyish wonder and astonishment; but, after all, he was forced to admit that the President, though a tall specimen of humanity, looked very much like the rest of mankind — to borrow a phrase from one of his illustrious predecessors.

Tom was too tired to wonder long at the grandeur of the Capitol, and the simple magnificence of the President. The tents were pitched, and the weary men were allowed a season of rest. In a couple of days, however, our soldier boy was "as good as new. "

"Come, Tom, it is about time for you too see something of the city, " said Ben Lethbridge, one afternoon, after the regiment had become fairly settled in its new quarters.

"I should like to take a tramp. There are lots of congressmen here, and I should like to know what they look like, " replied Tom. "I haven't been outside the lines since we came here. "

"I have; and I'm going again! Fred and I mean to have a good time to-day. Will you go? "

"Have you got a pass? "

The Soldier Boy; or, Tom Somers in the Army

"A pass! What a stupid! What do you want of a pass? You can't get one. They won't give any."

"Then we can't go, of course."

"Bah! What a great calf you are! Don't you want to cry again?"

"Ben, you needn't say cry to me again as long as you live," added Tom. "If you do, I'll give you something to cry for."

Tom did not like the style of remark which the other had adopted. He was angry, and, as he spoke, his fist involuntarily clinched, and his eye looked fierce and determined.

"Come, come, Tom; don't bristle up so. If you are a man, just show that you are, and come along with us."

"I say, Ben, I want to know who's a baby or a calf, you or I, before we go, I won't stand any more of your lip."

"Will you go with us?" demanded Ben, who was rather disposed to dodge the issue.

"What do you mean by calling me a calf and a baby? And this isn't the first time you've done it."

"Don't you know that every man in the regiment has been all over the city, and without any pass? When I ask you to go, you begin to talk about a pass."

"I choose to obey orders," replied Tom.

"O, you daresn't go with us."

"Come along!" said Tom, who had not yet learned to bear the taunts of his companion.

"Get your pail."

Tom got his pail, and was immediately joined by Fred and Ben, each of whom was also supplied with a pail. There was no water to be had within the camp ground, and the men were obliged to bring it in pails from the hydrants in the street. A pail, therefore, was quite as good as a written document to enable them to pass the guard.

The party thus provided had no difficulty in passing the sentinels. At a convenient place outside the line, they concealed the pails, and, for three hours, roamed at will over the city.

"Now, Tom, you wanted to see the congressmen? " said Ben, after they had "done" the city pretty thoroughly.

"Yes, but I have seen them at the Capitol. "

"But don't you want to get nearer to them, and hear them talk? "

"Well, I should like to. "

"Come with us, then. "

Ben led the way down the avenue, and entered a building not far from the railroad station. After passing through a long, narrow entry, they ascended a flight of stairs, at the head of which the conductor gave two raps. The door was opened by a negro, and they were invited to enter. At a table in the middle of the room was seated a foppish-looking man who held in his hand a silver box. As he turned it, Tom saw that it contained a pack of cards.

"Where are your congressmen? " asked the soldier boy, whose eyes had been opened by the appearance of the cards.

"They will be here pretty soon, " replied Ben.

The foppish man looked at his watch, and declared they would come in the course of five or ten minutes. He then took the cards out of the box, and, after shuffling them, returned them to their place. Fred placed a "quarter" on the table; the gambler put another by its side, and drew out a card from the silver case. Tom did not understand the game; but his companion put the quarters in his pocket.

"See that, Tom! " said he. "Got any money? "

"If I have I shall keep it. "

"Put down a quarter, and make another. "

"No, sir! I'm no gambler! " replied Tom, with emphasis.

"Quite respectable, I assure you, " added the blackleg at the table.

"I'm going, " said Tom, decidedly.

"Baby! " sneered Ben. "Afraid to play! "

"I *won't* play! I'm going. "

The negro opened the door, and he passed out. Contrary to his expectation, he was followed by Fred and Ben.

"Baby is afraid of cards! " sneered Ben, as they passed through the long entry.

"Afraid of cards, but not afraid of you, " replied Tom, as he planted a heavy blow between the eyes of his companion.

Ben Lethbridge returned the blow, and it cost him another, and there was a prospect of quite a lively skirmish in the entry; but Fred Pemberton interposed his good offices, and effected a compromise, which, like most of the political compromises, was only the postponement of the conflict.

"I told you not to call me 'baby, ' again, " said Tom, as they passed out of the building. "I will convince you before I am done that I'm not a baby. "

Ben found it convenient to offer no reply to this plain statement of facts, and the three soldiers made their way back to the camp, and, having obtained their pails and filled them with water at the hydrants, they passed the guard without a question.

CHAPTER XII.

ON TO RICHMOND.

It so happened that Ben Lethbridge, probably satisfied that it was not the fist of a baby which had partially blackened both of his eyes, and produced a heavy pain under his left ear, did not demand the satisfaction which was needed to heal his wounded honor. The matter was duly discussed in the tent of Tom's mess; but our soldier boy, while he professed to be entirely satisfied, was willing to meet Ben at such time and place as he desired, and finish up the affair.

The other party was magnanimous, and declared that he too was satisfied; and old Hapgood thought they had better proceed no further with the affair, for both of them might be arrested for disorderly conduct.

"I am satisfied, Ben; but if you ever call me a baby or a calf again, it will all have to be settled over again, " said Tom, as he laid aside his musket, which he had been cleaning during the conversation.

"I don't want to quarrel with you, Tom, " replied Ben, "but I wish you would be a little more like the rest of the fellows. "

"What do you mean by that? I am like the rest of the fellows. "

"You wouldn't play cards. "

"Yes, I will play cards, but I won't gamble; and there isn't many fellows in the company that will. "

"That's so, " added Hapgood. "I know all about that business. When I went to Mexico, I lost my money as fast as I got it, playing cards. Don't gamble, boys. "

"I won't, for one, " said Tom, with emphasis.

"Are you going to set up for a soldier-saint, too? " sneered Ben, turning to the old man.

"I'm no saint, but I've larned better than to gamble. "

"I think you'd better stop drinking too, " added Ben.

"Come, Ben, you are meaner than dirt, " said Tom, indignantly.

Old Hapgood was a confirmed toper. The people in Pinchbrook said he was a good man, but, they used to add, with a shrug of the shoulders, "pity he drinks. " It was a sad pity, but he seemed to have no power over his appetite. The allusion of Ben to his besetting sin was cruel and mortifying, for the old man had certainly tried to reform, and since the regiment left Boston, he had not tasted the intoxicating cup. He had declared before the mess that he had stopped drinking; so his resolution was known to all his companions, though none of them had much confidence in his ability to carry it out.

"I didn't speak to you, Tom Somers, " said Ben, sharply.

"You said a mean thing in my presence. "

"By and by we shall be having a prayer meeting in our tent every night. "

"If you are invited I hope you will come, " added Tom, "for if prayers will do any body any good, they won't hurt you. "

"If you will take care of yourself, and let me alone, it's all I ask of you. "

"I'm agreed. "

This was about the last of the skirmishing between Tom and Ben. The latter was a little disposed to be bully; and from the time the company left Pinchbrook, he had been in the habit of calling Tom a baby, and other opprobrious terms, till the subject of his sneers could endure them no longer. Tom had come to the conclusion that he could obtain respectful treatment only by the course he had adopted. Perhaps, if he had possessed the requisite patience, he might have attained the same result by a less repulsive and more noble policy.

The regiment remained in Washington about a fortnight. The capital was no longer considered to be in danger. A large body of troops had been massed in and around the city, and the rebels' boast that they would soon capture Washington was no longer heeded. Fear and anxiety had given place to hope and expectation. "On to Richmond! " was the cry sounded by the newspapers, and repeated by the people. The army of newly-fledged soldiers was burning with eagerness to be led against the rebels. "On to Richmond! " shouted citizens and soldiers, statesmen and politicians. Some cursed and some deprecated the cautious slowness of the old general who had never been defeated.

"On to Richmond! " cried the boys in Tom's regiment, and none more earnestly than he.

"Don't hurry old Scott. He knows what he is about. I know something about this business, for I've seen old Scott where the bullets flew thicker'n snow flakes at Christmas, " was the oft-repeated reply of Hapgood, the veteran of Company K.

The movement which had been so long desired and expected was made at last, and the regiment struck its tents, and proceeded over Long Bridge into Virginia. The first camp was at Shuter's Hill, near Alexandria.

"Now we are in for it, " said Tom Somers, when the mess gathered in their tent after the camp was formed. "I hope we shall not remain here long. "

"Don't be in a hurry, my brave boy, " said old Hapgood. "We may stop here a month. "

"I hope not. "

"Don't hope anything about it, Tom. Take things as they come. "

But the impatience of the soldier boy was soon relieved; for at daylight on the morning of the 16th of July, the regiment was routed out, the tents were struck, and at nine o'clock they took up the line of march to the southward. It was "on to Richmond, " in earnest, now, and merrily marched the men, who little knew what trials and sufferings, what scenes of blood and death, lay in their path.

The little colonel's command had been put in Franklin's brigade, which formed a part of Heintzelman's division; but little did Tom or his fellow-soldiers know of anything but their own regiment. The "sacred soil" of Virginia seemed to be covered with Federal soldiers, and whichever way he turned, columns of troops might be seen, all obedient to the one grand impulse of the loyal nation—"On to Richmond."

The great wagons, gun carriages, and caissons rolling slowly along, the rattling drums, with here and there the inspiring strains of a band, the general officers, with their staffs, were full of interest and excitement to the soldier boy; and though the business before him was stern and terrible, yet it seemed like some great pageant, moving grandly along to celebrate, rather than win, a glorious triumph.

The novelty of the movement, however, soon wore away, and it required only a few hours to convince the inexperienced soldiers in our regiment that it was no idle pageant in which they were engaged. The short intervals of rest which were occasionally allowed were moments to be appreciated. All day long they toiled upon their weary way, praying for the night to come, with its coveted hours of repose. The night did come, but it brought no rest to the weary and footsore soldiers.

Tom was terribly fatigued. His knapsack, which had been light upon his buoyant frame in the morning, now seemed to weigh two hundred pounds, while his musket had grown proportionally heavy. Hour after hour, in the darkness of that gloomy night, he trudged on, keeping his place in the ranks with a resolution which neither the long hours nor the weary miles could break down.

"I can't stand this much longer," whined Ben Lethbridge. "I shall drop pretty soon, and die by the roadside."

"No, you won't," added Hapgood. "Stick to it a little while longer; never say die."

"I can't stand it."

"Yes, you can. Only think you can, and you can," added the veteran.

"What do they think we are made of? We can't march all day and all night. I wish I was at home."

"I wish I hadn't come," said Fred Pemberton.

"Cheer up! cheer up, boys. Stick to it a little longer, " said the veteran.

It was three o'clock the next morning before they were permitted to halt, when the boys rolled themselves up in their blankets, and dropped upon the ground. It was positive enjoyment to Tom, and he felt happy; for rest was happiness when the body was all worn out. A thought of the cottage and of his mother crossed his mind, and he dropped asleep to dream of the joys of home.

Short and sweet was that blessed time of rest; for at four o'clock, after only one brief hour of repose, the regiment was turned out again, and resumed its weary march to the southward. But that short interval of rest was a fountain of strength to Tom, and without a murmur he took his place by the side of his grumbling companions. Ben and Fred were disgusted with the army, and wanted to go back; but that was impossible.

Again, for weary hours, they toiled upon the march. They passed Fairfax, and encamped near the railroad station, where a full night's rest was allowed them. By the advice of Hapgood, Tom went to a brook, and washed his aching feet in cold water. The veteran campaigner gave him other useful hints, which were of great service to him. That night he had as good reason to bless the memory of the man who invented sleep as ever Sancho Panza had, and every hour was fully improved.

At six o'clock, the next morning, the regiment marched again. Tom's legs were stiff, but he felt so much better than on the preceding day, that he began to think that he could stand any thing. In the early part of the afternoon his ears were saluted by a new sound—one which enabled him more fully than before to realize the nature of the mission upon which he had been sent. It was the roar of cannon. On that day was fought the battle of Blackburn's Ford; and when the regiment reached its halting-place at Centreville, the story of the fight was told by enthusiastic lips. Massachusetts men had stood firm and resolute before the artillery and musketry of the rebels, and every man who heard the story was proud that he hailed from the Old Bay State, and panted for the time when he might show himself worthy of his origin, and true to the traditions of the past.

The regiment lay in camp the two following days, and the men had an opportunity to recover in some measure from the fatigues of their first severe march. Visions of glory and victory were beginning to dawn upon them. They had listened to the cannon of the enemy, and they knew that the rebels were not many miles distant in front of them. A few days, perhaps a few hours, would elapse before the terrible conflict would commence. Some of those manly forms must soon sleep in the soldier's grave; some of those beating hearts must soon cease to beat forever; but still the brave and the true longed for the hour that would enable them to "strike home" for the nation's salvation.

CHAPTER XIII.

THE BATTLE OF BULL RUN.

"Tumble out! Tumble out! " shouted the sergeant, who was in the mess with the soldiers we have introduced. "Reveille! Don't you hear it? "

"But it isn't morning, " growled Ben Lethbridge.

"I haven't been asleep more than an hour or two, " snarled Fred Pemberton.

"Shut up your heads, and turn out! " said the sergeant.

It was the morning of the eventful twenty-first of July, and it was only two o'clock when the regiment was roused from its slumbers; but there was no great hardship in this fact, for most of the men had been sleeping the greater portion of the time during the preceding two days. Tom Somers was ready to take his place in the line in a few moments.

"Come, fellows, hurry up, " said he to his tardy companions. "The time has come, and, I tell you, there'll be music before many hours. "

"Where are we going, Tom? Have you any idea? " asked Fred.

"Going down to Manassas Junction, I suppose. That's where the rebels are. "

"Do you suppose we shall get into a fight? " asked Ben.

"I don't know; I hope so. "

"So do I, " returned Ben, faintly; "but I don't like to be broke of my rest in this way. "

Tom, full of excited anticipations in regard to the events of the day, laughed heartily at this reply, and left the tent. The regiment was formed in line, but there were two vacancies in the section to which he belonged. Fred and Ben had answered to their names at roll call.

On some pretence they had asked permission to leave the line for a few moments, and that was the last that had been seen of them.

"Where do you suppose they are? " said Tom to Hapgood.

"I don't know. I hain't got much confidence in Ben's pluck, and I shouldn't wonder if he had run away. "

"But that is desertion. "

"That's just what you may call it; and I've seen men shot for it. "

The regiment remained in line several hours before the order came to move. At daylight, while the men were still standing in the road, four soldiers, attended by a staff officer, conducted the two missing men of Company K into the presence of the regiment.

"These men say they belong to your regiment, " said the officer, saluting the little colonel.

Captain Benson immediately claimed them, and Fred and Ben were ordered into the ranks.

"Cowards—are you? " said the captain. "You shall take your places in the ranks, and at the right time we will settle this case. "

"I enlisted without my father's consent, and you can't hold me if I don't choose to stay, " replied Fred Pemberton.

"Next time you must ask your father before you come. It is too late to repent now. "

"I'm going home. "

"No, you're not. Sergeant, if either of those men attempt to leave the ranks again, shoot them! " said the captain.

Fred and Ben took their places in the ranks amid the laughter and jeers of the company.

"Who's the baby now? " said Bob Dornton.

"You have disgraced the company," added old Hapgood. "I didn't think you would run away before the battle commenced."

"I shall keep both eyes on you, my boys, and if you skulk again, I'll obey orders—by the Lord Harry, I will!" said the sergeant, as he glanced at the lock of his musket. "Company K isn't going to be laughed at for your cowardice."

At six o'clock the order came for the brigade to march. It now consisted of only three regiments, for the time of one, composed of three months' men, had expired while at Centreville; and though requested and importuned to remain a few days longer, they basely withdrew, even while they were on the very verge of the battlefield. This regiment left, and carried with it the scorn and contempt of the loyal and true men, who were as ready to fight the battles of their country on one day as on another.

The men knew they were going to battle now, for the enemy was only a few miles distant. The soldier boy's heart was full of hope. He knew not what a battle was; he could form no adequate conception of the terrible scene which was soon to open upon his view. He prayed and trusted that he might be able to do his duty with courage and fidelity. To say that he had no doubts and fears would be to say that he was not human.

As the brigade toiled slowly along, he tried to picture the scene which was before him, and thus make himself familiar with its terrors before he was actually called to confront them. He endeavored to imagine the sounds of screaming shells and whistling bullets, that the reality, when it came, might not appall him. He thought of his companions dropping dead around him, of his friends mangled by bayonets and cannon shot; he painted the most terrible picture of a battle which his imagination could conjure up, hoping in this manner to be prepared for the worst.

The day was hot, and the sun poured down his scorching rays upon the devoted soldiers as they pursued their weary march. They were fatigued by continued exertion, and some of the weary ones, when the sun approached the meridian, began to hope the great battle would not take place on that day. Tom Somers, nearly worn out by the tedious march, and half famished after the scanty breakfast of hard bread he had eaten before daylight, began to feel that he was in no condition to face the storm of bullets which he had been imagining.

No orders came to halt at noon, though the crowded roads several times secured them a welcome rest: but on marched the weary soldiers, till the roar of cannon broke upon their ears; and as they moved farther on, the rattling volleys of musketry were heard, denoting that the battle had already commenced. These notes of strife were full of inspiration to the loyal and patriotic in the columns. A new life was breathed into them. They were enthusiastic in the good cause, and their souls immediately became so big that what had been body before seemed to become spirit now. They forgot their empty stomachs and their weary limbs. The music of battle, wild and terrible as it was to these untutored soldiers, charmed away the weariness of the body, and, to the quickstep of thundering cannon and crashing musketry, they pressed on with elastic tread to the horrors before them.

Tom felt that he had suddenly and miraculously been made over anew. He could not explain the reason, but his legs had ceased to ache, his feet to be sore, and his musket and his knapsack were deprived of their superfluous weight.

"God be with me in this battle! " he exclaimed to himself a dozen times. "God give me strength and courage! "

Animated by his trust in Him who will always sustain those who confide in him, the soldier boy pressed on, determined not to disgrace the name he bore. The terrible sounds became more and more distinct as the regiment advanced, and in about two hours after the battle had opened, the brigade arrived at the field of operations. One regiment was immediately detached and sent off in one direction, while the other two were ordered to support a battery on a hill, from which it was belching forth a furious storm of shells upon the rebels.

The little colonel's sword gleamed in the air, as he gave the order to march on the double-quick to the position assigned to him.

"Now, Tom, steady, and think of nothing but God and your country," said old Hapgood, as the regiment commenced its rapid march. "I know something about this business, and I can tell you we shall have hot work before we get through with it. "

"Where are the rebels? I don't see any, " asked Tom, who found that his ideas of the manner in which a battle is fought were very much at fault.

"You will see them very soon. They are in their breastworks. There! Look down there! " exclaimed the veteran as the regiment reached a spot which commanded a full view of the battle.

Tom looked upon the fearful scene. The roar of the artillery and the crash of the small arms were absolutely stunning. He saw men fall, and lie motionless on the ground, where they were trampled upon by the horses, and crushed beneath the wheels of cannon and caisson. But the cry was, that the army of the Union had won the field, and it inspired him with new zeal and new courage.

Scarcely had the remnant of the brigade reached the right of the battery, before they were ordered to charge down the valley, by Colonel Franklin, the acting brigadier. They were executing the command with a dash and vigor that would have been creditable to veterans, when they were ordered to cross the ravine, and support the Eire Zouaves. The movement was made, and Tom soon found himself in the thickest of the fight. Shot and shell were flying in every direction, and the bullets hissed like hailstones around him.

In spite of all his preparations for this awful scene, his heart rose up into his throat. His eyes were blinded by the volumes of rolling smoke, and his mind confused by the rapid succession of incidents that were transpiring around him. The pictures he had painted were sunlight and golden compared with the dread reality. Dead and dying men strewed the ground in every direction. Wounded horses were careering on a mad course of destruction, trampling the wounded and the dead beneath their feet. The hoarse shouts of the officers were heard above the roar of battle. The scene mocked all the attempts which the soldier boy had made to imagine its horrors.

In front of the regiment were the famous Eire Zouaves, no longer guided and controlled by the master genius of Ellsworth. They fought like tigers, furiously, madly; but all discipline had ceased among them, and they rushed wildly to the right and the left, totally heedless of their officers. They fought like demons, and as Tom saw them shoot down, hew down, or bayonet the hapless rebels who came within their reach, it seemed to him as though they had lost their humanity, and been transformed into fiends.

As soon as the regiment reached its position, the order was given to fire. Tom found this a happy relief; and when he had discharged his musket a few times, all thoughts of the horrors of the scene forsook him. He no longer saw the dead and the dying; he no longer heard the appalling roar of battle. He had become a part of the scene, instead of an idle spectator. He was sending the bolt of death into the midst of the enemies of his country.

"Bravo! Good boy, Tom, " said old Hapgood, who seemed to be as much at ease as when he had counselled patience and resignation in the quiet of the tent. "Don't fire too high, Tom. "

"I've got the idea, " replied the soldier boy. "I begin to feel quite at home. "

"O, you'll do; and I knew you would from the first. "

The shouts of victory which had sounded over the field were full of inspiration to the men; but at the moment when the laurels seemed to be resting securely upon our banners, the rebel line moved forward with irresistible fury. Tom, at one instant, as he cast his eye along the line, found himself flanked on either side by his comrades; at the next there was a wild, indescribable tramp and roar, and he found himself alone. The regiment was scattered in every direction, and he did not see a single man whom he knew. There was a moving mass of Federal soldiers all around him. The Zouaves had been forced back, and the cry of victory had given place to the ominous sounds which betokened a defeat, if not a rout.

The rebels had been reënforced, and had hurled their fresh legions upon our exhausted troops, who could no longer roll back the masses that crowded upon them. The day was lost.

Tom, bewildered by this sudden and disastrous result, moved back with the crowds around him. Men had ceased to be brave and firm; they were fleeing in mortal terror before the victorious battalions that surged against them.

"It's all up with us, my lad, " said a panting Zouave. "Run for your life. Come along with me. "

Tom followed the Zouave towards the woods, the storm of bullets still raining destruction around them.

CHAPTER XIV.

AFTER THE BATTLE.

Tom Somers floated with the tide of humanity that was setting away from the scene of disaster and defeat. The panic that prevailed was even more fearful than the battle, for wounded and dying men were mercilessly trodden down by the feet of the horses, and run over by the wheels of the cannon and the baggage wagons. Though the battle was ended, the rebels still poured storms of shot and shell into the retreating, panic-stricken host.

Tom did not know where to go, for there were panic and death on all sides of him. The soldiers were flying in every direction, some of them into the very arms of their remorseless enemies. But the woods seemed to promise the most secure retreat from the fury of the Black Horse Cavalry, which was now sweeping over the battle-field. The Zouave ran in this direction, and our soldier boy followed him. Now that the excitement of the conflict was over, the enthusiasm which had buoyed him up began to subside. The day was lost; all hopes of glory had fled; and a total defeat and rout were not calculated to add much strength to his over-tasked limbs.

He was nearly used up, and it was hard work to run—very hard work; and nothing but the instinct of self-preservation enabled him to keep the tall and wiry form of the Zouave in sight. They reached the ravine, where the water was about three feet deep. The shot, and shell, and bullets still fell in showers around them, and occasionally one of the luckless fugitives was struck down. They crossed the stream, and continued on their flight. An officer on horseback dashed by them, and bade them run with all their might, or they would be taken.

"For Heaven's sake, get me some water! " said a rebel, who was wounded in the leg, to a Zouave, who passed near him.

"You are a rebel, but I will do that for you, " replied the Zouave; and he gave him a canteen filled with water.

The rebel drank a long, deep draught, and then levelled his musket at the head of his Samaritan enemy and fired. This transaction had occupied but a moment, and Tom saw the whole. His blood froze with horror at the unparalleled atrocity of the act. The Zouave, whom Tom had followed, uttered a terrible oath, and snatching the musket from the hands of the soldier boy, he rushed upon the soulless miscreant, and transfixed him upon the bayonet. Uttering fierce curses all the time, he plunged the bayonet again and again into the vitals of the rebel, till life was extinct.

"Boy, I used to be human once, " said the Zouave, when he had executed this summary justice upon the rebel; "but I'm not human now. I'm all devil. "

"What a wretch that rebel was! " exclaimed Tom, who seemed to breathe freer now that retribution had overtaken the viper.

"A wretch! Haven't you got any bigger word than that, boy? He was a fiend! But we mustn't stop here. "

"I thought the rebels were human. "

"Human? That isn't the first time to-day I've seen such a thing as that done. Come along, my boy; come along. "

Tom followed the Zouave again; but he was too much exhausted to run any farther. Even the terrors of the Black Horse Cavalry could not inspire him with strength and courage to continue his flight at any swifter pace than a walk.

"I can go no farther, " said he, at last.

"Yes, you can; pull up! pull up! You will be taken if you stop here. "

"I can't help it. I can go no farther. I am used up. "

"Pull up, pull up, my boy! "

"I can't. "

"But I don't want to leave you here. They'll murder you—cut your throat, like a dog. "

"I will hide myself in the bushes till I get a little more strength. "

"Try it a little longer. You are too good a fellow to be butchered like a calf, " added the generous Zouave.

But it was no use to plead with him, for exhausted nature refused to support him, and he dropped upon the ground like a log.

"Poor fellow! I would carry you in my arms if I could. "

"Save yourself if you can, " replied Tom, faintly.

The kind-hearted fireman was sorry to leave him, but he knew that one who wore his uniform could expect no mercy from the rebels. They had been too terrible upon the battle-field to receive any consideration from those whom they had so severely punished. He was, therefore, unwilling to trust himself to the tender mercies of the cavalry, who were sweeping the fields to pick up prisoners; and after asking Tom's name and regiment, he reluctantly left him.

Tom had eaten nothing since daylight in the morning, which, added to the long march, and the intense excitement of his first battle-field, had apparently reduced him to the last extremity. Then, for the first time, he realized what it was to be a soldier. Then he thought of his happy home—of his devoted mother. What must she not suffer when the telegraph should flash over the wires the intelligence of the terrible disaster which had overtaken the Union army! It would be many days, if not weeks or months, before she could know whether he was dead or alive. What anguish must she not endure!

He had but a moment for thoughts like these before he heard the sweep of the rebel cavalry, as they dashed down the road through the woods. He must not remain where he was, or the record of his earthly career would soon be closed. On his hands and knees he crawled away from the road, and rolled himself up behind a rotten log, just in season to escape the observation of the cavalrymen as they rode by the spot.

Here and there in the woods were the extended forms of Federals and rebels, who had dragged their wounded bodies away from the scene of mortal strife to breathe their last in this holy sanctuary of nature, or to escape from the death-dealing shot, and the mangling wheels that rumbled over the dead and the dying. Close by the soldier boy's retreat lay one who was moaning piteously for water. Tom had filled his canteen at a brook on the way, and he crawled up to the sufferer to lave his dying thirst. On reaching the wounded man, he found that he was a rebel, and the fate of the Zouave who had done a similar kindness only a short time before presented itself to his mind.

"Water! Water! For the love of God, give me a drop of water, " moaned the dying soldier.

Tom thought of the Zouave again, and had almost steeled his heart against the piteous cry. He turned away.

"Water! Water! If you are a Christian give me some water, " groaned the sufferer.

Our soldier boy could no longer resist the appeal. He felt that he could not be loved on earth or forgiven in heaven if he denied the petition of the dying rebel; but before he granted it, he assured himself that the sufferer had no dangerous weapon in his possession. The man was deadly pale; one of his arms hung useless by his side; and he was covered with blood. He was a terrible-looking object, and Tom felt sick and faint as he gazed upon him.

Placing his canteen at the lips of the poor wretch, he bade him drink. His frame quivered as he clutched the canteen with his remaining hand. The death damp was on his forehead; but his eye lighted up with new lustre as he drank the grateful beverage.

"God bless you! God bless you! " exclaimed he as he removed the canteen from his lips. "You are a Yankee, " he added, as he fixed his glazing eyes upon Tom's uniform. "Are you wounded? "

"No; I am worn out. I have eaten nothing since daylight, and not much then. I am used up. "

"Put your hand in my haversack. There is something there, " gasped the dying man.

Tom bent over him to comply with the invitation; but, with a thrill of horror, he started back, as he listened to the death-rattle in the throat of the rebel, and saw his eyes fixed and lustreless in death. It was an awful scene to the inexperienced youth. Though he had seen hundreds fall in the battle of that day, death had not seemed so ghastly and horrible to him as now, when he stood face to face with the grim monster. For a few moments he forgot his own toil-worn limbs, his craving hunger, and his aching head.

He gazed upon the silent form before him, which had ceased to suffer, and he felt thankful that he had been able to mitigate even a single pang of the dying rebel. But not long could he gaze, awe-struck, at the ghastly spectacle before him, for he had a life to save. The words of the sufferer—his last words—offering him the contents of his haversack recurred to him; but Tom's sensibilities recoiled at the thought of eating bread taken from the body of a dead man, and he turned away.

"Why shouldn't I take it? " said he to himself. "It may save my life. With rest and food, I may escape. Pooh! I'll not be a fool! "

Bending over the dead man, he resolutely cut the haversack from his body, and then returned to the log whose friendly shelter had screened him from the eyes of the rebel horsemen. Seating himself upon the ground, he commenced exploring the haversack. It contained two "ash-cakes, " a slice of bacon, and a small bottle. Tom's eyes glowed with delight as he gazed upon this rich feast, and, without waiting to say grace or consider the circumstances under which he obtained the materials for his feast, he began to eat. Ash-cake was a new institution to him. It was an Indian cake baked in the ashes, probably at the camp-fires of the rebels at Manassas. It tasted very much like his mother's johnny-cake, only he missed the fresh butter with which he had been wont to cover the article at home.

The soldier boy ate the bacon, and ate both of the cakes, though each of the latter was about the size of a saucer. It was a large meal, even for a growing boy; but every mouthful seemed to put a new sinew into his frame. While he was eating, he drew the cork from the bottle. It contained whiskey. Tom had heard that there was virtue in whiskey; that it was invigorating to a tired man, and he was tempted, under these extremely trying circumstances, to experiment upon the beverage. He would certainly have been excusable if he had done so; but our hero had a kind of horror of the article, which would not let him even taste it. He was afraid that he should acquire a habit which would go with him through life, and make him what Hapgood and others whom he knew were—a torment to themselves, and a nuisance to their fellow-beings. Putting the cork in the bottle, he threw it upon the ground.

With his renewed strength came renewed hope; but he did not deem it prudent to wander about the woods at present: therefore he threw himself on the ground under the protecting log to obtain the repose he so much needed.

He thought of home, and wondered whether he should ever see the cottage of his parents again; and while he was thinking, overcome by the excitement and fatigue of the day, he dropped asleep. It was strange that he could do so, consciously environed by so many perils; but he had in a measure become callous to danger, and he slept long and deep.

When he awoke, it was dark and silent around him. The roar of battle had ceased, and the calm of death seemed to have settled upon the scene of strife. Tom's bones still ached; but he was wonderfully refreshed by the nap he had taken. He had no idea of the time, and could not tell whether he had slept one hour or six. He was strong enough to walk now, and the first consideration was to escape from the vicinity of the rebel camps; but he had no conception of where he was, or what direction would lead him to the Federal lines.

A kind Providence had watched over him thus far; had spared his life in the fury of battle; had fed him in the wilderness, like Elijah of old; and restored his wasted strength. He could only trust to Providence for guidance, and, using his best judgment in choosing the direction, he entered upon the difficult task of finding his way out of the woods. He had walked an hour or more, when, suddenly, three men sprung up in the path before him.

"Halt! Who comes there?" demanded one of them.

"Friend!" replied Tom; though he had a great many doubts in regard to the truth of his assertion.

"Advance, friend, and give the countersign!"

But the soldier boy had no countersign to give. He had fallen upon a rebel picket post, and was made a prisoner.

CHAPTER XV.

TOM A PRISONER.

Tom could not exactly understand how he happened to be made a prisoner. He had certainly moved with extreme caution, and he wondered that he had not received some intimation of the presence of the enemy before it was too late to retreat. But, as we have before hinted, Tom was a philosopher; and he did not despair even under the present reverse of circumstances, though he was greatly disconcerted.

"Who are you? " demanded one of the rebel soldiers, when they had duly possessed his body, which, however, was not a very chivalrous adventure, for the prisoner was unarmed, his gun having been thrown away by the friendly Zouave, after he had so terribly avenged his murdered companion.

"I'm a soldier, " replied Tom, greatly perplexed by the trials of his difficult situation.

As yet he did not know whether he had fallen into the hands of friend or foe, for the night was cloudy and dark, and he could not see what uniform the pickets wore.

"What do you belong to? " demanded the spokesman of the picket trio.

"I belong to the army, " answered Tom, with admirable simplicity.

Our soldier boy, as the reader already knows, had been well "brought up. " He had been taught to tell the truth at all times; and he did so on the present occasion, very much to the confusion, no doubt, of the rebel soldiers, who had not been brought up under the droppings of the sanctuary in a New England village.

"B'long to the army—do you? " repeated Secesh, who must have thought Tom a very candid person.

"Yes, sir, I belong to the army, " added the prisoner.

"I s'pose you won't mind telling us what army you belong to, 'cause it mought make a difference in our calculations, " added the spokesman.

Tom did not know but that it might make some difference in his calculations, and for this reason he was exceedingly unwilling to commit himself before he ascertained upon which side his questioners belonged.

"Can you tell me where I am? " asked Tom, resolved to use a little strategy in obtaining the desired information.

"May be I can, " replied the picket.

"Will you do so? "

"Sartin, stranger—you are in the woods, " added Secesh; whereat his companions indulged in a wholesome chuckle, which assured Tom that they were human, and his hopes rose accordingly.

"Thank you, " replied Tom, with infinite good nature.

"You say you belong to the army, and I say you are in the woods, " said the soldier, repeating the double postulate, so that the essence of the joke should by no possibility fail to penetrate the cerebellum of his auditor.

Tom was perfectly willing to acknowledge that he was in the woods, both actually and metaphorically, and he was very much disturbed to know how he should get out of the woods—a problem which has puzzled wiser heads than his, even in less perplexing emergencies. He was fearful that, if he declared himself to be a Union soldier, he should share the fate of others whom he had seen coolly bayoneted on that eventful day.

"Now, stranger, s'pose you tell me what army you b'long to; then I can tell you where you are, " continued the soldier.

"What do you belong to? " asked Tom, though he did not put the question very confidently.

"I belong to the army; " and the two other pickets honored the reply with another chuckle. "You can't fool old Alabammy. "

There was no further need of fooling "Old Alabammy, " for the worthy old gentleman, symbolically represented by the rebel soldier, had kindly done it himself; and Tom then realized that he was in the hands of the enemy. It is true, the balance of the picket trio laughed heartily at the unfortunate slip of the tongue made by their companion, but Tom was in no condition to relish the joke, or he might perhaps have insinuated himself into the good graces of the jolly Secesh by repeating Pat's mysterious problem—"Tell me how many cheeses there are in the bag, and I'll give ye the whole five; " for, though this is an old joke in the civilized parts of the world, it is not at all probable that it had been perpetrated in the benighted regions of Secessia.

The announcement of the fact that he was in the hands of the foe, as we have before intimated, left Tom in no condition to give or take a joke. His heart was suddenly deprived of some portion of its ordinary gravity, and rose up to the vicinity of his throat. He drew sundry deep and long breaths, indicative of his alarm; for though Tom was a brave boy, —as these pages have already demonstrated,—he had a terrible idea of the tender mercies of the rebels. His first impulse was to break away from his captors, and run the risk of being overtaken by a trio of musket balls; for death from the quick action of a bullet seemed preferable to the fate which his fears conjured up if he should be taken by the bloodthirsty rebels. But the chances were too decidedly against him, and he reluctantly brought his mind to the condition of philosophical submission.

"Well, stranger, which army do you b'long to? " said the spokesman of the picket trio, when he had fully recovered his self-possession.

"I belong to the United States army, " replied Tom, desperately.

"That means the Yankee army, I s'pose. "

"Yes, sir; you call it by that name. "

"Then you are my prisoner. "

"I surrender because I can't help myself. "

"Hev you nary toothpick or bone-cracker in your pockets? "

"Any what? " replied Tom, whose dictionary seemed to be at fault.

"Nary pistol, knife, or any thing of that sort?"

"Nothing but my jackknife."

"Any plunder?"

"We piled up our knapsacks and haversacks before we went into the fight. Here is my canteen half full of water; I gave the other half to one of your soldiers, when he was dying of his wounds."

"Did ye?"

"Now will you be kind enough to tell me where I am?"

"You are inside the lines of our army, about three miles below Centreville," replied one of the pickets.

"What time is it?"

"Nigh upon nine o'clock, I should say. One of you fellers must take this prisoner to headquarters," he continued, speaking to his companions.

Tom was very agreeably surprised to find that his captors did not propose to hang, shoot, or bayonet him; and the Southern Confederacy rose a few degrees in his estimation. Certainly the men who had taken him were not fiends, and he began to hope that his situation as a prisoner would not be so terrible as his fancy had pictured it.

One of the men was deputed to conduct him to the officer of the guard; and he walked along by the side of the soldier through the woods, in the direction from which he had just come.

"Can you tell me how the battle went at last?" asked Tom, as they pursued their way through the forest.

"We whipped you all to pieces. Your army hasn't done running yet. We shall take Washington to-morrow, and Jeff Davis will be in the White House before the week is out."

"Have you taken many prisoners?" asked Tom, who could not dispute the position of the rebel soldier.

"About fifty thousand, I b'lieve, " replied Secesh, with refreshing confidence.

Tom indulged in a low whistle, but his companion could not tell whether it was an expression of regret or incredulity. If they had stood on an equality, Tom would probably have suggested that the figures should be interpreted "over the left"—an idiosyncrasy in language which he had imported from Pinchbrook, but which may not be wholly unintelligible to our young readers.

From his conductor he obtained some particulars of the battle and its result, which were afterwards more fully set forth in General Beauregard's official report, and which would have read better on the pages of Sinbad the Sailor than in the folios of a military despatch. But the Secesh soldier's "facts and figures" were comforting to Tom, who still had a stronger interest in the condition of the good cause, after the heavy blow it had received, than he had in his own individual welfare. Like too heavy a dose of poison, the magnitude of the stories refuted and defeated them. The soldier boy listened in respectful silence, but he was utterly incredulous. It was even possible that the Union army had won a victory, after all, though he was not very sanguine on this point.

He was ultimately conducted to the headquarters of the regiment to which his captors belonged, and then turned into a lot with about twenty others, who were strongly guarded. Tom joined his companions in misery, most of whom, worn out by the fatigues of the day, were sleeping soundly upon the ground. Only two or three of them were awake; but these were strangers to him, and he was unable to obtain any information from them concerning any of his friends in the regiment.

It began to rain shortly after Tom joined his fellow-prisoners; but there was no shelter for them. They had neither blankets nor great coats, yet this did not seem to disturb them. Our soldier boy threw himself upon the ground, but the nap he had taken under the side of the log set his eyes wide open for a time. He could only think of home, his mother and sisters, and John, by this time snugly coiled away in the bed where he had been wont to dream of the glories of war. He had cast his fears to the winds when he found that his captors did not intend to butcher him, and he could not help thinking that his situation might have been worse.

Those with whom he had spoken told him they had eaten nothing since morning; and in this respect he was far better off than his companions were. The only thing that troubled him was the thought of the anguish which his mother must suffer, when she heard of the battle. When the regiment should be gathered together again, he would be reported as "missing, " and this would be a terrible word to her, for it meant killed, wounded, or a prisoner. If he could only assure her that he still lived and was uninjured, he would have been happy—happy in spite of the drenching rain—happy in spite of the prospective dungeon, and the hardships to which he might be subjected. He felt that he had faithfully performed his duty. When he began to be drowsy, he settled himself in the most comfortable place he could find on the ground, and thanked God that he had been spared his life through the perils of that awful day, and more fervently that he had been enabled to do his duty like a good soldier; and then, with the Giver of all Good, the Fountain of all Mercy, in his heart, he fell asleep.

He slept several hours, and waked up to find himself as thoroughly soaked as though he had just come out of the river. There was no help for it, and it was no use to grumble. After walking to and fro for half an hour, he lay down again, and, between sleeping and waking, finished the night; uncomfortably, it is true, and yet without any positive suffering. There were hundreds, if not thousands, who were enduring the agony of fearful wounds through that long night; who were lying alone and uncared for where they had fallen in the deadly strife; who were dying every hour, away from their homes and friends, and with no kind hand to minister to their necessities, with no sweet voice of a loved one to smooth their passage down to the dark, cold grave.

Tom thought of these, for he had seen them in his path, and he felt that he had no cause to complain—that he ought to be cheerful and happy. At the dawn of the day he and his fellow-prisoners were marched to Sudley Church, where they were to be confined until they could be sent to Richmond. Here Tom found a captain belonging to his regiment; but neither could give any information to the other in regard to their friends.

"I shall not stay here long, " said the captain, in a whisper, when they had become better acquainted. "I intend to leave to-night. "

"Can't I go with you? " asked Tom.

"You can go, but we had better not go together."

Tom thought for a while, and determined upon an attempt to escape. During the day, he carefully examined the premises, and decided upon his mode of operations.

CHAPTER XVI.

A PERPLEXING QUESTION.

Tom Somers, who had had some experience, in a small way, in the kind of business now before him, was filled with hope when he had adopted his plan. He was a resolute and energetic young man, and to resolve upon any thing was almost equivalent to doing it. There were a great many difficulties in the way of success, it is true; but, nothing daunted by these, he determined to persevere. The church in which the prisoners were confined was carefully guarded on the exterior, and the sentinels carried loaded muskets in their hands—so that the affair before him was more hazardous and trying than that of escaping from the attic chamber of Squire Pemberton's house in Pinchbrook.

If he succeeded in making his way out of the church and eluding the guard which surrounded it, even then his trials would only have commenced; for there were many miles of hostile country between him and Washington, whither he supposed the Federal army had been driven. The captain who intended to escape at the same time gave him some information which would be of service to him in finding his way to the Potomac. He charged him particularly to follow the railroad, which would conduct him to Alexandria, in the vicinity of which he would probably find the regiment.

At dark the prisoners disposed of themselves as well as they could for the night. Tom saw the captain go through all the forms of preparing for a comfortable lodging, and he did the same himself. For hours he lay ruminating upon his purpose. When it was midnight, he thought it was time for him to commence the enterprise. He worked himself along on the floor till he reached the principal entrance. The door was open, as it had been all day, to enable the guards to obtain an occasional view of the prisoners.

The sentinels were evidently in no condition to discharge their duties with fidelity, for they had been marching and fighting for two or three days, and were nearly exhausted. Leaning against the door, Tom discovered a musket, which the careless guard had left there. On the floor in the entry lay two rebel soldiers. They had stretched themselves across the threshold of the door, so that no one could pass in or out of the church without stepping over them.

Tom carefully rose from his recumbent posture, and took possession of the musket. Then, with the utmost prudence, he stepped over the bodies of the sleeping soldiers; but with all his circumspection, he could not prevent one of his shoes from squeaking a little, and it required only a particle of noise to rouse the guard.

"Who goes there? " demanded one of them, springing to his feet.

"Is this the way you do your duty? " replied Tom, as sternly as though he had been a brigadier general.

"Who are you? " said the soldier, apparently impressed by the words and the tones of him who reproved his neglect.

"Who am I, you sleepy scum! I'll let you know who I am in about ten minutes, " added Tom, as he passed out at the front door of the church.

"Give me back my gun — won't you? " pleaded the confused sentinel.

"I'll give it back to you at the court-martial which will sit on your case to-morrow. "

"Who goes there? " challenged one of the sentinels on the outside.

"Who goes there! " added Tom, in a sneering tone. "Have you waked up? Where were you five minutes ago, when I passed this post? There won't be a prisoner left here by morning. The long roll wouldn't wake up such a stupid set of fellows. "

"Stop, sir! " said the astonished sentinel. "You can't pass this line. "

"Can't I, you stupid fool? I have passed it while you were asleep. "

"I haven't been asleep. "

"Where have you been, then? " demanded Tom with terrible energy.

"Been here, sir. "

"I'll court-martial the whole of you! "

"Stop, sir, or I'll fire at you! " added the soldier, as Tom moved on.

"Fire at me! Fire, if you dare, and I'll rid the army of one unfaithful man on the spot!" said the soldier boy, as he raised the musket to his shoulder.

"Don't fire, you fool!" interposed one of the men whom Tom had roused from his slumbers in the entry. "Don't you see he is an officer?"

"I'll teach you how to perform your duty!" added Tom, as he walked away.

The soldier, governed by the advice of his companion, offered no further objection to the departure of Tom; and he moved off as coolly as though he had just been regularly relieved from guard duty. He had walked but a short distance before he discovered the camp of a regiment or brigade, which, of course, it was necessary for him to avoid. Leaving the road, he jumped over the fence into a field—his first object being to place a respectful distance between himself and the enemy.

The scene through which he had just passed, though he had preserved the appearance of coolness and self-possession, had been exceedingly trying to his nerves; and when the moment of pressing danger had passed, he found his heart up in his throat, and his strength almost wasted by the excitement. He felt as one feels when he has just escaped a peril which menaced him with instant death. It was singular that the soldier had not fired, but the fact that he did not convinced Tom that there is an amazing power in impudence.

For half an hour, he pursued his way with haste and diligence, but without knowing where he was going—whether he was moving toward Richmond or Washington. As the musket which he had taken from the church was not only an encumbrance, but might betray him, he threw it away, though, thinking some means of defence might be useful, he retained the bayonet, and thrust it in his belt. Thus relieved of his burden, he walked till he came to a road. As there was no appearance of an enemy in any direction, he followed this road for some time, and finally it brought him to the object of his search—the railroad.

But then came up the most perplexing question he had yet been called upon to decide. To that railroad, as to all others, there were, unfortunately, two ends—one of which lay within the Federal lines, and the other within the rebel lines. If Tom had been an astronomer, which he was not, the night was too cloudy to enable him to consult the stars; besides, some railroads are so abominably crooked that the heavenly orbs would hardly have been safe pilots. He did not know which was north, nor which was south, and to go the wrong way would be to jump out of the frying pan into the fire.

Tom sat down by the side of the road, and tried to settle the difficult question; but the more he thought, the more perplexed he became — which shows the folly of attempting to reason when there are no premises to reason from. He was, no doubt, an excellent logician; but bricks cannot be made without straw.

"Which way shall I go? " said Tom to himself, as he stood up and peered first one way and then the other through the gloom of the night.

But he could not see Washington in one direction, nor Richmond in the other, and he had not a single landmark to guide him in coming to a decision.

"I'll toss up! " exclaimed he, desperately, as he took off his cap and threw it up into the air. "Right side up, this way — wrong side, that way; and may the fates or the angels turn it in the proper way. "

He stooped down to pick up the cap, and ascertain which way it had come down. It came down right side up, and Tom immediately started off in the direction indicated. Although he had no confidence in the arbitrament of the cap, he felt relieved to find the question disposed of even in this doubtful manner.

He kept both eyes wide open as he advanced, for if he had taken the wrong way a few miles of travel would bring him to the main camp of the rebels in the vicinity of Manassas Junction. He pursued his lonely journey for some time without impediment, and without discovering any camp, either large or small. He gathered new confidence as he proceeded. After he had walked two or three hours upon the railroad, he thought it was about time for Fairfax station to heave in sight, if he had chosen the right way — or for the rebel camps to appear if he had chosen the wrong way. With the first place he was familiar, as his regiment had encamped a short distance from it.

He was sorely perplexed by the non-appearance of either of these expected points. The country began to look wilder and less familiar as he proceeded. The region before him looked rugged and mountainous, and the dark outlines of several lofty peaks touched the sky in front of him. But with the feeling that every step he advanced placed a wider space between him and his captors at Sudley church, he continued on his way till the gray streaks of daylight appeared behind him.

This phenomenon promised to afford him a gleam of intelligence upon which to found a correct solution of his course. Tom knew that, in the ordinary course of events, the sun ought to rise in the east and set in the west. If he was going to the north, the sun would rise on his right hand—if to the south, on his left hand. The streaks of light grew more and more distinct, and the clouds having rolled away, he satisfied himself where the sun would appear. Contrary to both wings of his theory, the place was neither on his right nor his left, for it was exactly behind him. But his position might be upon a bend of the railroad whose direction did not correspond with the general course of the road. For half an hour longer, therefore, he pursued his way, carefully noting every curve, until he was fully convinced that his course was nearer west than north. The sun rose precisely as had been laid down in the programme, and precisely where he expected it would rise.

It was clear enough that he was not moving to the south; and, satisfied that he was in no danger of stumbling upon Richmond, his courage increased, and he plodded on till he discovered a small village—or what would be called such in Virginia—though it contained only a few houses. As he still wore the uniform of the United States army, he did not deem it prudent to pass through this village; besides, he was terribly perplexed to know what station it could be, and what had become of Fairfax. Though he must have passed through the country before, it did not look natural to him.

Leaving the railroad, he took to the fields, intending to pass round the village, or conceal himself in the woods till he could go through it in safety. After walking diligently for so many hours, Tom was reminded that he had a stomach. His rations on the preceding day had not been very bountiful, and he was positively hungry. The organ which had reminded him of its existence was beginning to be imperative in its demands, and a new problem was presented for solution—one which had not before received the attention which it deserved.

In the fields and forest he found a few berries; but all he could find made but a slight impression upon the neglected organ. If Tom was a philosopher, in his humble way, he was reasonable enough to admit that a man could not live without eating. At this point, therefore, the question of rations became a serious and solemn problem; and the longer it remained unsolved the more difficult and harassing it became.

After he had rested all the forenoon in a secluded spot, without interruption from man or beast, he decided to settle this question of rations once for all. If impudence had enabled him to pass a line of rebel sentries, it ought to furnish him with a dinner. Leaving his hiding place, he walked till he discovered a small house, at which he determined to apply for something to eat.

CHAPTER XVII.

DINNER AND DANGER.

The house at which Tom applied for food evidently did not belong to one of the "first families, " or, if it did, the owner's fortunes had become sadly dilapidated. It was built of rough boards, with a huge stone chimney, which was erected on the outside of the structure. The humblest fisherman in Pinchbrook Harbor would have thought himself poorly accommodated in such a rough and rickety mansion.

If Tom's case had not been growing desperate, he would not have run the risk of showing himself to any person on the "sacred soil" who was "to the manor born; " but his stomach was becoming more and more imperative in its demands, and he knocked at the front door with many misgivings, especially as his exchequer contained less than a dollar of clear cash.

The inmates were either very deaf or very much indisposed to see visitors; and Tom, after he had knocked three times, began to think he had not run any great risk in coming to this house. As nobody replied to his summons, he took the liberty to open the door and enter. The establishment was even more primitive in its interior than its exterior, and the soldier boy could not help contrasting it with the neat houses of the poor in his native town.

The front door opened into a large room without the formality of an entry or hall. In one corner of the apartment stood a bed. At one side was a large fireplace, in which half a dozen sticks of green wood were hissing and sizzling in a vain attempt to make the contents of an iron pot, which hung over them, reach the boiling point. No person was to be seen or heard on the premises, though the fire and the pot were suggestive of humanity at no great distance from the spot.

A door on the back side of the room was open, and Tom looked out in search of the occupants of the house. In the garden he discovered the whole family, consisting of a man and his wife, a girl of twelve, and a boy of ten. The man was digging in the garden, and the rest of the troupe seemed to be superintending the operation. The head of the family was altogether the most interesting person to Tom, for he must either shake hands or fight with him. He did not look like a giant in intellect, and he certainly was not a giant in stature. With the bayonet still in his belt, Tom was not afraid of him.

"How are you, people? " said Tom, as he walked towards the family, who with one accord suspended all operations, and gave their whole attention to the stranger.

"How are ye, yourself? " replied the man, rather gruffly.

"Do you keep a hotel? " demanded Tom, who concealed the anxiety of his heart under a broad grin.

"I reckon I don't. What do you want here? "

"I want something to eat, " replied Tom, proceeding to business with commendable straight-forwardness.

"We hain't got nothin' here, " said the man, sourly. "That ain't what ye come fur, nuther. "

"Must have something to eat. I'm not very particular, but I must have something. "

"You can't hev it 'bout yere, no how. That ain't what ye come fur, nuther. "

"If you know what I came for better than I do, suppose you tell me what it is, " added Tom, who was a little mystified by the manner of the man.

"You air one of them soger fellers, and you want me to 'list; but I tell yer, ye can't do nothin' of the sort. I'll be dog derned if I'll go. "

"I don't want you to go, " protested Tom. "I'm half starved and all I want is something to eat. "

"Yer don't reelly mean so. "

"Yes, I do. "

"Where d'yer come from? "

"From down below here. Have you seen any soldiers pass through this place?"

"I reckon I hev; but they hain't seen me; and I reckon they won't see me very soon;" and the man chuckled at his own cleverness in keeping clear of recruiting officers.

"I don't want you, and if you will give me something to eat, you will get rid of me very quick."

"Betsey, you kin feed the feller, if yer like, and I'll go over and see whar the hogs is."

The man dropped his shovel, and began to move off towards the woods, probably to see whether Tom would attempt to detain him. At the same time "Betsey" led the way into the house, and the visitor paid no further attention to the master.

"We hain't got much to eat in the house," said the woman, as they entered the room. "There's some biled pork and pertaters in the pot, and we've got some bread, sech as 'tis."

"It will do me very well. I'm hungry, and can eat any thing," replied Tom.

The woman placed a tin plate on the table, and dished up the contents of the kettle on the fire. She added some cold hoe cake to the dinner, and Tom thought it was a feast fit for a king. He took a seat at the table, and made himself entirely at home. The food was coarse, but it was good, and the hungry soldier boy did ample justice to the viands. The boy and girl who had followed him into the house, stood, one on each side of him, watching him in speechless astonishment.

"Where did yer come from?" asked the woman, when Tom had about half finished his dinner.

"From down below," replied Tom, rather indefinitely.

"Don't b'long in these yere parts, I reckon?"

"No, marm."

"Where are ye gwine?"

"Going to join my regiment."

"Where is yer rigiment?"

"That's more than I know, marm."

"How long yer been travelling?" persisted the woman, who was perhaps afraid that the guest would eat up the whole of the family's dinner, if she did not make some kind of a feint to attract his attention.

"Only a few days, marm."

"Kin yer till me what all thet noise was about day 'fore yesterday?"

"Yes, marm; it was a big battle."

"Gracious me! Yer don't say so! Whar was it?"

"Down below Centreville."

"Which beat?"

"The Confederates drove the Yankees off the field," answered Tom, suspending business long enough to glance at the woman, and see how the intelligence was received.

"Yer don't! Then they won't want my old man."

Tom was unable to determine whether his hostess was Union or "Secesh" from her words or her looks. He could not inform her whether they would want her old man or not. When he had eaten all he could, he proposed like an honest youth to pay for what he had eaten; but Betsey had the true idea of southern hospitality, and refused to receive money for the food eaten beneath her roof. She had a loaf of coarse bread, however, in which she permitted Tom to invest the sum of six cents.

"I am very much obliged to you, marm; and I shall be glad to do as much for you, any time," said Tom, as he went towards the front door.

As he was about to open it, his ears were startled by an imperative knock on the outside. He stepped back to one of the two windows on the front of the house, where he discovered an officer and two "grayback" soldiers. The ghost of his grandmother would not have been half so appalling a sight, and he retreated to the back door with a very undignified haste.

"Gracious me! " exclaimed the lady of the house. "Who kin thet be? "

"An officer and two soldiers, " replied Tom, hastily.

"Then they are arter my old man! " said she, dropping into the only chair the room contained.

"Don't say I'm here, marm, and I'll help your husband, if they catch him. Tell them he has gone off to be absent a week. "

"He'd be absent more'n thet if he knowed them fellers was arter him."

The woman moved towards the front door, and Tom through the back door; but as he was about to pass into the garden, he caught a glimpse of one of the graybacks in the rear of the house. For a moment his case seemed to be hopeless; but he retreated into the room again, just as the woman opened the front door to admit the officer. He could not escape from the house, and his only resource was to secure a hiding place within its walls. There were only two which seemed to be available; one of these was the bed, and the other the chimney. If any search was made, of course the soldiers would explore the bed first; and the chimney seemed the most practicable.

There was no time for consideration, for the woman had already opened the door, and was answering the questions of the Confederate officer; so Tom sprang into the fireplace, and, by the aid of the projecting stones, climbed up to a secure position. The chimney was large enough to accommodate half a dozen boys of Tom's size. The fire had gone out, and though the stones were rather warm in the fireplace, he was not uncomfortable.

The fears of the lady of the house proved to be well grounded this time, for the party had actually come in search of her "old man; "

and what was more, the officer announced his intention not to leave without him.

"He's gone away fur a week, and he won't be hum before the fust of August, no how, " said the woman resolutely, and adopting Tom's suggestion to the letter.

"All nonsense, woman! He is about here, somewhere, and we will find him. "

"You may, if you kin. "

The officer then went out at the back door, as Tom judged by his footsteps, and the woman asked one of the children what had become of the other soldier man. The boy said he was up chimney. She then told them not to tell the officer where he was.

"What shell I do? " said she, placing herself before the fireplace.

"Don't be alarmed. He will keep out of their way, " replied Tom.

"But the officer man said he was gwine to stay 'bout yere till he gits hum, " moaned the poor woman.

"He will not do any such thing. Your husband has the woods before him, and he won't let them catch him. "

"Deary me! I'm 'feared they will. "

"Where are they now? "

"They're gone out to look for him. "

The officer and his men returned in a few moments, having satisfied themselves that the proprietor of the place was not on the premises.

"Now we'll search the house, " said the officer; and Tom heard them walking about in the room.

Of course the militia man could not be found, and the officer used some very unbecoming language to express his disapprobation of the skulker, as he called him.

"Woman, if you don't tell me where your husband is, I'll have you arrested, " said he, angrily.

"I don't know myself. He's gone off over the mountains to git some things. Thet's all I know about it, and if yer want to arrest me, yer kin. "

But the officer concluded that she would be a poor substitute for an able bodied man, and he compromised the matter by leaving one of the privates, instructing him not to let the woman or the children leave the house, and to remain till the skulker returned.

This was not very pleasant information for Tom who perceived that he was likely to be shut up in the chimney for the rest of the day, and perhaps be smoked or roasted out at supper time. Climbing up to the top of his prison house, he looked over, and saw the officer and one private disappear in the woods which lay between the house and the railroad. Looking over the other way, he saw the coveted recruit approaching the house from beyond the garden.

CHAPTER XVIII.

THE REBEL SOLDIER.

Tom Somers was not very well satisfied with his situation, for the soldier who had been left in possession of the house was armed with a musket, and the prospect of escaping before night was not very flattering. The patriarch of the family, who had such a horror of recruiting officers, was approaching, and in a few moments there would be an exciting scene in the vicinity.

Independent of his promise made to the woman to help her husband, if she would not betray him, Tom deemed it his duty to prevent the so-called Confederate States of America from obtaining even a single additional recruit for the armies of rebellion and treason. Without having any personal feeling in the matter, therefore, he was disposed to do all he could to assist his host in "avoiding the draft. " What would have been treason in New England was loyalty in Virginia.

The unfortunate subject of the Virginia militia law was unconsciously approaching the trap which had been set for him. He had, no doubt, come to the conclusion, by this time, that the hungry soldier boy was not a recruiting officer, or even the corporal of a guard sent to apprehend him, and he was returning with confidence to partake of his noonday meal. Tom, from his perch at the top of the chimney, watched him as he ambled along over the rough path with his eyes fixed upon the ground. There was something rather exciting in the situation of affairs, and he soon found himself deeply interested in the issue.

The unhappy citizen owing service to the Confederate States climbed over the zigzag fence that enclosed his garden, and continued to approach the rude dwelling which the law had defined to be his castle. Tom did not dare to speak in tones loud enough to be heard by the innocent victim of the officer's conspiracy, for they would have betrayed his presence to the enemy. Sitting upon the top stones of the chimney, he gesticulated violently, hoping to attract his attention; but the man did not look up, and consequently could not see the signals.

He had approached within ten rods of the back door of the house, when Tom, fearing his footsteps might attract the attention of the soldier, ventured to give a low whistle. As this was not heeded, he repeated the signal when the man was within two or three rods of the house; but even this was not noticed, and throwing his head forward, so that the sound of his voice should not descend the chimney, he spoke.

"Halloo! " said he.

The man suddenly stopped, and looked up. Tom made signals with his hands for him to leave; but this mute language appeared not to be intelligible to him.

"Consarn yer picter, what are yer doin' up thar? " said the proprietor of the castle, in tones which seemed to Tom as loud as the roar of the cannon at Bull Run.

"Hush! Hush! " replied Tom, gesticulating with all his might, and using all his ingenuity to invent signs that would convey to the militiaman the idea that he was in imminent danger.

"You be scotched! " snarled the man. "What are yer doin'? What ails yer? "

"They are after you! " added Tom, in a hoarse whisper.

The fellow most provokingly refused to hear him, and Tom thought his skull was amazingly thick, and his perceptions amazingly blunt.

"Now you come down from thar, " said he, as he picked up a couple of stones. "You act like a monkey, and I s'pose yer be one. Now make tracks down that chimley. "

But instead of doing this, Tom retreated into his shell, as a snail does when the moment of peril arrives. The soldier in the house was not deaf; and if he had been, he could hardly have helped hearing the stentorian tones of his victim. Instead of going out the back door, like a sensible man, he passed out at the front door, and in a moment more Tom heard his voice just beneath him.

"Halt! " shouted the soldier, as he brought his musket to his shoulder. "Your name is Joe Burnap. "

"That's my name, but I don't want nothin' o' you, " replied the embarrassed militiaman, as he dropped the stones with which he had intended to assault Tom's citadel.

"I want something of you, " replied the soldier. "You must go with me. Advance, and give yourself up. "

"What fur? " asked poor Joe.

"We want you for the army. You are an enrolled militiaman. You must go with me. "

"Ill be dog derned if I do, " answered Joe Burnap, desperately.

"If you attempt to run away, I'll shoot you. You shall go with me, dead or alive, and hang me if I care much which. "

Joe evidently did care. He did not want to go with the soldier; his southern blood had not been fired by the wrongs of his country; and he was equally averse to being shot in cold blood by this minion of the Confederacy. His position was exceedingly embarrassing, for he could neither run, fight, nor compromise. While matters were in this interesting and critical condition, Tom ventured to raise his head over the top of the chimney to obtain a better view of the belligerents. Joe stood where he had last seen him, and the soldier was standing within three feet of the foot of the chimney.

"What ye going to do, Joe Burnap? " demanded the latter, after waiting a reasonable time for the other to make up his mind.

"What am I gwine to do? " repeated Joe, vacantly, as he glanced to the right and the left, apparently in the hope of obtaining some suggestion that would enable him to decide the momentous question.

"You needn't look round, Joe; you've got to come or be shot. Just take your choice between the two, and don't waste my time. "

"I s'pose I can't help myself, " replied Joe. "I'll tell ye what I'll do. I want to fix up things about hum a little, and I'll jine ye down to the Gap to-morrow. "

"No you don't, Joe Burnap! " said the soldier, shaking his head.

"Then I'll jine ye to-night, " suggested the strategist.

"My orders are not to return without you, and I shall obey them. "

Mrs. Burnap, who had followed the soldier out of the house, stood behind him wringing her hands in an agony of grief. She protested with all a woman's eloquence against the proceedings of the soldier; but her tears and her homely rhetoric were equally unavailing. While the parties were confronting each other, the soldier dropped his piece, and listened to the arguments of Joe and his wife. When he turned for a moment to listen to the appeals of the woman, her husband improved the opportunity to commence a retreat. He moved off steadily for a few paces, when the enemy discovered the retrograde march, and again brought the gun to his shoulder.

"None of that, Joe, " said the soldier, sternly. "Now march back again, or I'll shoot you; " and Tom heard the click of the hammer as he cocked the piece. "I've fooled long enough with you, and we'll end this business here. Come here, at once, or I'll put a bullet through your head. "

"Don't shoot! Don't shoot! For mercy's sake don't shoot, " cried Mrs. Burnap.

"I'll give him one minute to obey the order; if he don't do it then, I'll fire. That's all I've got to say. "

Tom saw by the soldier's manner that he intended to execute his threat. He saw him brace up his nerves, and otherwise prepare himself for the bloody deed. But Tom did not think that Joe had the stubbornness or the courage, whichever it might be called, to run the risk of dodging the bullet. He foresaw, too, that, if Joe gave himself up, his hiding place would be exposed, and the soldier would have two prisoners to conduct back to his officer, instead of one. It was therefore high time for him to do something for his own protection, if not for that of his host.

The necessity of defending himself, or of doing something to cover his retreat in an emergency, had been anticipated by Tom, and he had made such preparations as the circumstances would admit. His first suggestion was to dart his bayonet down at the rebel soldier, as he had seen the fishermen of Pinchbrook harpoon a horse mackerel; but the chances of hitting the mark were too uncertain to permit him to risk the loss of his only weapon, and he rejected the plan. He adopted the method, however, in a modified, form, deciding to use the material of which the chimney was constructed, instead of the bayonet. The stones being laid in clay instead of mortar, were easily detached from the structure, and he had one in his hands ready for operations.

"Come here, Joe Burnap, or you are a dead man, " repeated the soldier, who evidently had some scruples about depriving the infant Confederacy of an able-bodied recruit.

Tom Somers, being unembarrassed by any such scruples, lifted himself up from his hiding place, and hurled the stone upon the soldier, fully expecting to hit him on the head, and dash out his brains. The best laid calculations often miscarry, and Tom's did in part, for the missile, instead of striking the soldier upon the head, hit him on the right arm. The musket was discharged, either by the blow or by the act of its owner, and fell out of his hands upon the ground.

Now, a stone as big as a man's head, does not fall from the height of fifteen feet upon any vulnerable part of the human frame without inflicting some injury; and in strict conformity with this doctrine of probabilities, the stone which Tom hurled down upon the rebel, and which struck him upon the right arm, entirely disabled that useful member. The hero of this achievement was satisfied with the result, though it had not realized his anticipations. Concluding that the time had arrived for an effective charge, he leaped out of the chimney upon the roof of the house, descended to the eaves, and then jumped down upon the ground.

The soldier, in panic and pain, had not yet recovered from the surprise occasioned by this sudden and unexpected onslaught. Tom rushed up to him, and secured the musket before he had time to regain his self-possession.

"Who are you? " demanded the soldier, holding up the injured arm with his left hand.

"Your most obedient servant, " replied Tom, facetiously, as he placed himself in the attitude of "charge bayonets. " "Have you any dangerous weapons about your person? "

"Yes, I have, " replied the soldier, resolutely, as he retreated a few steps, and attempted to thrust his left hand into the breast pocket of his coat.

"Hands down! " exclaimed Tom, pricking his arm with the bayonet attached to the musket. "Here, Joe Burnap! "

"What d' yer want? " replied the proprietor of the house, who was as completely "demoralized" by the scene as the rebel soldier himself.

"Put your hand into this man's pocket, and take out his pistol. If he resists, I'll punch him with this, " added Tom, demonstrating the movement by a few vigorous thrusts with the bayonet.

With some hesitation Joe took a revolver from the pocket of the soldier, and handed it to Tom.

"Examine all his pockets. Take out everything he has in them, " added Tom, cocking the revolver, and pointing it at the head of the prisoner.

Joe took from the pockets of the rebel a quantity of pistol cartridges, a knife, some letters, and a wallet.

"Who's this fur? " asked Joe, as he proceeded to open the wallet, and take therefrom a roll of Confederate "shin-plasters. "

"Give it back to him. "

"But this is money. "

"Money! " sneered Tom. "A northern beggar wouldn't thank you for all he could carry of it. Give it back to him, and every thing else except the cartridges. "

Joe reluctantly restored the wallet, the letters, and the knife, to the pockets from which he had taken them. Tom then directed him to secure the cartridge box of the soldier.

"You are my prisoner, " said Tom; "but I believe in treating prisoners well. You may go into the house, and if your arm is much hurt, Mrs. Burnap may do what she can to help you. "

The Soldier Boy; or, Tom Somers in the Army

The prisoner sullenly attended the woman into the house, and Tom followed as far as the front door.

"Now, what am I gwine to do?" said Joe. "You've got me into a right smart scrape."

"I thought I had got you out of one," replied Tom. "Do you intend to remain here?"

"Sartin not, now. I must clear."

"So must I; and we have no time to spare. Get what you can to eat, and come along."

In ten minutes more, Tom and Joe Burnap were travelling towards the mountains.

CHAPTER XIX.

THROUGH THE GAP.

Joe Burnap was perfectly familiar with the country, and Tom readily accepted him as a guide; and, as they had a common object in view, neither had good cause for mistrusting the other. They walked, without stopping to rest, till the sun set behind the mountains towards which they were travelling.

"I reckon we needn't hurry now, " said Joe, as he seated himself on a rock.

"I don't think there is any danger of their catching us, " replied Tom, as he seated himself beside his fellow-traveller. "Can you tell me where we are? "

"I reckon I can. There ain't a foot of land in these yere parts that I hain't had my foot on. I've toted plunder of all sorts through these woods more'n ten thousand times. "

"Well, where are we? " asked Tom, whose doubts in regard to the locality had not yet been solved.

In the pressure of more exciting matters, he had not attempted to explain why he did not come to Fairfax station while following the railroad.

"If we keep on a little while longer, I reckon we shall come to Thoroughfare Gap, " answered Joe.

"But where do you live? What town is your house in? " asked Tom, who had never heard of Thoroughfare Gap before.

"Haymarket is the nearest town to my house. "

"What railroad is that over there? " asked Tom, who was no nearer the solution of the question than he had been in the beginning.

"That's the Manassas Gap Railroad, I reckon, " replied Joe, who seemed to be astonished at the ignorance of his companion.

"Just so," added Tom, who now, for the first time, comprehended where he was.

When he left Sudley church, he walked at random till he came to the railroad; but he had struck the Manassas Gap Railroad instead of the main line, and it had led him away from the great body of the rebels, though it also conducted him away from Washington, where he desired to go. He was perplexed at the discovery, and at once began to debate the question whether it was advisable for him to proceed any farther in this direction.

"I suppose you are a Union man—ain't you?" said Tom, after he had considered his situation for some time.

Instead of answering this question, Joe Burnap raised his eyes from the ground, and fixed his gaze intently upon Tom. He stared at him for a moment in doubt and silence, and then resumed his former attitude.

"You don't want to fight for the south," added Tom; "so I suppose you don't believe in the Southern Confederacy."

"I don't want to fight for nuther of 'em," replied Joe, after a moment of further consideration. "If they'll only let me alone, I don't keer which beats."

His position was certainly an independent one, and he appeared to be entirely impartial. The newspapers on either side would not have disturbed him. Patriotism—love of country—had not found a resting place in his soul. Tom had not, from the beginning, entertained a very high respect for the man; but now he despised him, and thought that a rebel was a gentleman compared with such a character. How a man could live in the United States, and not feel an interest in the stirring events which were transpiring around him, was beyond his comprehension. In one word, he so thoroughly despised Joe Burnap, that he resolved, at the first convenient opportunity, to get rid of him, for he did not feel safe in the company of such a person.

"Now which side do you fight fur?" asked Joe, after a long period of silence.

"For the Union side," replied Tom, promptly.

"What are yer doin' here, then? "

"I was in the battle below, and was taken prisoner, got away, and I want to get to Washington. "

"I reckon this ain't the way to git thar, " added Joe.

"I doubt whether I can get there any other way. "

Just then, Tom would have given all the money he had in the world, and all that the government owed him, for a good map of Virginia — or even for a knowledge of geography which would have enabled him to find his way by the safest route to Washington. But he had been a diligent scholar in school, and had faithfully improved the limited opportunities which had been afforded him. His mind could recall the map of Virginia which he had studied in school, but the picture was too faint to be of much practical benefit to him.

He had treasured up some information, derived from the newspapers, in regard to the Manassas Gap Railroad. He knew that it passed through the Blue Ridge, at the western base of which flowed the Shenandoah River: this emptied into the Potomac, which would certainly conduct him to Washington. In following these two rivers, he should have to describe nearly a circle, which was not an encouraging fact to a boy on foot, with no resources, and in an enemy's country.

If he returned by the way he came, the country was filled with rebel soldiers, and he could hardly expect to pass through their lines without being captured. Difficult and dangerous as the route by the Shenandoah appeared, he decided to adopt it.

Joe Burnap proposed that they should have supper and opened the bag which he had filled with such eatables as he could hastily procure on leaving home. They ate a hearty meal, and then resumed their walk for another hour.

"I reckon we'd better stop here, " said Joe. "The Gap's only half a mile from here, and it's too arly in the night to go through thar yet. Thar's too many soldiers goin' that way. "

"What time will you go through? " asked Tom.

"Not afore midnight."

"Then I'll turn in and take a nap. I didn't sleep any last night."

"I'm agreed," replied Joe, who seemed to be indifferent to every thing while he could keep out of the rebel army.

Tom coiled up his body in the softest place he could find, and went to sleep. Exhausted by fatigue and the want of rest, he did not wake for many hours. He came to his senses with a start, and jumped upon his feet. For a moment, he could not think where he was; but then came the recollection that he was in the country of his enemies—a wanderer and a fugitive.

He looked about him in search of his travelling companion; but the fact that he could not see him in the night was no argument that he was not near him. He supposed Joe had chosen a place to sleep in the vicinity, and thinking he might not wake in season to pass through the Gap before daylight, he commenced a search for him. He beat about the place for half an hour, calling his companion by name; but he could not see him, and no sound responded to the call but the echoes of his own voice.

The independent Virginia farmer had anticipated Tom's intention to part company with him, and, by this time, perhaps, had passed through the Gap. The soldier boy was not quite ready to dispense with the services of his guide, inasmuch as he did not even know where the Gap was, or in what direction he must travel to reach it. While he was debating his prospects, an enterprising rooster, in the distance, sounded his morning call. This assured him that he must be near some travelled road, and, taking the direction from the fowl, he resumed his journey.

A short walk brought him out of the woods, and, in the gray light of the dawn, he discovered a house. As he did not care to make any new acquaintances, he avoided the house, and continued his travels till he arrived at a road. As it was too early in the morning for people to be stirring, he ventured to follow the highway, and soon perceived an opening in the mountains, which he doubted not was the Gap.

At sunrise he arrived at another house, which suddenly came into view as he rounded a bend in the road. Near it were several negroes engaged in various occupations. As he passed the house, the negroes all suspended operations, and stared at him till he was out of sight. He soon reached the Gap; but he had advanced only a short distance before he discovered a battery of light artillery stationed on a kind of bluff, and whose guns commanded the approaches in every direction.

Deeming it prudent to reconnoitre before he proceeded any farther, he also ascertained that the Gap was picketed by rebel infantry. Of course it was impossible to pass through under these circumstances, and he again took to the woods. The scanty supply of food which he had purchased from Mrs. Burnap was now produced, and he made an economical breakfast. Finding a secluded place, he stretched himself upon the ground, and went to sleep. Though he slept till the sun had passed the meridian, the day was a very long one.

When it was fairly dark, he resolved to attempt the passage of the Gap, for he was so tired of inaction that peril and hardship seemed preferable to doing nothing. Returning to the road, he pursued his way with due diligence through the narrowing defile of the mountains, till he suddenly came upon a sentinel, who challenged him. Before he started from his hiding place, Tom had carefully loaded the revolver which he had taken from the rebel soldier; and, as he walked along, he carried the weapon in his hand, ready for any emergency that might require its use.

The guard questioned him, and Tom replied that he had fought in the battle down below, and had a furlough to go home and see his father, who was very sick.

"Where's your furlough? " demanded the soldier.

"In my pocket. "

"Let me see it. "

"Here it is, " replied Tom, producing an old letter which he happened to have in his pocket.

The sentinel took the paper, unfolded it, and turned it over two or three times. It was too dark for him to read it if he had been able to do so, for all the rebel soldiers are not gifted in this way.

"I reckon this won't do, " he added, after patiently considering the matter. "Just you tote this paper up to the corporal thar, and if he says it's all right, you kin go on. "

"But I can't stop to do all that. Here's my pass, and I want to go on. My father may die before I get home. "

"What regiment do you b'long to? " asked the guard, who evidently did not wish to disoblige a fellow-soldier unnecessarily.

"The Second Virginia, " replied Tom, at a venture.

"Where does your father live? " continued the sentinel.

"Just beyond the Gap, if he's living at all. "

"What town? "

Tom was nonplussed, for he did not know the name of a single place on the route before him; and, of course, he did not dare to answer the question.

"About five or six miles from here, " he answered.

"Is it Salem or White Plains? " demanded the soldier, whose cunning was inferior to his honesty.

"White Plains, " added Tom, promptly accepting the suggestion.

"What's the matter with your father? "

"I don't know; he was taken suddenly. "

"Pears like your uniform ain't exactly our sort, " added the soldier.

"Mine was all used up, and I got one on the battle-field. "

"I wouldn't do that. It's mean to rob a dead man of his clothes. "

"Couldn't help it—I was almost naked, " replied Tom, who perfectly agreed with the rebel on this point.

"You kin go on, Old Virginny, " said the soldier, whose kindly sympathy for Tom and his sick father was highly commendable.

The soldier boy thanked the sentinel for his permission, of which he immediately availed himself. Tom did not yet realize the force of the maxim that "all is fair in war, " and his conscience gave a momentary twinge as he thought of the deception he had practised upon the honest and kind-hearted rebel. He was very thankful that he had not been compelled to put a bullet through his head; but perhaps he was more thankful that the man had not been obliged to do him a similar favor.

The fugitive walked, with an occasional rest, till daylight the next morning. He went through three or four small villages. After passing through the Gap, he had taken the railroad, as less likely to lead him through the more thickly settled parts of the country. Before him the mountains of the Blue Ridge rose like an impassable wall, and when the day dawned he was approaching Manassas Gap. He had walked twenty-five miles during the night, and prudence, as well as fatigue, required him to seek a place of rest.

CHAPTER XX.

DOWN THE SHENANDOAH.

In that wild mountain region, Tom had no difficulty in finding a secluded spot, where there was no probability that he would be molested. He had been in a state of constant excitement during the night, for the country was full of soldiers. The mountaineers of Virginia were rushing to the standard of rebellion. They were a wild, rude set of men, and they made the night hideous with their debauchery. Tom succeeded in keeping out of the way of the straggling parties which were roaming here and there; but he was filled with dread and anxiety lest he should, at the next moment, stumble upon a camp, or a squad of these marauders.

The nook in the mountains which he had chosen as his resting place was a cleft in the rocks, concealed by the overhanging branches of trees. Here he made his bed, as the sun rose, and, worn out with fatigue and anxiety, he dropped asleep.

When he awoke, the sun was near the meridian. He rose and walked out a short distance from his lodging place, and listened for any sounds which might indicate the presence of an enemy. All was still; silence deep and profound reigned through the solitudes of the mountains. Tom returned to his place of concealment, and after eating the remainder of the food he had brought with him, he stretched himself upon the ground, and went to sleep again. He had nothing else to do, and he needed all the rest he could obtain. It was fortunate for him that he had self-possession enough to sleep—to banish his nervous doubts and fears, and thus secure the repose which was indispensable to the success of his arduous enterprise.

It was after sundown when he finished his second nap. He had slept nearly all day, —at least ten hours, —and he was entirely refreshed and restored. He was rather stiff in some of his limbs when he got up; but he knew this would wear off after a little exercise. He had no supper with which to brace himself for the night's work; so he took a drink from the mountain stream, and made his way back to the railroad. But it was too early then to commence the passage of the Gap, and he sat for a couple of hours by the side of the road, before he ventured to resume his journey.

While he was passing through the narrow gorge in the mountains, he met several persons, on foot and on horseback; but as he was armed with a pistol, he did not turn out for them; but when a party of soldiers approached, he sought a hiding place by the side of the road until they were out of hearing. When he had passed through the Gap, he came to a road crossing the track, and after debating the question thoroughly, he decided to abandon the railroad, and pursued his course by the common highway towards the North.

Continuing his journey diligently for a time longer, he came to another road, branching off to the left from the one he had chosen, which required further consideration. But his conclusion was satisfactory, and he continued on the same road, which soon brought him to a more thickly settled country than that through which he had been travelling.

By this time Tom's stomach began to be rebellious again, and the question of rations began to assume a serious aspect. He was not suffering for food, but it was so much more comfortable to travel upon a full stomach than an empty one, that he could not pass a dwelling house without thinking of the contents of the cellar and closets. It was perfectly proper to forage on the enemy; but he could not eat raw chicken and geese, or the problem of rations would have been effectually settled by a demonstration on the hen-coops of the Shenandoah valley.

He came to a halt before a large mansion, which had the appearance of belonging to a wealthy person. Its larder and kitchen cupboards, he doubted not, were plentifully supplied with the luxuries of the season; and Tom thought he might as well obtain his provisions now, as wait till he was driven to desperation by hunger. He entered the front gate of the great house, and stepped upon the veranda in front of it. The windows reached down to the floor. He tried one of them, and found that it was not fastened. He carefully raised the sash and entered.

Tom was determined to put himself upon his impudence on the present occasion; but he satisfied himself that his revolver was in condition for instant use before he proceeded any farther. Passing from the front room to an apartment in the rear, he found a lamp and matches, and concluded that he would have some light on the subject, which was duly obtained. Leaving this room, he entered another, which proved to be the kitchen. A patient search revealed to him the lurking place of a cold roast chicken, some fried bacon, bread, and crackers.

Placing these things on the table, he seated himself to partake of the feast which the forethought of the occupants had provided for him. Tom began to be entirely at home, for having thrown himself on his impudence now; he did not permit any doubts or fears to disturb him; but the handle of his pistol protruded from between the buttons of his coat. He ate till he had satisfied himself, when he happened to think that the coffee pot he had seen in the closet might contain some cold coffee; and he brought it out. He was not disappointed, and even found sugar and milk. He poured out a bowl of the beverage, and, having prepared it to his taste, was about to conclude the feast in this genteel style, when he heard footsteps in the adjoining entry.

Tom determined not to be cheated out of his coffee, and instead of putting himself in a flurry, he took the bowl in one hand and the pistol in the other. The door opened, and a negro timidly entered the room.

"Well, sar!" said the servant, as he edged along the side of the room. "Hem! Well, sar!"

Tom took no notice of him, but continued to drink his coffee as coolly as though he had been in his mother's cottage at Pinchbrook.

"Hem! Well, sar!" repeated the negro, who evidently wished to have the interloper take some notice of him.

But the soldier boy refused to descend from his dignity or his impudence. He finished the bowl of coffee as deliberately as though the darkey had been somewhere else.

"Well, sar! Who's you, sar?"

"Eh, Blackee?"

"Who's you, sar?"

"Good chicken! Good bread! Good bacon!" added Tom. "Are the folks at home, Blackee?"

"No, sar; nobody but de women folks, sar. Who's you, sar?"

"It don't make much difference who I am. Where's your master?"

"Gone to Richmond, sar. He's member ob Congress."

"Then he's in poor business, Blackee," said Tom, as he took out his handkerchief, and proceeded to transfer the remnants of his supper to its capacious folds.

"Better luff dem tings alone, sar."

But Tom refused to "luff dem alone," and when he had placed them on the handkerchief, he made a bundle of them.

"Golly, sar! I'll tell my missus what's gwine on down here," added the servant, as he moved towards the door.

"See here, Blackee," interposed Tom, pointing his pistol at the negro; "if you move, I'll put one of these balls through your skull."

"De Lud sabe us, massa! Don't shoot dis nigger, massa."

"Hold your tongue then, and mind what I say."

"Yes, massa," whined the darkey, in the most abject tones.

"Now come with me, Blackee, and if you open your mouth, one of these pills shall go down your throat."

Tom flourished his pistol before the negro, and led the way to the window by which he had entered the house. Passing out upon the veranda, he cautiously conducted the terrified servant to the road; and when they had gone a short distance, he halted.

"Now, Blackee, what town is this?" demanded Tom.

"Leeds Manor, sar," replied the trembling negro.

"How far is it to the Shenandoah River?"

"Only two or tree miles, massa. Now let dis chile go home again."

"Not yet."

"Hab mercy on dis nigger dis time, and sabe him."

"I won't hurt you, if you behave yourself."

Tom questioned him for some time in regard to the river, and the towns upon its banks; and when he had obtained all the information in regard to the valley which the servant possessed, he resumed his journey, driving the negro before him.

"Spare dis chile, massa, for de sake ob de wife and chil'n," pleaded the unwilling guide.

"I tell you I won't hurt you if you behave yourself," replied Tom. "You'll have the whole place down upon me in half an hour, if I let you go now."

"No, massa; dis nigger won't say one word 'bout you, nor de tings you took from de house—not one word, massa. Spare dis chile, and luff him go home."

But Tom compelled him to walk before him till they came to the river. The place was called Seaburn's Ford.

"Now, Blackee, if anybody wants me, tell them I've gone to Winchester," said Tom, when he had ordered his escort to halt.

"No, massa, I won't say one word," replied the servant.

"If you do, I'll shoot you the very next time I see you—depend upon that. You can go now."

The negro was not slow to avail himself of this privilege, and ran off, evidently expecting a bullet from the revolver would overtake him before he had gone far, for he glanced fearfully over his shoulder, begging his captor not to shoot him.

Tom stood upon the bank of the Shenandoah. The negro had told him that he was about thirty miles from Harper's Ferry, which he knew was in possession of General Patterson's forces. Attached to a tree on the shore was a small flat-bottomed boat, which attracted the attention of the soldier boy. Tom was accustomed to boats, and the sight of this one suggested a change of programme, for it would be much easier to float down the stream, than to walk the thirty miles.

This was a point which needed no argument; and unfastening the painter of the boat, he jumped in, and pushed off. Seating himself in the stern, with the paddle in his hand, he kept her head with the current, and swept down the rapid stream like a dreamy youth just starting upon the voyage of life.

Like the pilgrim on the sea of time, Tom was not familiar with the navigation of the Shenandoah, and he had neither chart nor compass to assist him. The current was very swift, and once in a while the bateau bumped upon a concealed rock, or bar of sand. Fortunately no serious accident occurred to him, though he found that the labor of managing the boat was scarcely less than that of walking.

There was one consolation about it; he was in no danger of missing the road, and he was not bothered by Confederate soldiers or inquisitive civilians. His light bark rushed on its way down the stream, without attracting the notice of any of the inhabitants, if any were abroad at that unseemly hour of the night. The difficulties of the navigation were overcome with more or less labor, and when the day dawned, Tom made up his mind that he had done a good night's work; and choosing a secluded nook by the side of the river, he hauled up his boat, intending to wait for the return of darkness.

The place he had chosen appeared to be far from any habitation, and he ate his breakfast in a very hopeful frame of mind. Though he was not very tired or very sleepy, yet for the want of something better to do, he felt compelled to go to sleep, hoping, as on the previous day, to dispose of the weary hours in this agreeable manner. His pastime, however, was soon interrupted by loud shouts and the tramp of men, not far from the spot where he lay. A hurried examination of the surroundings assured him that he had chosen a resting place near one of the fords of the river, over which a rebel regiment was then passing.

CHAPTER XXI.

THE PROBLEM OF RATIONS.

The ford over which the rebel regiment was passing was only a few rods distant from the place where Tom had concealed himself and his boat. When he discovered the soldiers, he was thrilled with terror; and, fully believing that his hour had come, he dropped upon the ground, to wait, in trembling anxiety, the passage of the troops. It was a regiment of Virginia mountaineers, clothed in the most fantastic style with hunting-shirts and coon-skin caps. They yelled and howled like so many wildcats.

From his hiding place on the bank of the stream, he obtained a good view of the men, as they waded across the river. He was fearful that some of them might stray from the ranks, and stumble upon his place of refuge; but a kind Providence put it into their heads to mind their own business, and Tom gathered hope as the yells of the mountaineers grew indistinct in the distance.

"This is no place for me, " said Tom to himself, when the sounds had died away in the direction of the Blue Ridge. "A whole army of them may camp near that ford, and drive me out of my hiding place. "

Jumping into the bateau again, he waited till he was satisfied no carriage or body of troops was in the vicinity; and then plying the paddle with the utmost vigor, he passed the ford. But then he found that the public highway ran along the banks of the river, which exposed him to increased risk of being seen. A couple of vehicles passed along the road while he was in this exposed situation; but as the occupants of them seemed to take no notice of him, he congratulated himself upon his escape, for presently the boat was beneath the shadows of the great trees. Finding a suitable place, he again hauled up, and concealed himself and the bateau.

As all danger seemed to have passed, Tom composed his nerves, ate his dinner, and went to sleep as usual; but his rest was not so tranquil as he had enjoyed in the solitudes of the mountains. Visions of rebel soldiers haunted his dreams, and more than once he started up, and gazed wildly around him; but these were only visions, and there was something more real to disturb his slumbers.

"Hi! Who are you? " exclaimed a wildcat soldier, who had penetrated the thicket without disturbing the sleeper.

Tom started up, and sprang to his feet. One of the tall mountaineers, whom he had seen crossing the ford, stood before him; and the reality was even more appalling than the vision.

"Who mought you be? " demanded the tall soldier, with a good-natured grin upon his greasy face.

"Faith! I believe I've been asleep! " said Tom, rubbing his eyes, and looking as innocent as a young lamb.

"You may bet your life on thet, my boy, " replied the rebel, laughing. "Hi! Jarvey! " added he, apparently addressing a companion at no great distance from the spot.

Heavy footsteps announced the approach of Jarvey, who soon joined them. He was not less than six feet three inches in height, and, with two such customers as these, Tom had no hope except in successful strategy. He had no doubt they had obtained information of him from the persons in the vehicles, and had come to secure him. He fully expected to be marched off to the rebel regiment, which could not be far off.

"Who is he, Sid? " asked Jarvey, when he reached the spot.

"Dunno. Say, who are ye, stranger? "

"Who am I? Tom Somers, of course. Do you belong to that regiment that stopped over yonder last night? " asked Tom, with a proper degree of enthusiasm. "Don't you know me? "

"Well, we don't. "

"Didn't you see me over there? That's a bully regiment of yours. I'd like to join it. "

"Would you, though, sonny? " said Sid, laughing till his mouth opened wide enough for a railroad train to pass in.

"Wouldn't I, though! " replied Tom. "If there's any big fighting done, I'll bet your boys do it. "

"Bet your life on thet," added Jarvey. "But why don't you jine a regiment?"

"Don't want to join any regiment that comes along. I want to go into a fighting regiment, like yours."

"Well, sonny, you ain't big enough to jine ours," said Sid, as he compassionately eyed the young man's diminutive proportions.

"The old man wouldn't let me go in when I wanted to, and I'm bound not to go in any of your fancy regiments. I want to fight when I go."

"You'll do, sonny. Now, what ye doing here?"

"I came out a-fishing, but I got tired, and went to sleep."

"Where's your fish-line?"

"In the boat."

"What ye got in that handkerchief?"

"My dinner," replied Tom. "Won't you take a bite?"

"What ye got?"

"A piece of cold chicken and some bread."

"We don't mind it now, sonny. Hev you seen any men with this gear on in these yere parts?" asked Jarvey, as he pointed to his uniform.

"Yes, *sir*," replied Tom, vigorously.

"Whar d'ye see 'em, sonny?"

"They crossed the ford, just above, only a little while ago."

"How many?"

"Two," replied Tom, with promptness.

"Where's the other?" asked Jarvey, turning to his companion.

"He's in these yere woods, somewhar. We'll fotch 'em before night. You say the two men crossed the ford—did ye, sonny?"

"Yes, half an hour ago. What is the matter with them?"

"They're mean trash, and want to run off. Now, sonny, 'spose you put us over the river in your boat."

"Yes, *sir*!" replied Tom, readily.

The two wildcats got into the bateau, nearly swamping it by their great weight, and Tom soon landed them on the other side of the river.

"Thank'e, sonny," said Jarvey, as they jumped on shore. "If you were only four foot higher, we'd like to take you into our regiment. You'll make a right smart chance of a soldier one of these yere days. Good by, sonny."

"Good by," answered Tom, as he drew a long breath, indicative of his satisfaction at being so well rid of his passengers.

He had fully persuaded himself that he should be carried off a prisoner to this wildcat regiment, and he could hardly believe his senses when he found himself again safely floating down the rapid tide of the Shenandoah. His impudence and his self-possession had saved him; but it was a mystery to him that his uniform, or the absence of his fish-line, or the answers he gave, had not betrayed him. The mountaineers had probably not yet seen a United States uniform, or they would, at least, have questioned him about his dress.

Tom ran down the river a short distance farther before he ventured to stop again, for he could not hope to meet with many rebel soldiers who were so innocent and inexperienced as these wildcats of the mountains had been. When the darkness favored his movements, he again embarked upon his voyage. Twice during the night his boat got aground, and once he was pitched into the river by striking upon a rock; but he escaped these and other perils of the navigation with nothing worse than a thorough ducking, which was by no means a new experience to the soldier boy. In the morning, well satisfied with his night's work, he laid up for the day in the safest place he could find.

The Soldier Boy; or, Tom Somers in the Army

On the second day of his voyage down the river, the old problem of rations again presented itself for consideration, for the ham and chicken he had procured at Leed's Manor were all gone. There were plenty of houses on the banks of the river, but Tom had hoped to complete his cruise without the necessity of again exposing himself to the peril of being captured while foraging for the commissary department. But the question was as imperative as it had been several times before, and twelve hours fasting gave him only a faint hint of what his necessities might compel him to endure in twenty-four or forty-eight hours. He did not consider it wise to postpone the settlement of the problem till he was actually suffering for the want of food.

On the third night of his voyage, therefore, he hauled up the bateau at a convenient place, and started off upon a foraging expedition, intending to visit some farmer's kitchen, and help himself, as he had done on a former occasion. Of course, Tom had no idea where he was; but he hoped and believed that he should soon reach Harper's Ferry.

After making his way through the woods for half a mile, he came to a public road, which he followed till it brought him to a house. It was evidently the abode of a thrifty farmer, for near it were half a dozen negro houses. As the dwelling had no long windows in front, Tom was obliged to approach the place by a flank and rear movement; but the back door was locked. He tried the windows, and they were fastened. While he was reconnoitring the premises, he heard heavy footsteps within. Returning to the door, he knocked vigorously for admission.

"Who's thar?" said a man, as he threw the door wide open.

"A stranger, who wants something to eat," replied Tom, boldly.

"Who are ye?"

"My name is Tom Somers," added the soldier boy, as he stepped into the house. "Can you tell me whether the Seventh Georgia Regiment is down this way?"

"I reckon 'tis; least wise I don't know. There's three rigiments about five mile below yere."

"I was told my regiment was down this way, and I'm trying to find it. I'm half starved. Will you give me something to eat? "

"Sartin, stranger; I'll do thet. "

The man, who was evidently the proprietor of the house, brought up the remnant of a boiled ham, a loaf of white bread, some butter, and a pitcher of milk. Tom ate till he was satisfied. The farmer, in deference to his amazing appetite probably, suspended his questions till the guest began to show some signs of satiety, when he pressed him again as vigorously as though he had been born and brought up among the hills of New England.

"Where d'ye come from? " said he.

"From Manassas. I lost my regiment in the fight; and the next day I heard they had been toted over this way, and I put after them right smart, " answered Tom, adopting as much of the Georgia vernacular as his knowledge would permit.

"Walk all the way? "

"No; I came in the keers most of the way. "

"But you don't wear our colors, " added the farmer, glancing at Tom's clothes.

"My clothes were all worn out, and I helped myself to the best suit I could find on the field. "

"What regiment did ye say ye b'longed to? " queried the man, eying the uniform again.

"To the Seventh Georgia. Perhaps you can tell me where I shall find it. "

"I can't; but I reckon there's somebody here that can. I'll call him. "

Tom was not at all particular about obtaining this information. There was evidently some military man in the house, who would expose him if he remained any longer.

The Soldier Boy; or, Tom Somers in the Army

"Who is it, father? " asked a person who had probably heard a part of the conversation we have narrated; for the voice proceeded from a bed-room adjoining the apartment in which Tom had eaten his supper.

"A soldier b'longing to the Seventh Georgia, " answered the farmer. "That's my son; he's a captain in the cavalry, and he'll know all about it. He can tell you where yer regiment is, " added he, turning to Tom, who was edging towards the door.

"I'm very much obliged to you for my supper, " said the fugitive, nervously. "I reckon I'll be moving along. "

"Wait half a second, and my son will tell you just where to find your regiment. "

"The Seventh Georgia? " said the captain of cavalry, entering the room at this moment with nothing but his pants on. "There's no such regiment up here, and hasn't been. I reckon you're a deserter. "

"No, *sir!* I scorn the charge, " replied Tom, with becoming indignation. "I never desert my colors. "

"I suppose not, " added the officer, glancing at his uniform; "but your colors desert you. "

Tom failed to appreciate the wit of the reply, and backed off towards the door, with one hand upon the stock of his revolver.

"Hold on to him, father; don't let him go, " said the officer, as he rushed back into his chamber, evidently for his pistols or his sabre.

"Hands off, or you are a dead man; " cried Tom, as he pointed his revolver at the head of the farmer.

In another instant, the captain of cavalry reappeared with a pistol in each hand. A stunning report resounded through the house, and Tom heard a bullet whistle by his head.

CHAPTER XXII.

THE PICKET GUARD.

It was sufficiently obvious to Tom that, on the present occasion, the suspicions of his host were awakened. It is possible that, if he had depended upon his impudence, he might have succeeded in deceiving the Confederate officer; but his evident intention to retire from the contest before an investigation could be had, proved him, in the estimation of the captain, to be either a spy or a deserter, and shooting him was preferable to losing him.

The officer fired quick, and with little attention to the important matter of a steady aim; and Tom had to thank his stars for the hasty shot, for, though it went within a few inches of his head, "a miss was as good as a mile, " and the brains of our hero remained intact and complete. But he was not willing to be the subject of any further experiments of this description, and without waiting further to express his gratitude to the host for the bountiful supper he had eaten, he threw open the door, and dashed off at the top of his speed.

The revolver he carried was a very good implement with which to bully a negro, or an unarmed farmer; but Tom had more confidence in his legs than in his skill as a marksman, and before the captain could transfer the second pistol from his left to his right hand, he had passed out of the house, and was concealed from his pursuers by the gloom of the night. He felt that he had had a narrow escape, and he was not disposed to trifle with destiny by loitering in the vicinity of the house.

He had not proceeded far before he heard a hue and cry behind him; and if the captain of cavalry had not stopped to put on his boots, it is more than possible that our humble volume might have contained a chapter or two upon prison life in Richmond. Undoubtedly it was quite proper for the officer to put on his boots before he went out; a decent regard for his individual sanitary condition, and a reasonable horror of ague and rheumatism, would have induced him to do it, even at the risk of losing a Federal prisoner, or a rebel deserter, as the case might be. At any rate, if Tom had known the cause of the delay, he would freely have forgiven him for wasting his time in healthful precautions.

The Soldier Boy; or, Tom Somers in the Army

The fugitive retraced his steps to the river by the same route he had taken in approaching the hospitable roof of the farmer. As nearly as he could judge by the sounds that reached him from the distance, the officer and his father were gathering up a force to hunt down the fugitive. Tom jumped into the bateau, and pushed off. Keeping under the shadow of the bank of the river, he plied his paddle vigorously, and by the time his pursuers arrived at the river, he was a couple of miles from the spot. He could hear a shout occasionally in the deep silence of the night, but with the distance between him and the enemy, he felt entirely secure. The danger had passed, and he floated leisurely on his voyage, buoyant as his light bark, and hopeful as the dream of youth.

Hour after hour, in the gloom of the solemn night, he was borne by the swift tide towards the lines of the loyal army. The day was dawning, and he was on the lookout for a suitable place to conceal himself, until the friendly shades of night should again favor his movements. After the experience of the former night near the ford, he was very cautious in the selection of a hiding place. It is not always safe to be fastidious; for while Tom was rejecting one location, and waiting for another to appear, the river bore him into a tract of very open country, which was less favorable than that through which he had just been passing.

The prospect began to make him nervous; and while he was bitterly regretting that he had not moored the boat before, he was startled to hear a sharp, commanding voice on the bank at his left.

"Who comes there? Halt!"

Tom looked up, and discovered a grayback, standing on the shore, very deliberately pointing his musket at him.

"Who comes there?" demanded the picket; for at this point were stationed the outposts of the rebel force in the Shenandoah valley.

"Friend!" replied Tom.

"Halt, then!"

"I would, if I could," answered Tom, as hastily as possible.

"Halt, or I'll fire!"

"I tell you I can't halt," replied Tom, using his paddle vigorously, as though he was trying to urge the bateau to the shore. "Don't fire! For mercy's sake, don't fire."

Tom appeared to be intensely frightened at the situation in which he was placed, and redoubled his efforts apparently to gain the bank of the stream; but the more he seemed to paddle one way, the more the boat went the other way. However much Tom appeared to be terrified by the peril that menaced him, it must be confessed that he was not wholly unmoved.

"Stop your boat, quick!" said the soldier, who had partially dropped his musket from its menacing position.

"I can't stop it," responded Tom, apparently in an agony of terror. "I would go ashore if I could."

"What's the matter?"

"The water runs so swift, I can't stop her; been trying this two hours."

"You will be inside the Yankee lines in half an hour if you don't fetch to," shouted the picket.

"Gracious!" exclaimed Tom, redoubling his efforts.

But it was useless to struggle with the furious current, and Tom threw himself into the bottom of the boat, as if in utter desperation. If Niagara Falls, with their thundering roar and fearful abyss, had been before him, his agony could not have been more intense, as judged from the shore.

By this time, the sentinel on the bank had been joined by his two companions, and the three men forming the picket post stood gazing at him, as he abandoned himself to the awful fate of being captured by the blood-thirsty Yankees, to whose lines the relentless current of the Shenandoah was bearing him.

When Tom was first challenged by the grayback, the boat had been some twenty rods above him; and it had now passed the spot where he stood, but the rebels were still near enough to converse with him.

The Soldier Boy; or, Tom Somers in the Army

Tom heard one of them ask another who he was. Of course neither of them knew who he was, or where he came from.

"Try again!" shouted one of the pickets. "The Yankees will have you in a few minutes."

Tom did make another ineffectual effort to check the progress of the bateau, and again abandoned the attempt in despair. The rebels followed him on the bank, encouraging him with words of cheer, and with dire prophecies of his fate if he fell into the hands of the cruel Yankees.

"Can't you help me?" pleaded Tom, in accents of despair. "Throw me a rope! Do something for me."

Now, this was a suggestion that had not before occurred to the picket guard, and Tom would have been infinitely wiser if he had not put the idea of assisting him into their dull brains; for it is not at all probable that they would have thought of such a thing themselves, for the south, especially the poor white trash, are not largely endowed with inventive genius.

"Save me! Save me!" cried Tom, as he saw the rebels engaged in a hasty consultation, the result of which was, that two of them started off upon the run in a direction at right angles with the stream.

"Try again! Stick to it!" shouted the picket left on the shore.

"I can't do any more; I'm all tired out," replied Tom, throwing himself for the fourth time in the bottom of the boat, the very picture of despair.

The picture was very much exaggerated and over-drawn; but as long as the bullet from the rebel's musket did not come his way, Tom was satisfied with his acting, and hopeful for the future. The man on the shore, full of sympathy for the distressed and exhausted voyager, walked and ran so as to keep up with the refractory barge, which seemed to be spitefully hurling its agonized passenger into the Federal lines, where death and dungeons lurked at every corner.

While this exciting drama was in progress, the stream bore Tom to a sharp bend in the river, where the current set in close to the shore. His attentive guardian on the bank ran ahead, and stationed himself at this point, ready to afford any assistance to the disconsolate navigator which the circumstances might permit.

"Now's your chance! " shouted he. "Gosh all whittaker! put in now, and do your pootiest! "

Tom adopted this friendly advice, and "put in" with all his might; but the more he "put in, " the more he put out—from the shore, whither the inauspicious eddies were sweeping him. If Tom had not been born in Pinchbrook, and had a home by the sea, where boating is an appreciated accomplishment, he would probably have been borne into the arms of the expectant rebel, or received in his vitals the ounce of cold lead which that gentleman's musket contained. As it was, he had the skill to do what he seemed not to be doing. Mr. Johnny Reb evidently did not suspect that Tom was "playing 'possum, " as the Tennessee sharpshooters would have expressed it. The voyager's efforts appeared to be made in good faith; and certainly he applied himself with a degree of zeal and energy which ought to have overcome the inertia of a small gunboat.

The bateau approached the point not more than a rod from the waiting arms of the sympathizing grayback. As it passed, he waded a short distance into the water, and stretched forth his musket to the unhappy voyager. Tom threw down his paddle, and sprang with desperate energy to obtain a hold upon the gun. He even succeeded in grasping the end of the bayonet. For a moment he pulled so hard that it was doubtful whether the bateau would be hauled ashore, or Secesh drawn into the deep water.

"Hold on tight, my boy! Pull for your life! " shouted the soldier, highly excited by the probable success of his philanthropic efforts.

"Save me! Save me! " groaned Tom, as he tugged, or seemed to do so, at the bayonet.

Then, while the united exertions of the saver and the saved, in anticipation, were on the very point of being successful, the polished steel of the bayonet unaccountably slipped through the fingers of Tom, and the bateau was borne off towards the opposite shore.

"Save me! Save me, " cried Tom again, in tones more piteous than ever.

"What d'ye let go fur? " said the grayback, indignantly, as his musket, which he had held by the tip end of the stock, dropped into the water, when Tom let go of the bayonet.

The soldier indulged in a volley of peculiarly southern oaths, with which we cannot disfigure our page, even in deference to the necessity of painting a correct picture of the scene we have described. Tom had a vein of humor in his composition, which has already displayed itself in some of the rough experiences of his career; and when he saw the rebel soldier deprived of all power to make war upon him, either offensive or defensive, he could not resist the temptation to celebrate the signal strategical victory he had obtained over the picket guard. This triumphal demonstration was not very dignified, nor, under the circumstances, very prudent or sensible. It consisted in placing the thumb of his right hand upon the end of his nose, while he wiggled the four remaining digital appendages of the same member in the most aggravating manner, whistling Yankee Doodle as an accompaniment to the movement.

If Secesh did not understand the case before, he did now; and fishing up his musket, he emptied the water out of the barrel, and attempted to fire it. Luckily for Tom, the gun would not go off, and he swept on his way jubilant and joyous.

CHAPTER XXIII.

THE END OF THE VOYAGE.

Tom Somers's voyage down the Shenandoah was, in many respects, a type of human life. He experienced the various reverses, the trials and hardships, which attend all sojourners here below. He triumphed over all obstacles, and when he had completely outwitted the grayback who had labored so diligently to save him from his impending fate, he was at the zenith of prosperity. He had vanquished the last impediment, and the lines of the Union army — the haven of peace to him — were only a short distance from the scene of his victory.

Prosperity makes men arrogant and reckless, and I am sorry to say that it had the same effect upon Tom Somers. If he had been content modestly to enjoy the victory he had achieved, it would have been wiser and safer for him; but when Fortune was kind to him, he mocked her, and she turned against him.

When he had passed out of the reach of the rebel soldier, whose musket had been rendered useless for the time being, Tom believed that he was safe, and that he had fairly escaped from the last peril that menaced him on the voyage. But he was mistaken; for as the current swept the bateau around the bend of the river, he discovered, to his astonishment and chagrin, the two secesh soldiers, who had left the picket post some time before, standing at convenient distances from each other and from the shore, in the water, ready to rescue him from the fate before him. The place they had chosen was evidently a ford of the river, where they intended to check the boat in its mad career down the stream. They were painfully persistent in their kind intentions to save him from the horrible Yankees, and Tom wished they had been less humane and less enthusiastic in his cause.

As soon as Tom perceived this trap, he regretted his imprudence in betraying himself to the soldier from whom he had just escaped. His sorrow was not diminished, when, a few minutes later, he heard the shouts of the third soldier, who, by hard running across the fields, had reached the ford before him.

"Shoot him! Shoot him! He's a Yankee! " bellowed the grayback on the shore.

Tom was appalled at these words, and wondered how the soldier could have found out that he was a Yankee; but when he recalled the fact that he had entertained him with Yankee Doodle at their last meeting, the mystery became less formidable.

"Shoot him! He's a Yankee! " shouted Secesh on the bank of the stream.

"We've left our guns on shore, " replied Secesh in the water.

"I'm very much obliged to you for that, " said Tom to himself, as he grasped his paddle, and set the boat over towards the right bank of the river.

No doubt the rebels in the water, when they saw with what facility the boatman moved the bateau in the swift tide, as compared with his futile efforts farther up the stream, were fully satisfied of the truth of their companion's assertion. Tom decided to run the gauntlet between the right bank and the soldier nearest to that shore. He paddled the bateau with all his vigor, until he had obtained the desired position.

The graybacks in the water, realizing that they were engaged on an errand of peace and humanity, had left their muskets on shore. They were, therefore, comparatively harmless; but the one on shore had reached the ford, and picking up one of the muskets of his companions, without threat or warning, fired. It was lucky for Tom that he was not a Tennessee sharpshooter, nor a Texas ranger, for the shot passed harmlessly over him. The soldier dropped the gun, and picked up the other, which he instantly discharged, and with better aim than before, for the ball struck the bateau, though not within four feet of where Tom stood.

"Don't waste your powder, if you can't shoot better than that, " shouted one of the soldiers in the water. "You'll hit us next. "

"Stop him, then! Stop him! " replied the grayback on the shore. "Kill him if you can. "

Tom was paddling with all his might to pass the ford before the soldier nearest to him should reach a position in which he could intercept the boat. The rebel was an enterprising fellow, and the soldier boy's chances were growing amazingly small. Secesh had actually reached a place where he could make a dash at the boat. There he stood with a long bowie-knife between his teeth, and with both hands outstretched, ready to seize upon the unfortunate bark. He looked grim and ferocious, and Tom saw that he was thoroughly in earnest.

It was a trying situation for a boy of Tom's years, and he would fain have dodged the issue. That bowie-knife had a wicked look, though it was mild and tame compared with the savage eye of the rebel who held it. As it was a case of life and death, the fugitive braced himself up to meet the shock. Taking his position in the stern of the boat, he held the paddle in his left hand, while his right firmly grasped his revolver. It was either "kill or be killed, " and Tom was not so sentimental as to choose the latter rather than the former, especially as his intended victim was a secessionist and a rebel.

"Keep off, or you are a dead man, " shouted Tom, as he flourished his pistol so that his assailant could obtain a fair view of its calibre, and in the hope that the fellow would be willing to adopt a politician's expedient, and compromise the matter by retiring out of range.

"Tew kin play at that game. This yere tooth-pick will wipe you out, " coolly replied the fellow, as he made a spring at the boat.

"Stand off! " screamed Tom, as he raised the pistol, and fired.

It was a short range, and Tom would have been inexcusable if he had missed his aim. The rebel struck his chest with his right hand, and the bowie knife dropped from his teeth; but with his left hand he had grasped the gunwale of the boat, and as he sunk down in the shallow water, he pulled the bateau over on one side till the water poured in, and threatened to swamp her. Fortunately the wounded man relaxed his hold, the boat righted, and Tom commenced paddling again with all his strength and skill.

The other soldier in the water, as soon as he discovered where Tom intended to pass, hastened over to assist his associate. The shouts of their companion on shore had fully fired their southern hearts, and both of them were ten times as zealous to kill or capture a Yankee, as they had been to save a Virginian. When the wounded man clutched the boat, the other was not more than ten feet from him, but farther down the stream. His associate fell, and he sprang forward to engage in the affray.

"Stand off, or you are a dead man! " yelled Tom, with emphasis, as he plied his paddle with renewed energy, for he saw that the man could not reach him.

The bateau passed them both, and Tom began to breathe easier. The second rebel, finding he could not capture or kill the detested Yankee, went to the assistance of his companion. The soldier boy suspended his exertions, for the danger seemed to be over, and gazed with interest upon the scene which was transpiring in the water just above him. He was anxious to know whether he had killed the rebel or not. There was something awful in the circumstances, for the soldier boy's sensibilities were too acute to permit him to take a human life, though it was that of an enemy, without producing a deep impression upon his mind. Perhaps, in the great battle in which he had been a participant, he had killed several rebels; if he had done so, he had not seen them fall. This was the first man he had consciously killed or wounded, and the fact was solemn, if not appalling, to the young soldier.

As the rebel raised his companion from the water he seemed to be dead, and Tom was forced to the conclusion that he had killed him. He had done the deed in self-defence, and in the strict line of duty. He could not be blamed even by his enemies for the act. He felt no exultation, and hoped from the bottom of his heart that the man was prepared to meet his Maker, into whose presence he had been so suddenly summoned.

Tom had heard the boys in Pinchbrook talk lightly about killing rebels, and he had talked so himself; but the reality was not so pleasant as it had seemed at a distance. He was sorry for the poor fellow, and wished he had not been obliged to kill him. It was terrible to him, even in battle, to take a human life, to slay a being created in the image of God, and for whom Christ lived and died.

While he was indulging in these sad reflections, he heard a bullet whistle near his head. The Secesh soldier on the shore had loaded up his companions' muskets, and was doing his best to bring down the lucky fugitive. His last shot was not a bad one, and Tom could not help thinking, if the grayback should hit him, that he would not waste any fine feelings over him. He did not like the sound of those whizzing bullets, and as he had never boasted of his courage, he did not scorn to adopt precautionary measures. The water was three inches deep in the bottom of the bateau; but Tom deemed it prudent to lie down there until the current should bear him out of the reach of the rebel bullets.

He maintained this recumbent posture for half an hour or more, listening to the balls that frequently whistled over his head. Once he ventured to raise his head, and discovered, not one man, but a dozen, on the shore, which accounted for the rapid firing he heard. When he looked up again, his bateau had passed round a bend, and he was no longer exposed to the fire of the enemy.

From his heart Tom thanked God for his escape. He was religiously grateful for the aid which Providence had rendered him, and when he thought how near he had stood to the brink of destruction, he realized how narrow the span between the Here and the Hereafter. And the moral of his reflections was, that if he stood so near to the open gate of death, he ought always to live wisely and well, and ever be prepared to pass the portals which separate time from eternity.

Tom's thoughts were sad and heavy. He could not banish from his mind the face of the rebel, as he raised his hand to his breast, where he had received his mortal wound. That countenance, full of hate and revenge, haunted him for weeks afterwards, in the solitude of his tent, and on his midnight vigils as a sentinel.

As he sat in the boat, thinking of the events of the morning, and listening to the mournful rippling of the waters, which, to his subdued soul, sounded like the requiem of his victim, he was challenged from the shore again.

"Who comes there! "

Tom jumped up, and saw a sentinel on the bank pointing his gun at him. He surveyed the form with anxious interest; but this time he had nothing to fear, for the soldier wore the blue uniform of the United States army.

"Friend, " replied he, as he grasped his paddle.

"Come ashore, or I'll put a bullet through you, " added the sentinel.

"Don't do it! " said Tom, with energy. "Can't you see the colors I wear. "

"Come ashore, then. "

"I will. "

The soldier boy worked his paddle with vigor and skill, and it was astonishing to observe with what better success than when invited to land by the grayback up the river. The guard assisted him in landing and securing his boat.

"Who are you? " demanded he, as he gazed at Tom's wet and soiled garments.

"I was taken prisoner at Bull Run, and came back on my own hook. "

"Perhaps you were, but you can't pass these lines, " said the soldier.

Tom was sent to the Federal camp, and passed from one officer to another, till he was finally introduced to General Banks, at Harper's Ferry. He was questioned in regard to his own adventures, the country he had passed through, and the troops of the enemy he had seen. When, to use his own expression, he had been "pumped dry, " he was permitted to rest a few days, and then forwarded to his regiment.

CHAPTER XXIV.

BUDD'S FERRY.

Though Tom Somers had been absent from the regiment only a fortnight, it seemed to him as though a year had elapsed since the day of the battle when he had stood shoulder to shoulder with his townsmen and friends. He had been ordered to report to the provost marshal at Washington, where he learned that his regiment was at Bladensburg, about six miles from the city. Being provided with the necessary pass and "transportation, " he soon reached the camp.

"Tom Somers! Tom Somers! " shouted several of his comrades, as soon as they recognized him.

"Three cheers for Tom Somers! " shouted Bob Dornton.

The soldier boy was a favorite in the company, and his return was sufficient to justify such a proceeding. The cheers, therefore, were given with tremendous enthusiasm.

"Tom, I'm glad to see you! " said old Hapgood, with extended hand, while his eyes filled with tears. "I was afeared we should never see you again. "

The fugitive shook hands with every member of the company who was present. His reception was in the highest degree gratifying to him, and he was determined always to merit the good will of his companions in arms.

"Now, fellows, tell us what the news is, " said Tom, as he seated himself on a camp stool before the tent of his mess.

"There are letters for you, Tom, in the hands of the orderly, " added one of his friends. "I suppose you have got a bigger story to tell than any of us, but you shall have a chance to read your letters first. "

These precious missives from the loved ones at home were given to him, and the soldier boy opened them with fear and trembling, lest he should find in them some bad news; but his mother and all the family were well. One of them was written since the battle, and it was evidently penned with deep solicitude for his fate, of which nothing had been heard.

Hapgood, who sat by him while he read his letters, assured him that his mother must know, by this time, that he was not killed, for all the men had written to their friends since the battle. The captain who had escaped from Sudley church had reported him alive and well, but he had no information in regard to his escape.

"We are all well, and every thing goes on about the same as usual in Pinchbrook, " wrote one of his older sisters. "John is so bent upon going to sea in the navy, that it is as much as mother can do to keep him at home. He says the country wants him, and he wants to go; and what's more, he must go. We haven't heard a word from father since he left home; but Captain Barney read in the paper that his vessel had been sunk in the harbor of Norfolk to block up the channel. We can only hope that he is safe, and pray that God will have him in his holy keeping.

"Squire Pemberton was dreadful mad because his son went into the army. He don't say a word about politics now. "

In a letter from John, he learned that Captain Barney had advanced the money to pay the interest on the note, and that Squire Pemberton had not said a word about foreclosing the mortgage. His brother added that he was determined to go into the navy, even if he had to run away. He could get good wages, and he thought it was a pity that he should not do his share towards supporting the family.

Tom finished his letters, and was rejoiced to find that his friends at home were all well and happy; and in a few days more, a letter from him would gladden their hearts with the intelligence of his safe return to the regiment.

"All well—ain't they? " asked Hapgood, as Tom folded up the letters and put them in his pocket; and the veteran could not fail to see, from the happy expression of his countenance, that their contents were satisfactory.

"All well, " replied Tom. "Where is Fred Pemberton? I haven't seen him yet. "

"In the hospital: he's sick, or thinks he is, " answered Hapgood. "Ben Lethbridge is in the guard house. He attempted to run away while we were coming over from Shuter's Hill."

"Who were killed, and who were wounded? I haven't heard a word about the affair, you know, " asked Tom.

"Sergeant Bradford was wounded and taken prisoner. Sergeant Brown was hit by a shell, but not hurt much. The second lieutenant was wounded in the foot, and—"

A loud laugh from the men interrupted the statement.

"What are you laughing at? " demanded Tom.

"He resigned, " added Bob Dornton, chuckling.

"You said he was wounded? "

"I didn't say so; the lieutenant said so himself, and hobbled about with a big cane for a week; but as soon as his resignation was accepted, he threw away his stick, and walked as well as ever he could. "

The boys all laughed heartily, and seemed to enjoy the joke prodigiously. Tom thought it was a remarkable cure, though the remedy was one which no decent man would be willing to adopt.

"How's Captain Benson? "

"He's better; he felt awful bad because he wasn't in that battle. The colonel has gone home, sick. He has more pluck than body. He was sun-struck, and dropped off his horse, like a dead man, on the field. It's a great pity he hasn't twice or three times as much body; if he had, he'd make a first-rate officer. "

It was now Tom's turn to relate his adventures; and he modestly told his story. His auditors were deeply interested in his narrative, and when he had finished, it was unanimously voted that Tom was a "trump; " which I suppose means nothing more than that he was a smart fellow—a position which no one who has read his adventures will be disposed to controvert.

The Soldier Boy; or, Tom Somers in the Army

A long period of comparative inactivity for the regiment followed the battle of Bull Run. General McClellan had been called from the scene of his brilliant operations in Western Virginia, to command the army of the Potomac, and he was engaged in the arduous task of organizing the vast body of loyal troops that rushed forward to sustain the government in this dark hour of peril.

While at Bladensburg the —th regiment with three others were formed into a brigade, the command of which was given to Hooker—a name then unknown beyond the circle of his own friends.

About the first of November the brigade was sent to Budd's Ferry, thirty miles below Washington, on the Potomac, to watch the rebels in that vicinity. The enemy had, by this time, closed the river against the passage of vessels to the capital, by erecting batteries at various places, the principal of which were at Evansport, Shipping Point, and Cockpit Point. Budd's Ferry was a position in the vicinity of these works, and the brigade was employed in picketing the river, to prevent the enemy on the other side from approaching, and also to arrest the operations of the viler traitors on this side, who were attempting to send supplies to the rebels.

It was not a very exciting life to which the boys of our regiment were introduced on their arrival at Budd's Ferry, though the rebel batteries at Shipping Point made a great deal of noise and smoke at times. As the season advanced the weather began to grow colder, and the soldiers were called to a new experience in military life; but as they were gradually inured to the diminishing temperature, the hardship was less severe than those who gather around their northern fireside may be disposed to imagine. Tom continued to be a philosopher, which was better than an extra blanket; and he got along very well.

It was a dark, cold, and windy night, in December, when Tom found himself doing picket duty near the mouth of Chickamoxon Creek. Nobody supposed that any rebel sympathizer would be mad enough to attempt the passage of the river on such a night as that, for the Potomac looked alive with the angry waves that beat upon its broad bosom. Hapgood and Fred Pemberton were with him, and the party did the best they could to keep themselves comfortable, and at the same time discharge the duty assigned to them.

"Here, lads," said old Hapgood, who, closely muffled in his great-coat, was walking up and down the bank of the creek to keep the blood warm in his veins.

"What is it, Hapgood?" demanded Fred, who was coiled up on the lee side of a tree, to protect him from the cold blast that swept down the creek.

"Hush!" said Hapgood. "Don't make a noise; there's a boat coming. Down! down! Don't let them see you."

Tom and Fred crawled upon the ground to the verge of the creek, and placed themselves by the side of the veteran.

"I don't see any boat," said Tom.

"I can see her plain enough, with my old eyes. Look up the creek."

"Ay, ay! I see her."

"So do I," added Fred. "What shall we do?"

"Stop her, of course." replied Tom.

"That's easy enough said, but not so easily done. We had better send word up to the battery, and let them open upon her," suggested Fred.

"Open upon the man in the moon!" replied Tom, contemptuously. "Don't you see she is under sail, and driving down like sixty? We must board her!"

Tom spoke in an emphatic whisper, and pointed to a small boat, which lay upon the shore. The craft approaching was a small schooner apparently about five tons burden. The secessionists of Baltimore or elsewhere had chosen this dark and tempestuous night to send over a mail and such supplies as could not be obtained, for love or money, on the other side of the Potomac. Of course, they expected to run the risk of a few shots from the Union pickets on the river; but on such a night, and in such a sea, there was very little danger of their hitting the mark.

The Soldier Boy; or, Tom Somers in the Army

Up the creek the water was comparatively smooth; but the little schooner was driving furiously down the stream, with the wind on her quarter, and the chances of making a safe and profitable run to the rebel line, those on board, no doubt, believed were all in their favor.

"We have no time to lose, " said Hapgood, with energy, as he pushed off the boat, which lay upon the beach. "Tumble in lively, and be sure your guns are in good order. "

"Mine is all right, " added Tom, as he examined the cap on his musket, and then jumped into the boat.

"So is mine, " said Fred; "but I don't much like this business. Do you know how many men there are in the schooner? "

"Don't know, and don't care, " replied Tom.

"Of course they are armed. They have revolvers, I'll bet my month's pay. "

"If you don't want to go, stay on shore, " answered Hapgood, petulantly. "But don't make a noise about it. "

"Of course I'll go, but I think we are getting into a bad scrape. "

Tom and Hapgood held a hurried consultation, which ended in the former's taking a position in the bow of the boat, while the other two took their places at the oars. The muskets were laid across the thwarts, and the rowers pulled out to the middle of the creek, just in season to intercept the schooner. Of course they were seen by the men on board of her, who attempted to avoid them.

"Hallo! " said Tom, in a kind of confidential tone. "On board the schooner there! Are you going over? "

"Yes. What do you want? " answered one of the men on board the vessel.

"We want to get over, and are afraid to go in this boat. Won't you take us over? "

"Who are you? "

"Friends. We've got a mail bag."

"Where did you get it?"

"In Washington."

By this time, the schooner had luffed up into the wind, and Tom directed his companions to pull again. In a moment the boat was alongside the schooner, and the soldier boy was about to jump upon her half-deck, when the rebel crew, very naturally, ordered him to wait till they had satisfied themselves in regard to his secession proclivities.

There were five men in the schooner, all of whom were seated near the stern. Tom did not heed the protest of the traitors, but sprang on board the schooner, followed by his companions.

"Now, tell us who you are before you come any farther," said one of the men.

"Massachusetts soldiers! Surrender, or you are a dead man," replied Tom, pointing his gun.

CHAPTER XXV.

IN THE HOSPITAL.

The night was very dark, so that the rebels in the boat could not distinguish the uniform of those who had applied for a passage on the schooner. Perhaps Tom Somers's experience in the Blue Ridge and on the Shenandoah had improved his strategic ability, so that his words and his manner seemed plausible. But as strategy and cunning always owe their success to the comparative stupidity of the victims, Tom and his companions gained the half-deck of the schooner more by the palpable blundering of her crew than through the brilliancy of their own scheme.

Tom did not stop, in the midst of the exciting enterprise, to determine the particular reason of his success, as we, his humble biographer, have done. He was on the enemy's ground, and confronting the enemy's forces, and logic was as much out of place as rebellion in a free republican country. He was closely followed by Hapgood, and at a later period by Fred Pemberton. The nerves of the latter were not remarkably steady, and as he stepped on board the schooner, he neglected to take the painter with him; and the consequence was, that the boat went adrift. It is good generalship to keep the line of retreat open; and Fred's neglect had deprived them of all means of retiring from the scene of action. The only alternative was to fight their way through, and find safety in success.

To Tom's reply, that the party were Massachusetts soldiers, the rebel who had acted as spokesman for the crew, uttered a volley of oaths, expressive of his indignation and disgust at the sudden check which had been given to their prosperous voyage.

"Surrender!" repeated Tom, in energetic tones.

Two of the rebels at the stern discharged their pistols in answer to the summons—a piece of impudence which our Massachusetts soldiers could not tolerate; and they returned the fire. The secessionists evidently carried revolvers; and a turn of the barrel enabled them to fire a second volley, which the soldiers were unable to do, for they had no time to load their guns.

"O!" groaned Fred, as he sunk down upon the half-deck. "I'm hit."

"We can't stand this, Hapgood," said Tom, fiercely, as he leaped into the midst of the party in the standing room. "Let's give them the bayonet."

"Give it to 'em, Tom!" replied the veteran, as he placed himself by the side of his young companion.

"Will you surrender?" demanded Tom, as he thrust vigorously with his bayonet.

"We surrender," replied one of the men; but it was not the one who had spoken before, for he had dropped off his seat upon the bottom of the boat.

"Give up your pistols, then," added Hapgood. "You look out for the boat, Tom, and I will take care of these fellows."

Tom sprang to the position which had been occupied by the spokesman of the party, and grasping the foresheet and the tiller of the boat, he soon brought her up to the wind. Seating himself in the stern, he assumed the management of the schooner, while Hapgood busied himself in taking the pistols from the hands of the rebels, and exploring their pockets, in search of other dangerous weapons.

"How are you, Fred?" shouted Tom, when the pressing business of the moment had been disposed of. "Are you much hurt?"

"I'm afraid my time's most up," replied he, faintly.

"Where are you hit?"

"In the face; the ball went through my head, I suppose," he added, in tones that were hardly audible, in the warring of the December blast.

"Keep up a good heart, Fred, and we will soon be ashore. Have you got an easy place?"

"No, the water dashes over me."

"Can't you move him aft, Hapgood?"

"Pretty soon; when I get these fellows fixed, " replied the veteran, who had cut the rope nearest to his hands, and was securing the arms of the prisoners behind them.

"There is no fear of them now. We have got two revolvers apiece, and we can have it all our own way, if they show fight. "

But Hapgood had bound the rebels by this time, and with tender care he lifted his wounded companion down into the standing room, and made him as comfortable as the circumstances would permit.

"Now, where are we, Hapgood? " asked Tom, who had been vainly peering ahead to discover some familiar object by which to steer. I can't see the first thing. "

"I don't know where we are, " replied Hapgood. "I never was much of a sailor, and I leave the navigating all to you. "

"I can navigate well enough, if I knew where we were, " added Tom, who had thus far been utterly unable to ascertain the "ship's position. "

During the brief struggle for the possession of the schooner, she had drifted some distance, which had caused the new commander to lose his bearings. The shore they had just left had disappeared, as though it had been swallowed up by an earthquake. No lights were allowed on shore, where they could be seen from the river, for they afforded so many targets to the artillerymen in the rebel batteries. The more Tom tried to discover a familiar object to steer by, the more it seemed as though the land and everything else had been cut adrift, and emigrated to foreign parts. Those who have been in a boat in a very dark night, or in a dense fog, will be able to appreciate the bewilderment of the skipper of the captured schooner.

"Look out, Tom, that you don't run us into some of those rebel batteries, " said Hapgood, after he had watched the rapid progress of the boat for a few moments. "A shot from a thirty-two pounder would be a pill we couldn't swallow. "

"No danger of that, Hapgood, " answered Tom, confidently.

"I don't know about that, my boy, " answered the veteran, in a tone heavy with dire anxiety.

"I know it. The schooner was running with the wind on her starboard quarter when we boarded her. We are now close-hauled, and of course we can't make the shore on the other side while we are on this tack."

Well, I don't know much about it, Tom, but if you say its all right, I'm satisfied; that' all. I'd trust you just as far as I would General McClennon, and you know we all b'lieve in him."

"What are you going to do with us?" asked one of the rebels, who began to exhibit some interest in the fate of the schooner.

"I suppose you will find good quarters in Fort McHenry," replied Tom. "Where do you belong?"

"In Baltimore."

"What are you doing here, then?"

"We go in for the South."

"Go in, then!" added Tom, laughing.

"You'll fetch up where all the rest of 'em do," said Hapgood.

"How's that fellow that was hit?" asked Tom, pointing to the rebel who lay in the middle of the standing room.

"I guess it's all right with him," replied Hapgood, bending over the silent form. "No; he isn't dead."

"I have it!" shouted Tom, suddenly crowding the helm hard-a-lee.

"What, Tom?"

"I see where we are. We are running up the river. I see the land on the weather bow."

The schooner was put about, and after running with the wind amidships for ten or fifteen minutes, Tom discovered the outline of Mrs. Budd's house, which was directly under the guns of the Union battery.

"Stand by the fore halliards, Hapgood," said Tom, as the boat came about again. "Let go!"

The foresail came down, and Tom sprang upon the pier, as the schooner came up under its lee. In a moment the boat was made fast. By this time the pickets appeared.

"Who comes there?" demanded the soldier.

"Friends!" replied Tom.

"Advance, friend, and give the countersign."

"Little Mac," whispered the soldier boy in the ear of the sentinel.

"Who are you?"

"Co. K." answered Tom.

"What's the row? The long roll was beat just now, and the whole regiment is in line. What was that firing?"

"We have captured this boat, and five prisoners, one of them wounded, if not dead."

"Bully for you," replied the picket.

They were soon joined by a squad of men, and Fred Pemberton and the wounded rebel were conveyed to the hospital, while the four prisoners were conducted to a secure place. Hapgood and Tom then hastened to the parade, where the regiment was drawn up, and reported the events which had just transpired. It was unanimously voted by officers and privates that the picket guard had done "a big thing," and they were warmly and generously commended for their skill and bravery.

Hapgood and Tom requested permission to go to the hospital and see their companion. They found that the surgeon had already dressed his wound.

"Will he die?" asked Tom, full of solicitude for his friend.

"Die! no; it's a mere scratch. The ball ploughed into his cheek a little way, " replied the surgeon. "It isn't a bad wound. He was more scared than hurt. "

"I am glad it is no worse, " said Captain Benson, who, with fatherly solicitude for his men, had come to the hospital as soon as the company was dismissed. "But what ails you, Tom? You look pale. "

"Nothing, captain. "

"Are you sure? "

"I don't think I am badly hurt. I believe one of those pistol balls grazed my side; but I hardly felt it. "

"Let me see, " said the surgeon.

The doctor opened Tom's coat, and his gray shirt was found to be saturated with blood.

"That's a worse wound than Pemberton's. Didn't you know it, Tom?"

"Well, of course I knew it; but I didn't think it was any thing, " replied Tom, apologetically. "I knew it wouldn't do to drop down, or we should all be in Dixie in half an hour. "

"You are my man for the present, " said the doctor, as he proceeded to a further examination of the wound.

Tom was hit in the side by one of the pistol bullets. As I have not the surgeon's report of the case, I cannot give a minute description of it; but he comforted Hapgood and the captain with the assurance that, though severe, it was not a dangerous wound.

"Tom Somers, there's a sergeant's warrant in Company K for one of you three men, " said Captain Benson, when the patient was comfortably settled upon his camp bed. "The colonel told me to give him the name of the most deserving man in my company. "

"Give it to Tom, " said Hapgood, promptly. "He led off in this matter, and ef't hadn't been for him, we should all have been on t'other side of the river, and p'raps on t'other side of Jordan, afore this time. And then, to think that the poor fellow stood by, and handled the boat like a commodore, when the life-blood was runnin' out of him all the time! It belongs to Tom. "

"Give it to Tom, " added Fred, who lay near the patient.

"No, Captain Benson, " interposed Tom, faintly. "Hapgood is an old soldier, and deserves it more than I do. Give it to him, and I shall be better satisfied than if you give it to me. "

"Tom Somers! " exclaimed old Hapgood, a flood of tears sliding down his furrowed cheeks, "I won't stand nothin' of the sort! I'd jump into the river and drownd myself before I'd take it, after what you've done. "

"You are both worthy of it, " added Captain Benson.

"Please give it to Hapgood, " pleaded Tom. "He first proposed going out after the little schooner. "

"Give it to Tom, cap'n. It'll help heal his wound, " said Hapgood.

"No; it would do me more good to have you receive it, " protested Tom.

"Well, here, I can't have this battle fought in the hospital, " interposed the surgeon. "They are good friends, captain, and whichever one you give it to, the other will be suited. You had better settle the case at head-quarters. "

"If you please, Captain Benson, I would like to have Hapgood stay with me to-night, if he can be spared. "

The veteran was promptly detailed for hospital duty, and the captain returned to his quarters to decide the momentous question in regard to the sergeant's warrant.

CHAPTER XXVI.

TOM IS SENTIMENTAL.

The little schooner which the picket guard had captured was loaded with valuable supplies for the rebels, which of course were confiscated without ceremony. The mail bag which was on board contained a great many letters from traitors in Baltimore, some of whom were exposed by the capture of their treasonable correspondence.

Tom's wound proved to be more serious than even the surgeon had anticipated; but the best care which it was possible to give in a military hospital was bestowed upon him. Old Hapgood, in recognition of his services on that eventful night, was permitted to be near the patient as much as the interests of the service would permit; and the old man was happy when seated by the rude couch of the soldier boy, ministering to his necessities, or cheering him with bright hopes of the future. A strong friendship had grown up between them, for Tom's kind heart and brave conduct produced a deep impression upon the old man.

"Here, Tom, " said Captain Benson, as he approached the sufferer, a few days after he entered the hospital, and laid a paper upon the bed. "Here's a prescription which the colonel says you must take."

"What is it? " asked Tom, with a faint smile.

"A sergeant's warrant. "

"Glory, glory, hallelujah, as we go marching on! " exclaimed old Hapgood, jumping up like a youth of sixteen, and swinging his cap above his head.

"Shut up, there! " shouted the hospital steward. "Don't you know any better than to make such a racket in this place? "

"I beg pardon, Jameson. I forgot where I was, " apologized the veteran. "The news was so good I couldn't help it. Our Tom is a sergeant now! "

"Not yet, Hapgood," replied Tom, feebly. "I can't accept it, Captain Benson; it belongs to Hapgood, sir, and I shall feel a great deal better if you put his name in place of mine."

"Don't do it, cap'n!" interposed the old man, vehemently. "Tom shall be a brigadier general if the war lasts one year more. I should feel like a whipped kitten if that warrant was altered."

"The matter has been fully and fairly considered at head-quarters, and there is no such thing as altering the decision now; so, Tom, you can put the stripes on your arm just as soon as you please."

Hapgood insisted, the surgeon insisted, and the captain insisted; and Tom was too sick to hold way with them in an argument, and his name was placed upon the roster of the company as a sergeant. He was proud of the distinction which had been conferred upon him, though he thought Hapgood, as an older and abler soldier, was better entitled to the honor than himself.

It was six weeks before Tom was able to enter upon the actual enjoyment of the well-merited promotion which he had won by his gallantry; but when he appeared before the company with the chevron of the sergeant upon his arm, he was lustily cheered by his comrades, and it was evident that the appointment was a very popular one. Not even the grumblers, of whom there is a full quota in every regiment, deemed it prudent to growl at the decision of the officers. If any one ventured to suggest that he was too young to be placed over older and stronger men, his friends replied, that men in the army were measured by bravery and skill, not by years.

If my young readers wish to know why Tom's appointment was so well received by his companions in arms, I can only reply, that he had not only been brave and cheerful in the midst of peril and hardship, but he was kind and obliging to his comrades. He had always been willing to help those that needed help, to sympathize with those in trouble, and generally to do all he could to render those around him happy.

Above all these considerations, Tom was a young man of high principle. He had obeyed his mother's parting injunction, often repeated in the letters which came to him from home, and had faithfully "read his Testament." Without being a hypocrite or a canting saint, Tom carried about with him the true elements of Christian character.

Tom had fought a greater battle than that in which he had been engaged at Bull Run a hundred times, in resisting the temptations which beset him from within and without. True to God and true to himself, he had won the victory. Though his lot was cast in the midst of men who swore, gambled, and drank liquor, he had shunned these vices, and loved the sinner while he hated the sin. Such a person could not fail to win the respect of his companions. Though he had been jeered at and insulted for being sober, honest, and pious, he had fought down and lived down all these vilifiers, and won their esteem.

It must be acknowledged that Tom's piety was of the robust type. He would not allow any man to insult him; and after the chastisement he had given Ben Lethbridge, not even those who were strong enough to whip him were disposed to trespass upon his rights and dignity. Perhaps Tom's creed needed a little revising; but he lived under martial law, which does not take cognizance of insults and revilings. He was willing to be smitten on the one cheek, and on the other also, for the good of his country, or even his friends, but not to be wantonly insulted.

The influence of Tom's principles was not confined to himself, for "a little leaven leaveneth the whole lump. " This was particularly true of Hapgood, who, more through Tom's preaching and practice than from any strength in his own character, had steadily maintained his purpose to abstain from intoxicating drinks, though occasional opportunities were presented for the indulgence of his darling vice. Tom and he read the Testament and other good books which were sent to the regiment, and both profited by them.

When the soldier boy was discharged from the hospital, the surgeon gave him a pair of woolen socks, from a case of them which had been sent by the friends of the soldier in Boston and its vicinity. He was very much in need of them, and from the depths of his heart he blessed the ladies who had done this good work. He unrolled the socks, and proceeded to pull one of them on. It was as good a fit as though his mother had knit it on purpose for him.

"God bless the lady that knit these socks! " exclaimed Tom, as he began to draw on the other.

"Amen!" replied Hapgood, who was watching the operation in full sympathy with his protege.

"Eh! what's this?" added Tom, for his foot had met with an obstruction in its passage down the leg.

He pulled off the sock, and thrusting his hand into it, took therefrom a letter enclosed in an envelope.

"See that, uncle?" said he, exhibiting the prize.

"What is it, Tom? Open it quick," replied Hapgood.

The soldier boy broke the envelope, and took from it a note enclosing a photograph. Tom looked at the picture with a feeling of pleasure, which would have caused the original of the miniature, the author of the note, and the author of the socks, to blush up to her eyes if she had beheld the expression of admiration which glowed upon the handsome, manly face of the young sergeant.

"By all that's lovely, isn't she a beauty!" exclaimed Tom, rapturously, as he glanced from the picture to Hapgood, who was looking over his shoulder.

"She's hahnsome, and no mistake," replied the veteran, with a grim smile.

"Well, she is!" added Tom, whose eyes were riveted to the photograph.

"Well, why don't you read the letter, Tom?" demanded the old soldier, after the young man had gazed with blushing cheek upon the sweet face of the author of his socks for full five minutes.

"I guess I will," said Tom; but he did not; for the picture seemed to be glory and beauty enough to satisfy him for the present.

"Read the letter, Tom!" shouted the veteran, after he had waited as long as the nature of the case seemed to require.

The soldier boy carefully placed the photograph in the envelope, and unfolded the letter. It was written in a beautiful hand, which looked as soft and delicate as the fair fingers which had penned the lines. He glanced at it as a whole, admired the penmanship, and the fairy-like symmetry that make up the *tout-ensemble* of the page, and was about to dissolve into another rhapsody, when Hapgood, who was not half so sentimental as the sergeant, became impatient to know the contents of the missive. Tom read it aloud to the stoical veteran; and though we cannot clothe its sweet words in the fairy chirography which transported our hero, and made the letter a dream of bliss to him, we shall venture to present it to our curious readers, stiffened and hardened into the dull, cold forms of the printer's art.

No. — —, RUTLAND STREET, BOSTON, *Nov.* 5, 1861.

MY DEAR SOLDIER: —

This is the first pair of socks I ever knit; and I send them to you with my blessing upon the brave defenders of my country. I hope they will keep your feet warm, and thus keep your heart warm towards God and our blessed land.

Grandma says I am a silly girl, and I suppose I am; but if you feel half as much interest in me as I do in the person who will wear the first pair of socks I ever knit, you will wish to know how I look; therefore I send you my photograph.

I very much desire to know whether my work has done any good; whether my socks are ever worn in a battle; and most of all, I desire to know how the noble fellow looks that wears them. Therefore I beg you to answer my letter, and also to send me your photograph, if you can conveniently.

Now, my dear soldier, be brave and true, and, above all, do not run away from the rebels with my socks on your feet. You may retreat when your officers order you to retire; but if you are a coward, and find yourself compelled to run away, please pull them off before you do so, for I should die with mortification if I thought I had knit a pair of socks for a Union soldier to run away in.

Truly yours, for our flag and our country.

LILIAN ASHFORD.

"Well, if that gal ain't a trump, then there ain't no snakes in Virginny!" exclaimed Hapgood. "She's got the true grit, and no mistake."

"That's so," replied the recipient of the gift, thoughtfully, as he bent down, and began to pull off the sock which encased his left foot.

"What are you doing?" demanded Hapgood, surprised at this new movement of his companion.

"I can't wear these socks yet, uncle," replied he.

"Why not?"

Don't she say she wants them worn in a battle?"

"Tom, you are a little fool!" added the veteran, petulantly. "Are you going with cold feet just to please a silly gal, whose head is as full of moonshine as an egg is of meat. Put on the socks, and keep your feet warm. If you don't, I'll write to her, and tell what a fool you are."

Tom did put them on, but he could not help feeling that uncle Hapgood, as he was familiarly called in the camp, did not understand and appreciate his sentiments. The socks seemed to be too precious to be worn in the vulgar mud of Maryland. To him there was something ethereal about them, and it looked a little like profanation to put any thing emanating from the fairy fingers of the original of that photograph, and the author of that letter, upon his feet.

"Now you act like a sensible fellow, as you are, Tom," said Hapgood, as the sergeant put on his army brogans.

"Well, uncle, one thing is certain: I never will run away from the rebels with these socks on," added Tom, with a rich glow of enthusiasm.

"If Gen'l McClennon don't stir his stumps pretty soon, you'll wear 'em out afore you git a chance to run away."

Tom, almost for the first time since he had been in the army, wanted to be alone. With those socks on, it seemed just as though he was walking the streets of the New Jerusalem, with heaven and stacks of silver-fringed and golden-tinged clouds beneath his feet, buried up to the eyes in floods of liquid moonshine.

If "grandma" really thought that Lilian Ashford was a silly girl, and if Lilian really supposed so herself, it must be added, in justification of her conduct, that she had given the soldier boy a new incentive to do his duty nobly, and kindled in his soul a holy aspiration to serve God and his country with renewed zeal and fidelity.

CHAPTER XXVII.

THE CONFEDERATE DESERTER.

While Tom was in the hospital, he received a letter from his sister, informing him that his brother John had actually entered the navy, and with his mother's consent. The news from home was so favorable, that the soldier boy was pleased to hear that Jack had realized his darling wish, and that he was now in his element.

Intelligence from home, accompanied with letters, papers, books, comforts, and luxuries of various kinds, reached him every two or three weeks; and when the news went back that Tom had been made a sergeant for gallant conduct, there was a great sensation in Pinchbrook. The letters which reached him after the receipt of this gratifying announcement contained all the gossip of the place in regard to the important event. Of course, Tom was delighted by these letters, and was more than ever determined to be diligent and faithful in the discharge of his duties, and never to disgrace the name he bore. He was confident his friends would never have occasion to blush for his conduct—including the original of the photograph, the author of the letter and of the socks.

Tom recovered from the effects of his wound, as we have before intimated, and took his place in the regimental line as a sergeant. January and February passed away without any very stirring events; but in the month of March came indications of activity. The rebels began to draw in their lines, by abandoning various points, till the nation was startled by the evacuation of their strongly fortified position at Manassas, and the forts in front of Budd's Ferry were suddenly left for the occupation of the Federal troops.

Hooker's men crossed the Potomac, and Tom was once more on the sacred soil of Virginia. Skirmishers were sent out in various directions, and though a deserted camp, which had been hastily abandoned, was found, there were no rebels to be seen. The Union boys were not disposed to leave their investigations at this interesting point, and they pursued their way still farther into the country. Somehow or other, Tom and his party did not receive the order to return, and the enterprising young hero continued his march in search of further adventures. It was altogether too tame for him and the congenial spirits in his section to retire without seeing a live rebel or two; and I am not sure, if their desire had not been gratified, that they would not have penetrated to Fredericksburg, and captured that citadel of rebellion in advance to General Augur, who visited the place in April.

As it was, they stumbled upon the pickets of a rebel force, and as soon as their uniform was identified they had the honor of being fired upon, though none of them had the honor of being killed in the midst of their virtual disobedience of orders. But their appearance created a panic among the Confederates, who had no means of knowing that they were not the pioneers of a whole division of Union troops, for General McClellan had removed the spell which bound the loyal army to its camps, and corps, divisions, and brigades were pushing forward into the dominion of the traitors.

The alarm was given, and Tom saw that he was rushing into a bad scrape; and as prudence is as much a requisite of the good soldier as bravery, he ordered his men to fall back. Rebels are very much like ill-natured curs, ever ready to pursue a retreating foe, or run away from an advancing one. The Confederates chased them, and as the legs of the former seemed to be in remarkably good condition, the sergeant came to the conclusion that it would not be safe to run too fast.

"Halt! " shouted he; and the men promptly obeyed the order.

They discharged their muskets, and then made a demonstration towards the enemy, who, obeying their instinct, ran away as fast as their legs would carry them. Taking advantage of this movement on their part, Tom again ordered a retreat.

"They are after us again, " said Hapgood. "I hope there ain't no cavalry within hearing. If there is, we may take a journey to Richmond. "

"They have stopped to load their guns, " replied Tom. "We will use our legs now. "

"See that, Tom! " said Hapgood, suddenly.

"What? "

"There's one of them rushing towards us all alone. "

"He has thrown up his gun. The others are yelling to him to come back. What does that mean? "

"He is a deserter; he wants to get away from them. There he comes. "

"Yes, and there comes the rest of them—the whole rebel army—more than a million of them, " said Fred Pemberton. "It's time for us to be going. "

"See! They are firing at him. Forward! " added Tom, leading the way.

The party rushed forward, for a short distance; but the dozen rebels had been reënforced, and it was madness to rush into the very teeth of danger. Tom ordered his men to halt and fire at will. The deserter, probably finding that he was between two fires, turned aside from the direct course he was pursuing, and sought shelter in the woods. The sergeant then directed his men to retire, for whether the retreat of the runaway rebel was covered or not, it was no longer safe to remain.

Fortunately the Confederates were more in doubt than the Unionists; and perhaps expecting to fall upon a larger body of the latter, they abandoned the pursuit, and returned to their posts. Nothing was seen of the deserter for some time, and Tom concluded that he had lost his way in the woods, or had missed the direction taken by the Federal scouts.

"He was a plucky fellow, any how, " said one of the men, "to attempt to run away in the very face of his companions. "

"Well, he timed it well, for he started just when their guns were all empty, " added another.

"I'm not sorry he missed us, " continued Hapgood. "I don't like a deserter, no how. It goes right agin my grain. "

"But he was running from the wrong to the right side, " replied Tom.

"I don't keer if he was. Them colors on t'other side were his'n. He chose 'em for himself, and it's mean to run away from 'em. If a man's go'n to be a rebel, let him be one, and stick to it. "

"You don't know any thing about it, uncle. Thousands of men have been forced into the rebel army, and I don't blame them for getting out of it the best way they can. I should do so. "

"That may be. Tom; that may be, " added the veteran, taking off his cap and rubbing his bald head, as though a new idea had penetrated it. "I didn't think of that. "

"He's a brave man, whoever he is, and whatever he is. "

"He must want to get away from 'em pretty bad, or he wouldn't have run that risk. I shouldn't wonder if they hit him. "

"Perhaps he is wounded, and gone into the woods there to die, " suggested Tom.

"Halloo! " shouted some one in the rear of them.

"There's your man, " said Hapgood.

"Halloo! " cried the same voice.

"Halloo, yourself! " shouted Hapgood in reply to the hail.

The party halted, and after waiting a few moments, the rebel deserter came in sight. He was apparently a man of fifty; and no mendicant of St. Giles, who followed begging as a profession, could have given himself a more wretched and squalid appearance, if he had devoted a lifetime to the study of making himself look miserable. He wore a long black and gray beard, uncut and unkempt, and snarled, tangled, and knotted into the most fantastic forms. His gray uniform, plentifully bedaubed with Virginia mud, was torn in a hundred places, and hung in tatters upon his emaciated frame. On his head was an old felt hat, in a terribly dilapidated condition. He wore one boot and one shoe, which he had probably taken from the common sewer of Richmond, or some other southern city; they were ripped to such an extent that the "uppers" went flipperty-flap as he walked, and had the general appearance of the open mouth of the mythic dragon, with five bare toes in each to represent teeth.

As he approached, the unthinking soldiers of the party indulged in screams of laughter at the uncouth appearance of the whilom rebel;

and certainly the character in tableau or farce need not have spoken, to convulse any audience that ever assembled in Christendom. Rip Van Winkle, with the devastations and dilapidations of five-and-twenty years hanging about him, did not present a more forlorn appearance than did this representative of the Confederate army.

"What are you laughing at? " demanded the deserter, not at all delighted with this reception.

"I say, old fellow, how long since you escaped from the rag-bag? " jeered one of the men.

"What's the price of boots in Richmond now? " asked another.

"Who's your barber? "

"Silence, men! " interposed Tom, sternly, for he could not permit his boys to make fun of the wretchedness of any human being.

"We'll sell you out for paper stock, " said Ben Lethbridge, who had just returned from three months' service in the Rip-Raps for desertion.

"Shut up, Ben! " added Tom.

"Dry up, all of you! " said Corporal Snyder.

"Who and what are you? " asked Tom, of the deserter.

"I'm a Union man! " replied the stranger with emphasis; "and I didn't expect to be treated in this way after all I've suffered. "

"They thought you were a rebel. You wear the colors of the rebel army, " answered the sergeant, willing to explain the rudeness of his men.

"Well, I suppose I do look rather the worse for the wear, " added the grayback, glancing down at the tattered uniform he wore. "I joined the rebel army, after I had tried every way in the world to get out of this infernal country; but I never fired a gun at a Union man. Seems to me, sergeant, I've seen you before somewhere. What's your name? Where did you come from? "

"Pinchbrook, Massachusetts; and most of us hail from the same place."

"Creation!" exclaimed the deserter. "You don't say so!"

"Your voice sounds familiar to me," added Tom; and for some reason his chest was heaving violently beneath his suddenly accelerated respiration.

As he spoke, he walked towards the dilapidated rebel, who had not ventured to come within twenty feet of the party.

"Did you say Pinchbrook?" demanded the stranger, who began to display a great deal of emotion.

"Pinchbrook, sir," added Tom; and so intensely was he excited, that the words were gasped from his lips.

"What's your name?"

"Thomas Somers," replied the sergeant.

"Tom!" screamed the deserter, rushing forward.

"Father!" cried Tom, as he grasped the hand of the phantom Confederate.

The soldiers of the party were transfixed with astonishment at this unexpected scene, and they stood like statues gazing at the meeting of father and son, till the final development of their relationship, when the muscles of their faces relaxed, and the expression of wonder gave place to joyous sympathy.

"Captain Somers, of Pinchbrook!" shouted old Hapgood; and the men joined with him in a roar of intense satisfaction, that made the woods ring.

CHAPTER XXVIII.

ON THE PENINSULA.

The scene between Captain Somers and his son was very affecting and very exciting; and if the soldiers had all been uncles and first cousins of the parties, they could not have manifested more interest on the joyous occasion. The father wept, and the son wept; for each, amid the terrible experience of these troublous times, had hardly expected to meet the other.

For several minutes they held each other by the hand, laughing and weeping alternately, and neither being able to express the intense emotions which agitated him. The men shouted and laughed in full sympathy with the reunited sire and son.

"I'm glad to see you, Tom, " said Captain Somers, as he wiped away the tears that were sliding down upon his grizzly beard. "I haven't cried before for thirty years; I'm ashamed of it, Tom, but I can't help it."

"I didn't expect to find you here, father, and clothed in the rebel uniform; but I'm glad to see you in any uniform, " replied the soldier boy.

"So you're in the army, Tom, " continued the father, gazing with satisfaction at the neat appearance of the sergeant.

"Yes, sir; I enlisted within a fortnight after we heard that the traitors had bombarded Fort Sumter. "

"I see you've got three stripes on your arm. "

"Yes, Cap'n Somers, " said Hapgood; "Tom was made a sergeant for gallant conduct on the river in December; and he deserved his promotion too. "

"I'm glad to see you with that uniform on your back, Tom; and glad to hear that you have behaved well. "

"I was in the battle of Bull Run, father, and was taken prisoner, but I got away. "

"Well, Tom, we'll hear about that bimeby, " said the old man, stopping and looking nervously into the face of his son. "I want to ask a great many questions, Tom, but I hardly dare to do it. You know I haven't heard a word from home since I left, and it's almost a year now. "

"You needn't be afraid, father; the folks are all well. I have got a heap of letters at the camp, and you shall read them all as soon as we get there. "

"Is your mother well, Tom? "

"First rate. "

"And John? "

"Yes, sir; but he's gone into the navy. He was bound to be in the fight any how. "

"John's a chip of the old block. He wanted to snuff the salt water afore he was a week old. John's a good sailor, and he ought to have a good lay wherever he goes, " added the father.

Captain Somers and Tom sat upon the ground for half an hour, until the fugitive from the rebel army was in some degree rested after the hard run he had had through the woods. The soldiers gathered around them, as much interested as though they had been members of the Somers family. Tom's father had a multitude of questions to ask about Pinchbrook and its people, all of which were answered to his satisfaction.

The sergeant thought it was time for the party to move on, and his father declared that he was able to walk any distance which would bring him nearer to the home of his wife and children. The order was given, and the little band resumed its march.

"How have you been all this time, father? " asked Tom, as he walked along by the side of Captain Somers.

"I've been pretty fairly most of the time. I'm tough and hardy, or I should have been dead afore this time. We've been half starved and half frozen in the camp; but I managed to live through it, hoping and expecting to get away from those rascally rebels. "

"Where have you been all the time?" asked Tom. "Have you been in the rebel army long?"

"About four months; but I may as well begin at the beginning, and tell you the whole story," added the captain. "I got to Norfolk all right, and was there when the news came up that the rebels had taken Sumter. Every body was mad, and I was as mad as the rest of them, though not exactly in the same way. I let on a little with my tongue, and came pretty near being tarred and feathered, and I think I should have been, if your uncle Wyman hadn't interfered."

"Did he settle with you, father?"

"After a while he did. He had some fifteen thousand dollars in New York, which had just been sent over from England, and as he was secesh, he was terribly afeard the Lincoln government would confiscate it; so he settled with me, and gave me a power of attorney to draw his money, pay myself, and take care of what was over. I've got the papers safe in my waistbands now."

"Good! Glory, hallelujah!" shouted Tom. "We can pay off old Pemberton now, for it goes against my grain to owe a dollar to a traitor. But if uncle Wyman is a rebel, and I suppose he is, I hope the government will confiscate what's over after you have paid yourself."

"Well, I don't know. We will see about that bimeby. He used me fair, and I don't wish him any harm; but I hate his principles. Well, just then, Tom, when I had got my accounts squared, the rascals took my vessel, and sunk it in the channel to keep the Union fleet out. My pipe was out then, and I couldn't do any thing more. I hung round the city of Norfolk till I saw there was no chance to get out in that direction; and then I left. I was up near Bull Run—the rebels call it Manassas—when the battle was fought; but our folks got licked so badly, that it was no use to try to get through there.

"I tried half a dozen times to crawl through, and had nearly starved to death in the woods; but some rebel cavalry pickets spied me out, called me a traitor, and sent me back. My money was all gone by this time, and I went over to Norfolk again. Your uncle Wyman told me I had better keep quiet where I was, for just as sure as his name was Somers, the North would all fall to pieces in less than six months. He expected the rebel army would be in New York afore long, and I should be a great deal better off where I was. He tried to get a pass to send me through the rebel lines, but he couldn't do it.

"Things went on in this way till your uncle Wyman went to Charleston on business, and I haven't seen him from that day to this. The rebels tried to make me go into their navy, but I wouldn't do it, of course; but when I couldn't do any other way, I went into the army, hoping I should be sent to the front, and find a chance to get away. I've been watching ever since, but I never happened to get within twenty miles of the Union pickets before. But here I am, and I'm perfectly satisfied with the past, though I've suffered a good deal in one way and another. "

By the time Captain Somers had finished his narrative, the party arrived at the camp. Tom was reprimanded very gently for detaching himself from the main body of the regiment; but when he reported the events of his excursion, as he had safely returned with his command, nothing more was said about his adventure.

At the camp the Union refugee was provided with comfortable clothing; his hair and beard were trimmed down to decent proportions, and he was otherwise purged of the barbarisms of the rebel camp. But even then he did not look like the stout, hearty, healthy Captain Somers who sailed from Boston in the Gazelle nearly a year before. He was haggard and emaciated from anxiety and semi-starvation.

Captain Somers was warmly welcomed by the members of Company K, who came from Pinchbrook; and when his physical wants had been satisfied, he was sent to General Hooker, to communicate to him such intelligence as he possessed in regard to the position and numbers of the rebel army. He remained at the camp but two days, at the end of which time he was sent to Washington, and from there hastened to his home in Pinchbrook. A letter from Tom, announcing the joyful intelligence of his return, had preceded him.

In ten days after parting with his father, the sergeant received a full and glowing account of the reception of Captain Somers, who became quite a lion in Pinchbrook for the time being. He received his money as he passed through New York, though not without the aid of a government order which he had procured in Washington, and only the amount that was actually due to him, for uncle Wyman's funds were then in process of being confiscated.

The only drawback upon his father's happiness was the absence of John, who had been drafted into a vessel bound to the South. He had not seen him for a year, and another year would probably elapse before he could expect to realize this pleasure. But the captain's patriotism had been intensified a hundred fold by his bitter experience in Virginia; and while his twin sons were gallantly serving their country in the army and the navy, he was willing to sacrifice the yearnings of his paternal heart, and he hoped and prayed that they might do their duty faithfully.

Tom's regiment remained on the Potomac but a short time after the event we have related. Sharper and sterner experience was before these tried soldiers, and the first indications of active service were greeted with joyous enthusiasm. Suddenly the camp was broken up, and the order to march given. The men wondered and speculated upon their destination, and though the prophets of the regiments gave them certain information in regard to the direction they were to take, most of them were incredulous. One declared they were going to Richmond by the way of Fredericksburg; another, by the way of Manassas; and a third was positive, from hints he had seen in the newspapers, that they were going down the valley of the Shenandoah, to take the capital of Rebeldom on the flank and rear.

While the prophets and wise men were speculating, the regiment marched on; and to the astonishment of all, and to the utter confusion of the seers, they were embarked in a transport—the steamer Napoleon—bound no one knew where. One regiment and half of another belonging to the brigade were huddled on board of this one steamer. Every foot of standing room was occupied, and, of course, the boys were not very comfortably quartered; but, as Tom expressed it, there was music ahead, and the brave hearts on board were ready to stand any thing if they could only get a fight out of the rebels. The mortification of their defeat at Bull Run still hung heavily on their spirits, and they were panting for an opportunity to retaliate upon the foe, and win the laurels they had lost upon that disastrous field.

The prophets, though their failure to foretell the coming event had cast them into disgrace, were still ready to volunteer an opinion. They declared that the transports were bound to North Carolina, to follow up Burnside's successes; but most of the men were content to wait till the future should develop itself.

The troops were eager for active duty, and if they could get into the field and strike a heavy blow at the rebellion, they did not care where it was. They had unbounded confidence in the young general who was to organize victory for them, and they were willing to obey orders, and leave every thing to him.

It "thundered all around" them. Roanoke, Pea Ridge, Newbern, Winchester, Donelson, were a succession of Union victories, which inspired them with zeal and courage to endure all hardships, and face any peril which might be in their path.

The transport descended the Potomac, and came to anchor in the bay, where they lay one day; the steamer then continued on her course, and landed her troops in Cheseman's Creek, an indentation of the peninsula between the York and James Rivers. After lying in camp a few days, they marched again, and Tom learned that the regiment was before Yorktown, which had been strongly fortified by the rebels to resist the advance of the Union army.

CHAPTER XXIX.

THE BATTLE OF WILLIAMSBURG.

What the army of the Potomac achieved and suffered before Yorktown, we must leave for the historian. Our soldier boy was only one hero among thousands who toiled in the soft mud of the early spring, who watched and waited for the tremendous events which have now passed into history, and whose actors will be honored and remembered by future generations.

Tom Somers bore his full share of the trials and hardships of that eventful period; and when McClellan's scientific engineering had driven the rebels from their strong works without a struggle to retain them, he moved forward with the gallant army. "On to Richmond! " again sounded along the lines, and the soldiers toiled through mud and mire, hoping and expecting to strike the final blow that would crush out the rebellion.

Yorktown was evacuated. The rebels were fleeing from their frowning batteries, and the order came for Hooker's division to join in the pursuit. At noon the brigade—now under command of General Grover commenced its forward movement.

"Rather rough, " said Hapgood, as the regiment struggled on through the mire. "Rather soft, I think, " replied Tom, laughing.

"I hope we haven't got to march far through this mud, " added Ben Lethbridge.

"That will depend upon how soon we come up with the rebels. If it rests with Hooker, I tell you he will get a fight out of the rebs, if such a thing is possible. "

After the regiment had marched five or six miles, the order came to halt; and the intelligence passed along the column that the cavalry had come up with the enemy, and were waiting the arrival of an infantry force to assist in the attack.

"Good! " shouted Tom. "We shall have a battle before night. "

"Perhaps not, " added Hapgood. "It takes the cat a good while to catch the mouse, even after she smells the critter. "

"Why don't we march? What are we stopping here for? " said Tom, impatiently.

"They say Smith's division has got in ahead of us. Keep cool, Tom; never be in a hurry for a battle. Some of us that stand here now won't be alive in twenty-four hours from now; for I don't believe the rebs are going to let us have it all our own way, " said the veteran.

"Nor I, " added Fred Pemberton. "I shall be killed in this fight. "

"How do you know, Fred? " demanded Hapgood, sternly.

"Of course I don't know, but I feel it in my bones that I shall fall in the first battle. "

"Your bones ain't no guide at all. I know something about this business, and I've seen croakers afore to-day. Don't talk about being killed, or even hit. Be ready to die, do your duty like a soldier, and leave all the rest to your Maker, " said the veteran, solemnly.

"I don't have any such feeling as that. I know I shan't be killed, " laughed Ben. "The bullet hasn't been cast yet that will stop my wind."

"Perhaps it has, my boy. It may be in some rebel soldier's cartridge box over yonder, even now. I tell you, boys, you don't know any thing about it. Just afore we went in at Cerry Gordy, a feller by my side said the same thing you did, Ben; and he was the first man that went down. I tried to pick him up, and do something for him, but he was stone dead. I tell you, Ben, you don't know any thing about it. Leave it all to the Almighty. "

"Pooh, uncle! " sneered Ben, trying to laugh down the solemn words of the old man. "Don't you think we'd better have a prayer meetin' before we go in? "

"I think we should fight the better for it, for he who trusts in God don't fear death. "

But it was evident that the words of Hapgood, especially the incident of Cerro Gordo, had made a deep impression upon the mind of the thoughtless young man. Though the division did not move for three hours, he was very silent and sober. He seemed to feel that he had been tempting Providence by his bold speech, and even expressed his regret to Tom for what he had said.

It was dark when the order to march was given. The night was exceedingly gloomy, and the rain poured down upon the devoted army, as it moved forward to do its great work. Hour after hour, in the deep darkness and the pouring rain, the men struggled through the mire, expecting every moment to be hurled upon the rebel battalions, or to meet the impetuous onset of the foe.

Between ten and eleven, when the men were nearly worn out by the exhausting labors of the march, they were ordered to halt in the road, and bivouac for the rest of the night. What a time and what a place for repose! They could only wrap themselves up in their wet blankets, and stretch themselves upon the ground, soaked with water, and with the rain still pouring down upon them. But they slept, and enjoyed their rest, for Nature was imperative in her demands.

At daylight the march was resumed; for the intrepid Hooker, ever faithful to the trust confided to him, was wholly in earnest. At half-past five the column was halted in the woods. The rebel works before Williamsburg were in sight, and General Hooker rode to the front to examine the position of the enemy.

In front of the rebel batteries, and on each side of the roads, the trees had been felled, in order to give the guns in the field works full play upon an approaching force.

"Hurrah! " shouted some of the boys on the right of the column. "Our brigade is to commence the attack. "

"How do you know? " growled Hapgood, who did not think a soldier ought to know any thing about the plan of the battle.

"We are ordered to move, " replied Tom. "I suppose that's all they know about it. "

The prophets on the right were correct this time, for the regiment was soon sent to the right of the road, and ordered to deploy as skirmishers. A battery was thrown forward in front of the felled timber; but before a gun could be fired, two officers and two privates were seen to fall before the unerring aim of the rebel sharpshooters, occupying the rifle pits which dotted the cleared land in front of the forts.

"That's a hot place, " said Ben Lethbridge.

"We shall all see hot work before the sun goes down to-night, " replied Tom. "But let us stand up to it like men. "

"That's the talk, Tom! " exclaimed Hapgood.

"Have you got those socks on, my boy? "

"I have, uncle; and I have the letter and the photograph in my pocket. "

"Good, Tom! After this day's work is over, you can write the lady a letter, and tell her that her socks have been in a battle. "

"And that I didn't run away in them. "

The roar of the guns in Fort Magruder interrupted the conversation. The gunners of the battery in front of them had been driven from their pieces; but it was almost instantly manned by volunteers, and a destructive fire poured into the works. Other batteries were brought up, and the fort was soon silenced. The roar of battle sounded all along the line; the thunder of cannon and the crash of musketry reverberated through the woods and over the plain, assuring the impatient troops that they were engaged in no trivial affair; that they were fighting a great battle, of which thousands yet unborn would read upon the pages of history.

Our regiment closed up its lines, and the gallant colonel gave the order to move forward in the direction of the field works. On, on, steadily and firmly marched the men of Massachusetts, through ditch and swamp, through mud and mire, loading, firing, and charging, as the enemy presented opportunity. The hot work of the day had commenced; for, from every bush, tree, and covert, which could conceal a man, the rebels poured a deadly fire into the ranks of the advancing Federals.

Tom stood as firm as a rock. The doubts and fears which beset him in his first battle had no existence on this day. So thoroughly had he schooled his mind to the fearful ordeal of carnage, that he felt quite at home. He was cool and determined, and continually encouraged those around him by his cheering words as well as by his example.

"Ben is down! " exclaimed Hapgood.

"Poor fellow! " replied Tom, without taking his eye off the foe in front.

"There goes Bob Dornton! " added Hapgood.

"Stand up to it, my men! " said Tom, firmly, for he had no time then to think of the fallen.

"Forward! " shouted the impetuous colonel, who, if he had never been popular with the men before, was rapidly establishing himself in their good graces by his unflinching heroism. "Forward! double quick! march! "

And on dashed the gallant regiment, mounting the enemy's lofty works, and driving the foe before them like sheep, at the point of the bayonet. This was the first experience of this exciting description which Tom had seen, and he entered into the spirit of it with a hearty zeal.

"Halt! " was the order, as a regiment filed out in front of them, with a flag of truce flying on its front. "Steady—don't fire, " repeated several officers along the line.

"What regiment are you? " shouted a person, as the flag came within speaking distance.

"What are you? " demanded an officer of the storming party.

"We're the Alabama eighth! "

"We are the Massachusetts —th, " replied our men.

"Then you are the villains we want! " returned the rebel, plentifully interlarding the sentence with oaths.

The flag of truce dropped, and the dastardly foe poured in a volley of musketry, before which a dozen of our brave boys fell, either killed or wounded.

"Fire! " yelled the colonel; and the order was obeyed with a will. "Charge bayonets! Forward—double quick—march! "

The men, burning with indignation at the treachery of the rebel horde, sprang forward to wreak their righteous vengeance upon the cowardly traitors. So impetuous was the charge, that the rebel regiment broke, and sought safety in flight.

"Down with them! " hoarsely screamed Tom, as the line swayed forward, and pursued the panic-stricken foe into the woods on the left. The even line was broken, and the boys scattered to do their work to the best advantage.

Tom's legs seemed to be in excellent condition, notwithstanding the toilsome marches of the last twenty-four hours; and he dashed forward into the woods followed by only a dozen choice spirits, whose enthusiasm was equal to his own. A squad of flying rebels in front of them was the object of their present anxiety, and they soon distanced their companions.

The rebels, seeing by how small a force they were pursued, rallied and formed line again.

"Give it to them! " cried Tom, as he led his little force upon the rebels.

"Hold on, Tom! " said Hapgood; "we have gone far enough. There's a rebel regiment forming behind us. "

"Can't help it, " said Tom, as he rushed forward, with the veteran by his side. "Give it to them! "

Tom and his men threw themselves upon the rebel squad, and a sharp fight ensued, in which the parties fought with bayonets, clubbed muskets, and even with the death grip upon each other's throats. The traitors could not stand it, and fled again.

The sergeant glanced behind him, and saw the rebel regiment formed ready to charge upon his own. He was cut off from his friends, with the enemy on his front and rear. Three of his men had fallen in the sharp encounter with the rebels, and most of them were wounded or bruised, and all of them out of breath. To add to the peril of the situation, the squad they had been pursuing were rallying and being reënforced by their fugitive companions.

"Bad, Tom, bad, " said Hapgood, who was puffing and blowing like a porpoise, as he ominously shook his head.

"Follow me! " said Tom, confidently, as he led the way in a direction at right angles with the advance of the party.

Our regiment had reformed again, and soon gave that in front of them enough to do. The rebels in their rear caused the sergeant's squad no little annoyance; but they continued on their course, loading and firing as they retreated.

CHAPTER XXX.

MORE OF THE BATTLE.

While Tom and his little command were working their way back to the Union lines, followed up by the disorganized band of rebels, a series of most unearthly yells swept over the field, for they had emerged from the woods. It was the rallying cry of the Confederate regiment which had formed in their rear. They were charging upon the Massachusetts —th; but they might as well have charged upon the Rock of Gibraltar, for presently Tom was delighted to see them retiring before the tremendous onslaught of his friends.

"Hurrah! " shouted he, forgetting the foe in his rear, and pressing forward to that on his front, at the same time changing his course so as to approach the right wing of the rebel regiment.

"Don't be rash, Tom, " said the old soldier, who never permitted the sergeant to leave his side.

"Follow me, boys! " roared Tom, breathless with excitement, as he started off on the double quick towards the breaking lines of the enemy.

"Here we are! " replied the gallant fellows behind him, pushing forward with a zeal equal to that of their leader, from whom they derived their inspiration. "Go in, sergeant, and we'll stand by you. "

But the bold soldier boy had discretion as well as gallantry; and he saw that if he threw his little force upon the rebel line, the whole party would be instantly annihilated. A covert of bushes fortunately lay on the right flank of the retreating regiment, and Tom ordered his men to conceal themselves behind it, until a favorable moment should arrive to take their places in the lines.

The men were glad enough to obtain a breathing spell; but, at such a tremendous moment as that, idleness would have been treason, for such a glorious opportunity to strike a heavy blow had not before occurred.

"Load up, and fire at will, " said Tom, as he charged his musket. "Don't throw your lead away either. "

"We are a dead shot here if we are any where, " added Hapgood, as he and the rest of the party hastily loaded their muskets.

Pop went Tom's piece first, and over went the rebel at the extreme right of the rebel regiment. There was no such thing as missing the mark, for they were on the flank of the Confederate line, which the united efforts of the officers could hardly preserve. The men in the covert fired when they were ready; and as they carefully observed the injunction of Tom not to waste their lead, every shot told upon the rebels.

The Confederate officers glanced nervously at the clump of bushes, which glowed with flashes of fire as the sergeant's little command poured in their volleys; but they were too closely pressed by the Federals in front to attempt to dislodge them. The rebel privates were not long in ascertaining what was so clear to their officers—that they were flanked, and were being shot down like sheep, from a quarter where they could not defend themselves. They had been slowly and doggedly retiring before the advancing Federals, disputing every inch of ground; but when they realized that the bolts of death were dropping among them from another direction, they could no longer endure that awful suspense which takes possession of the minds of men when they are suspended, as it were, between life and death.

Tom saw them waver, and he knew what it meant. The rebel line was just abreast of him, and he had seen at least a score of men fall before the deadly fire of his party.

"Give it to them, boys! They shake! " shouted Tom, as he delivered his fire again. "Pour in as fast as you can, but don't waste your powder. "

The men redoubled their exertions, and the rapidity of their fire was sensibly increased. The effect was soon perceptible in the rebel ranks; for the right of the line, probably supposing a company, if not a whole regiment, of sharp-shooters was concealed in the covert, suddenly broke and fled with the utmost precipitation, in spite of the gallant efforts of their officers to rally them.

The Federal regiment instantly took advantage of this partial panic, and charged furiously upon the rebel line. A desperate hand-to-hand encounter ensued, during which Tom and his companions emerged from their concealment, and ran along the rear of the victorious line. They soon satisfied themselves of what they had before believed — that the regiment was their own; and they lost no time in finding the company to which they belonged. They joined in the pursuit, which soon ended in the utter rout of the rebel force.

The position of the enemy's lines did not permit them to follow the advantage to any great extent, and the order was soon given to fall back. At this juncture the regiment, which had been constantly engaged for several hours, was relieved; and not too early in the day, for the men were completely exhausted by the furious onslaughts they had made.

"Who were those men in the bushes on the flank of the rebel regiment?" demanded the colonel, as he reined up his jaded horse in front of Company K.

"Sergeant Somers and others," replied Captain Benson.

"Somers again!" exclaimed the colonel.

"Yes, sir. They pursued the regiment into the woods — the one that showed the flag of truce — till they were separated from the rest of us." "Forward, Sergeant Somers," added the colonel.

Tom modestly stepped forward, and he would have blushed if his face had not been so reddened by his previous exertions as to leave no room for a deepening of its tint.

"You did a big thing, Sergeant Somers. You broke that rebel line by your steady fire. Sergeant Somers, I thank you and the men you commanded for your good service."

Tom bowed, and the regiment cheered. It was the proudest moment of his life to be thanked on the field, while the guns were roaring and the musketry rattling, for the good service he had rendered. It would form an excellent paragraph for his letter to Lilian Ashford, especially as he had more than once, in the perils of that exciting hour, thought of the socks he wore, and of the letter and the photograph which nestled in his breast pocket, and upon which his quick throbbing heart was beating the notes of glory and victory.

"We gave you up for lost, " said Captain Benson, as Tom returned to the line.

"We are safe, thank God! " replied Tom, "though three of our number fell in the woods, or on the field where we were chased by the rebels. "

"Sergeant Somers saved us, " added uncle Hapgood. "If he hadn't been as cool as cowcumber, and as stiff as the mainmast of a frigate, we should have been taken, every one of us. "

"Bravo, Tom! " said the captain.

"The men stood by me like heroes, or it would have been all up with the whole of us. They are good fellows, and they deserve as much credit as I do. "

The battle continued to rage with increasing fury, till the roar, and the crash, and the sweep of armed legions beggared description. Regiments and brigades advanced and fell back with the varying fortunes of the day, but as yet there was nothing to indicate the final result.

When the men of our regiment had recovered their breath, an order came for them to proceed to the left. On their arrival at the position assigned to them, they were immediately led to the front, where the batteries which had been pouring a hot fire into the enemy were in imminent danger of being surrounded. Indeed, the swoop of the rebel infantry upon the guns had already been made, and the cannoneers had been driven from their stations. With the colonel on the right, and the adjutant in command on the left, the regiment charged upon the foe, as it had twice before charged on that eventful day, with an enthusiasm bordering upon fury.

The rebels had even spiked one of the guns, and they maintained their position with an obstinacy which promised the annihilation of one or the other of the contending forces. A desperate strife ensued, in which the least perceptible advantage was gained by the Federals. But if they could do no more, they held the enemy in check, till the gunners could charge their pieces with grape and canister, which they poured into the rebels with the most deadly effect.

"Hurrah! " shouted Tom, as the rebels quaked before the withering storm of shot belched forth by the guns of the battery. "They shake! Give it to them! "

"Steady, my men! steady, " said Captain Benson. "The ammunition of the battery is expended, " he added, as the cannon ceased their work of destruction. "We must hold these pieces, and every man must do his duty. "

"Ay, ay, sir! " replied Tom, vigorously, and the cry was repeated through the company.

As soon as the guns were thus rendered useless, the enemy swept down upon the supports again, intent upon capturing the pieces. They advanced with that terrific yell which is enough of itself to frighten a nervous man, and with an impetuosity which nothing human could resist. Our regiment recoiled under the shock; but it was forced back by the sheer stress of numbers.

"Rally men! Rally, my brave fellows! " shouted the adjutant, in command of the left wing.

"Stand stiff! Roll them back! " roared the colonel.

"Steady, men! " added Captain Benson.

"Now, give it to them! " screamed Tom, as he plunged his bayonet into the vitals of the rebel in front of him, and pushed forward into the very midst of the foe.

The sergeant seemed suddenly to be endowed with the strength of a giant, and he held his own till Hapgood sprang to his assistance. The rest of the line, inspired by this daring conduct, rushed forward, and fell upon the foe with a fury that could not be resisted.

"Bravo! Bravo, Tom! " shouted the captain. "Go in, boys! " roared the lieutenant.

And the boys "went in, " and forced back the rebel line, and held the guns until another battery with a supply of ammunition arrived upon the ground to relieve them. The enemy was again repulsed, and the guns were saved by the unflinching heroism of our gallant

Massachusetts regiment—another paragraph for the letter to Lilian Ashford.

CHAPTER XXXI.

GLORY AND VICTORY.

The battle now raged more fiercely than ever, and hotter and hotter became the fire on every side. The shouts of the enemy indicated the arrival of reënforcements. "Johnston! " "Long-street! " resounded over the field, and roused the rebels to renewed activity. More certainly was the increase of the enemy's force determined by the gradual falling back of the brigade at the left of the road; but the men fought with desperate courage, and yielded not a foot of ground without enriching it with their best blood.

There were no signs of reënforcements for over exhausted troops, though a whole corps was within hearing of the booming guns that were slaughtering our outnumbered and exhausted brigades. On the field the aspect began to be dark and unpromising, and Tom prayed with all his soul that he might be spared the pain of beholding another defeat, another rout.

Our regiment was ordered to the support of the yielding brigade on the left. The woods were full of rebels, and the issue of the conflict in this part of the field was almost hopeless. The enemy seemed to be inspired by the slight advantage they had gained, and their yells were fiercer and more diabolical than ever, as they gathered themselves up for a desperate onslaught.

The Federal brigade was overmatched, and the result seemed to waver upon a balance; then the equilibrium was slightly disturbed, and the Union force fell back a little, but only a little, and doggedly resisted the advance of the foe. It needed but little to restore the equilibrium, and our regiment, after struggling through the mud with all attainable speed, arrived upon the spot when the prospect was so gloomy for the loyal cause.

The men were almost exhausted by the tremendous strain which had all day long been imposed upon their nervous systems, and by the physical exertion required of them. But the battle was going against the North, and they were ready again to make a desperate effort to redeem the field.

"One more of your Massachusetts charges, colonel, " said General Hooker, as the weary soldiers moved up to the endangered position.

"You shall have it, general. My men are always ready, though they are nearly used up. "

"Hancock and Kearney are close by, and if we can hold out a few minutes longer, all will be well with us. "

"We'll drive them back, general! " shouted the colonel.

"Go in, then! " added the gallant Hooker, waving his sword to encourage the soldiers. "Forward! You have no time to lose! "

The fiery colonel briefly stated to the regiment the nature of the work before them, admonished the men to do as they had done all day, and Massachusetts would be proud of them. A ringing cheer was the reply to the stirring words of the colonel, and the orders were given for the advance.

On went the brave fellows like a wall of iron, and precipitated themselves upon the rebels, buoyant with hope as they followed up their temporary advantage. The point of attack was all in their favor, and their exhilarating shouts as they sprang upon the foe kindled up the expiring enthusiasm of the yielding brigade to whose assistance they had come. The shock was terrible—more fearful and destructive than any which our boys had before experienced.

"Steady, my men! " shouted Captain Benson.

"Give it to them! " roared Tom, maddened to desperation by the awful strife around him, and by seeing so many of our men fall by his side.

"Stand up to it! " shouted the excited colonel. "They run! "

At this moment an inequality of the ground beneath the men of Company K placed them in a bad position, and the rebels in front of them, taking advantage of the circumstance, pressed forward, and actually broke through the line, trampling some of our soldiers beneath their feet, and transfixing them with their bayonets.

The Soldier Boy; or, Tom Somers in the Army

A terrible scene ensued at this gap in the ranks, for the whole rebel regiment began to press into the weak place. The breach was made by the side of our sergeant, so that he was not borne down by the pressure of the rebel battalion.

"Close up! " yelled Tom. "Close up! Hail, Columbia! and give it to them! "

Drawing a revolver which he had been permitted to retain after the capture of the contraband craft on the Potomac, he discharged its six barrels into the foremost of the assailants; and Hapgood and Fred Pemberton, who were armed in like manner from the same source, imitated the example of the sergeant.

"Now give them the bayonet, boys! " screamed Tom, hoarsely, as he plunged into the midst of the rebels.

The men on the other side of the gap pushed forward with equal energy, and the ranks closed up again over a pile of dead and wounded rebels, and Federals, who had fallen in that sharp encounter.

"Bravo! " shouted General Hooker, whose attention had been drawn to the break in the line. "Bravo, sergeant! You shall have a commission! Forward, my brave boys! Massachusetts sees you! "

"Up and at them, " cried Tom, as the rebels began to yield and break before the tremendous charge of our regiment.

The young sergeant's throat was raw with the shouting he had done, and his limbs were beginning to yield to the fatigues of the day; but the words of the commander of the division made him over new again, and his husky voice still rang along the line, full of new courage and new energy to his exhausted comrades. The rebels were driven back for the time, and fled before the iron masses that crowded upon them.

The regiment was recalled, and the weary troops, now almost decimated by the slaughter which had taken place in their ranks, were permitted to breathe once more.

"This is awful, " said the veteran of Company K, panting from the violence of his exertions. "I never saw any thing like this before. "

"Nor I," replied Tom, dropping upon the ground with exhaustion.

"I know something about this business. I thought Cerry Gordy was consid'able of a battle, but 'twas nothin' like this."

"It's awful," sighed Tom, as he thought of the good fellows he had seen fall upon the field.

"Heaps of our boys have gone down!"

"Attention—battalion!" came ringing with startling effect along the line, in the familiar tones of the intrepid colonel.

"If we win the day, we can afford to lose many. Victory or death!" shouted Tom, as he sprang to his feet, in obedience to the command. "More work for us!"

"How do you feel, Tom?" demanded the veteran, as they sprang into the line.

"All right," replied Tom, with a forced buoyancy of spirits.

"Are you sure, my boy?" continued the veteran, gazing with deep anxiety into the face of the sergeant.

"I'm first rate, uncle. I think I can stand it as long as any body else."

"You have done wonders to-day, Tom. I'm proud of you, but I'm afeared you are doing too much. If you are used up, it wouldn't be any disgrace for you to go to the rear. After what you've done, nobody will say a word. Don't kill yourself, Tom, but go to the rear."

"I go to the rear!" exclaimed Tom, with indignation.

"If you are disabled, I mean, of course," apologized the veteran.

"I'm not disabled. If I go to the rear with these socks on, it won't be till after the breath has left my body."

"Socks!" replied Hapgood, with a sneer. "I'm afeared that gal will be the death of you."

"I don't sulk in these socks," replied Tom, with a faint smile, as the regiment moved off on the double quick to some new position of peril.

"The rebels are flanking us!" shouted an officer in another command, as our regiment hurried forward to the endangered point.

"That's what we are wanted for," said Hapgood.

The enemy had nearly accomplished their purpose when our gallant colonel and his jaded force reached the left of the line, and in a few moments more would have poured a flanking fire into our devoted battalions, which were struggling with terrible energy to roll back the pressure in front of them.

The colonel had his men well in hand, and he manoeuvred them with consummate skill, so as to bring them advantageously to the work they were to perform. The regiment was hurled against the head of the flanking column, and the boys rushed forward with that dash and spirit which had characterized their conduct half a score of times before in various parts of the field.

Tom's muscles had become loose and soft after the long continued strain upon them, and if his soul had not been ten times as big as his body, he must have sunk under the exhaustion of the day. Another desperate onslaught was required of the men of our regiment, and commanding all his energies, Tom braced himself up once more for the fearful struggle.

"How do you feel now, Tom?" demanded the anxious veteran, as he bit off the cartridge, and rammed it home.

"First rate, uncle!" replied Tom, as the regiment poured a withering volley into the rebel line.

"For Heaven's sake, Tom, don't kill yourself," added the old man, as they loaded up again. "Your knees shake under you now."

"Do you think I'm afraid, uncle?" demanded the sergeant with a grim smile.

"No, no, Tom; of course I don't think any thing of the kind. I'm afeared you'll bust a blood-vessel, or something of that sort."

The Soldier Boy; or, Tom Somers in the Army

"If I do, I'll let you know, uncle."

"Charge bayonets! Double quick—march!" rang along the line.

"Have at them!" cried Tom, who was always the first to catch the orders of the commanding officer. "Down with them! Give 'em Yankee Doodle, Hail, Columbia, and the Red, White, and Blue."

The advancing column, shaken by the furious fire of our regiment, recoiled before the shock. Slowly the foe fell back, leaving heaps of their slain upon the hotly-contested ground. Our boys halted, and poured in another destructive volley.

The Confederate officers rallied their men, and, maddened by the check they had received, drove them forward to recover the lost ground.

"Once more, boys! Give it to 'em again," cried Tom, as the order to advance was repeated.

His words were only representations of his actions; for, as he spoke, he rushed on a little in front of his comrades, who, however, pressed forward to keep up with him. He did not exceed the orders of his superior, but he was one of the promptest to obey them. On dashed the regiment, and again the rebel line recoiled, and soon broke in spite of the admirable efforts of their officers to keep them steady.

"Kearney! Kearney! Kearney is here!" shouted the weary heroes in various parts of the field.

"Down with them!" roared Tom, as the inspiring words rang in his ears. "Down with them! Kearney has come, and the day is ours!"

He had scarcely uttered the words, and sprung forward, before he was seen to drop upon the ground, several paces in front of the line, though the undaunted old Hapgood was close by his side. The enemy had fled; the danger of being flanked was averted; and when Kearney's men dashed on the field, the sad-hearted veteran, assisted by Fred Pemberton, bore the silent form of the gallant sergeant to the rear.

Kearney and Hancock rushed gallantly to the rescue of the exhausted troops, and Hooker's division was ordered to the rear to act as a reserve. The strife raged with unabated fury as those who had borne the brunt of the battle slowly fell back to give place to the fresh legions.

Poor Tom was tenderly carried by the wiry veteran and his friends to the surgeon's quarters in the rear. There were tears in the eyes of the old man as he laid the silent form of his *protégé* upon the wet ground. There he sat by his charge, sorrowful beyond expression, till tremendous shouts rent the air. Tom opened his eyes.

"Glory and Victory! " shouted he, in husky tones, as he sprang to his feet.

CHAPTER XXXII.

HONORABLE MENTION.

The surgeon examined Tom's wound, and found that he had been struck by a bullet over the left temple. The flesh was torn off, and if the skull was not fractured, it had received a tremendous hard shock. It was probably done at the instant when he turned to rally the men of Company K, and the ball glanced under the visor of his cap, close enough to scrape upon his skull, but far enough off to save his brains. Half an inch closer, and the bullet would have wound up Tom's earthly career.

The shock had stunned him, and he had dropped like a dead man, while the profusion of blood that came from the wound covered his face, and his friends could not tell whether he was killed or not. He was a pitiable object as he lay on the ground by the surgeon's quarters; but the veteran soon assured himself that his young charge was not dead.

Hapgood washed the gore from his face, and did what he could in his unscientific manner; and probably the cold water had a salutary effect upon the patient, for when Hancock and Kearney had completed their work, and the cry of victory rang over the bloody field, he was sufficiently revived to hear the inspiring tones of triumph. Leaping to his feet, faint and sick as he was, he took up the cry, and shouted in unison with the victors upon the field.

But he had scarcely uttered the notes of glory and victory before his strength deserted him, and he would have dropped upon the ground if he had not been caught by Hapgood. He groaned heavily as he sank into the arms of his friend, and yielded to the faintness and exhaustion of the moment.

The surgeon said the wound was not a very bad one, but that the patient was completely worn out by the excessive fatigues of march and battle. In due time he was conveyed to the college building in Williamsburg, where hundreds of his companions in arms were suffering and dying of their wounds. He received every attention which the circumstances would permit. Hapgood, by sundry vigorous applications at headquarters, was, in consideration of his own and his *protégé's* good conduct on the battle field, permitted to remain with the patient over night.

The sergeant's skull, as we have before intimated, was not very badly damaged, as physical injuries were measured after the bloody battle of that day. But his wound was not the only detriment he had experienced in the trying ordeal of that terrible day. His constitution had not yet been fully developed; his muscles were not hardened, and the fatigues of battle and march had a more serious effect upon him than the ounce of lead which had struck him on the forehead.

The surgeon understood his case perfectly, and after dressing his wound, he administered some simple restoratives, and ordered the patient to go to sleep. On the night of the 3d of May, he had been on guard duty; on that of the 4th, he had obtained but three hours' sleep; and thus deprived of the rest which a growing boy needs, he had passed through the fearful scenes of the battle, in which his energies, mental and physical, had been tasked to their utmost. He was completely worn out, and in spite of the surroundings of the hospital, he went to sleep, obeying to the letter the orders of the surgeon.

After twelve hours of almost uninterrupted slumber, Tom's condition was very materially improved, and when the doctor went his morning round, our sergeant buoyantly proposed to join his regiment forthwith.

"Not yet, my boy, " said the surgeon, kindly. "I shall not permit you to do duty for at least thirty days to come, " he added, as he felt the patient's pulse.

"I feel pretty well, sir, " replied Tom.

"No, you don't. Your regiment will remain here, I learn, for a few days, and you must keep quiet, or you will have a fever. "

"I don't feel sick, and my head doesn't pain me a bit. "

"That may be, but you are not fit for duty. You did too much yesterday. They say you behaved like a hero, on the field. "

"I tried to do my duty, " replied Tom, his pale cheek suffused with a blush.

"Boys like you can't stand much of such work as that. We must fix you up for the next battle; and you shall go into Richmond with the rest of the boys."

"Must I stay in here all the time?"

"No, you may go where you please. I will give you a certificate which will keep you safe from harm. You can walk about, and visit your regiment if you wish."

"Thank you, doctor."

Hapgood had been compelled to leave the hospital before his patient waked, and Tom had not yet learned any thing in regard to the casualties of the battle. Armed with the surgeon's certificate, he left the hospital, and walked to the place where the steward told him he would find his regiment. Somewhat to his astonishment he found that he was very weak; and before he had accomplished half the distance to the camp, he came to the conclusion that he was in no condition to carry a knapsack and a musket on a long march. But after resting himself for a short time, he succeeded in reaching his friends.

He was warmly received by his companions, and the veteran of the company had nearly hugged him in his joy and admiration.

"Honorable mention, Tom," said Hapgood. "You will be promoted as true as you live."

"O, I guess not," replied Tom, modestly. "I didn't do any more than any body else. At any rate, you were close by my side, uncle."

"Yes, but I followed, and you led. The commander of the division says you shall be a lieutenant. He said so on the field, and the colonel said so to-day."

"I don't think I deserve it."

"I do; and if you don't get a commission, then there ain't no justice left in the land. I tell you, Tom, you shall be a brigadier if the war lasts only one year more."

"O, nonsense, uncle!"

"Well, if you ain't, you ought to be."

"I'm lucky to get out alive. Whom have we lost, uncle?"

"A good many fine fellows." replied Hapgood, shaking his head, sadly.

"Poor Ben dropped early in the day."

"Yes, I was afraid he'd got most to the end of his chapter afore we went in. Poor fellow! I'm sorry for him, and sorry for his folks."

"Fred Pemberton said he should be killed, and Ben said he should not, you remember."

"Yes, and that shows how little we know about these things."

"Bob Dornton was killed, too."

"No, he's badly hurt, but the surgeon thinks he will git over it. The cap'n was slightly wounded." And Hapgood mentioned the names of those in the company who had been killed or wounded, or were missing.

"It was an awful day," sighed Tom, when the old man had finished the list. "There will be sad hearts in Pinchbrook when the news gets there."

"So there will, Tom; but we gained the day. We did something handsome for 'Old Glory,' and I s'pose it's all right."

"I would rather have been killed than lost the battle."

"So would I; and betwixt you and me, Tom, you didn't come very fur from losing your number in the mess," added the veteran, as he thrust his little fingers into a bullet hole in the breast of Tom's coat. "That was rather a close shave."

"I felt that one, but I hadn't time to think about it then, for it was just as we were repelling that flank movement," replied Tom, as he unbuttoned his coat, and thrust his hand into his breast pocket. "Do you suppose she will give me another?" he added, as he drew forth the envelope which contained the letter and the photograph of the author of his socks.

A minie ball had found its way through the envelope, grinding a furrow through the picture, transversely, carrying away the chin and throat of the young lady. The letter was mangled and minced up beyond restoration. Tom had discovered the catastrophe when he waked up in the hospital, for his last thought at night, and his first in the morning, had been the beautiful Lilian Ashford. He was sad when he first beheld the wreck; but when he thought what a glorious assurance this would be of his conduct on the field, he was pleased with the idea; and while in his heart he thanked the rebel marksman for not putting the bullet any nearer to the vital organ beneath the envelope, he was not ungrateful for the splendid testimonial he had given him of his position during the battle.

"Of course she'll give you another. Won't she be proud of that picture when she gets it back?"

"If I had been a coward, I couldn't have run away with those socks on my feet."

Tom remained with the regiment several hours, and then, in obedience to the surgeon's orders, returned to the hospital, where he wrote a letter to his father, containing a short account of the battle, and another to Lilian Ashford, setting forth the accident which had happened to the picture, and begging her to send him another.

I am afraid in this last letter Tom indulged in some moonshiny nonsense; but we are willing to excuse him for saying that the thought of the beautiful original of the photograph and the beautiful author of his socks had inspired him with courage on the battle field, and enabled him faithfully to perform his duty, to the honor and glory of the flag beneath whose starry folds he had fought, bled, and conquered, and so forth. It would not be unnatural in a young man of eighteen to express as much as this, and, we are not sure that he said any more.

The next day Tom was down with a slow fever, induced by fatigue and over-exertion. He lay upon his cot for a fortnight, before he was able to go out again; but he was frequently visited by Hapgood and other friends in the regiment. About the middle of the month, the brigade moved on, and Tom was sad at the thought of lying idle, while the glorious work of the army was waiting for true and tried men.

Tom received "honorable mention" in the report of the colonel, and his recommendation, supported by that of the general of the division, brought to the hospital his commission as second lieutenant.

"Here's medicine for you, " said the chaplain, as he handed the patient a ponderous envelope.

"What is it, sir? "

"I don't know, but it has an official look. "

The sergeant opened it, and read the commission, duly signed by the governor of Massachusetts, and countersigned and sealed in proper form. Tom was astounded at the purport of the document. He could hardly believe his senses; but it read all right, and dated from the day of the battle in which he had distinguished himself. This was glory enough, and it took Tom forty-eight hours thoroughly to digest the contents of the envelope.

Lieutenant Somers! The words had a queer sound, and he could not realize that he was a commissioned officer. But he came to a better understanding of the subject the next day, when a letter from Lilian Ashford was placed in his hands. It was actually addressed to "Lieutenant Thomas Somers. " She had read of his gallant conduct and of his promotion on the battle field in the newspapers. She sent him two photographs of herself, and a sweet little letter, begging him to return the photograph which had been damaged by a rebel bullet.

Of course Tom complied with this natural request; but, as the surgeon thought his patient would improve faster at home than in the hospital, he had procured a furlough of thirty days for him, and the lieutenant decided to present the photograph in person.

CHAPTER XXXIII.

LIEUTENANT SOMERS AND OTHERS.

Tom Somers had been absent from home nearly a year; and much as his heart was in the work of putting down the rebellion, he was delighted with the thought of visiting, even for a brief period, the loved ones who thought of and prayed for him in the little cottage in Pinchbrook. I am not quite sure that the well-merited promotion he had just received did not have some influence upon him, for it would not have been unnatural for a young man of eighteen, who had won his shoulder-straps by hard fighting on a bloody field, to feel some pride in the laurels he had earned. Not that Tom was proud or vain; but he was moved by a lofty and noble ambition. It is quite likely he wondered what the people of Pinchbrook would say when he appeared there with the straps upon his shoulders.

Of course he thought what his father would say, what his mother would say, and he could see the wrinkled face of gran'ther Greene expand into a genial smile of commendation. It is quite possible that he had even more interest in his reception at No —— Rutland Street, when he should present himself to the author and finisher of those marvellous socks, which had wielded such an immense influence upon their wearer in camp and on the field. Perhaps it was a weakness on the part of the soldier boy, but we are compelled to record the fact that he had faithfully conned his speech for that interesting occasion. He had supposed every thing she would say, and carefully prepared a suitable reply to each remark, adorned with all the graces of rhetoric within his reach.

With the furlough in his pocket, Tom obtained his order for transportation, and with a light heart, full of pleasant anticipations, started for home. As he was still dressed in the faded and shattered uniform of a non-commissioned officer, he did not attract any particular notice on the way. He was enabled to pass through Baltimore, Philadelphia, and New York, without being bored by a public reception, which some less deserving heroes have not been permitted to escape. But the people did not understand that Tom had a second lieutenant's commission in his pocket, and he was too modest to proclaim the fact, which may be the reason why he was suffered to pass through these great emporiums of trade without an escort, or other demonstration of respect and admiration.

Tom's heart jumped with strange emotions when he arrived at Boston, perhaps because he was within a few miles of home; possibly because he was in the city that contained Lilian Ashford, for boys will be silly in spite of all the exertions of parents, guardians, and teachers, to make them sober and sensible. Such absurdities as "the air she breathes, " and other rhapsodies of that sort, may have flitted through his mind; but we are positive that Tom did not give voice to any such nonsense, for every body in the city was a total stranger to him, so far as he knew. Besides, Tom had no notion of appearing before the original of the photograph in the rusty uniform he wore; and as he had to wait an hour for the Pinchbrook train, he hastened to a tailor's to order a suit of clothes which would be appropriate to his new dignity.

He ordered them, was duly measured and had given the tailor his promise to call for the garments at the expiration of five days, when the man of shears disturbed the serene current of his meditations by suggesting that the lieutenant should pay one half of the price of the suit in advance.

"It is a custom we adopt in all our dealings with strangers, " politely added the tailor.

"But I don't propose to take the uniform away until it is paid for, " said Tom, blushing with mortification; for it so happened that he had not money enough to meet the demand of the tailor.

"Certainly not, " blandly replied Shears; "but we cannot make up the goods with the risk of not disposing of them. They may not fit the next man who wants such a suit. "

"I have not the money, sir; " and Tom felt that the confession was an awful sacrifice of dignity on the part of an officer in the army of the Potomac, who had fought gallantly for his country on the bloody fields of Williamsburg and Bull Run.

"I am very sorry, sir. I should be happy to make up the goods, but you will see that our rule is a reasonable one. "

Tom wanted to tell him that this lack of confidence was not a suitable return of a stay-at-home for the peril and privation he had endured for him; but he left in disgust, hardly replying to the flattering request of the tailor that he would call again. With his pride touched, he walked down to the railroad station to await the departure of the train. He had hardly entered the building before he discovered the familiar form of Captain Barney, to whom he hastened to present himself.

"Why, Tom, my hearty! " roared the old sea captain, as he grasped and wrung his hand. "I'm glad to see you. Shiver my mainmast, but you've grown a foot since you went away. But you don't look well, Tom. "

"I'm not very well, sir; but I'm improving very rapidly. "

"How's your wound? "

"O, that's almost well. "

"Sit down, Tom. I want to talk with you, " said Captain Barney, as he led the soldier boy to a seat.

In half an hour Tom had told all he knew about the battle of Williamsburg, and the old sailor had communicated all the news from Pinchbrook.

"Tom, you're a lieutenant now, but you haven't got on your uniform," continued Captain Barney.

"No, sir, " replied Tom, laughing. "I went into a store to order one, and they wouldn't trust me. "

"Wouldn't trust *you*, Tom! " exclaimed the captain. "Show me the place, and I'll smash in their deadlights. "

"I don't know as I blame them. I was a stranger to them. "

"But, Tom, you mustn't go home without a uniform. Come with me, and you shall be fitted out at once. I'm proud of you, Tom. You are one of my boys, and I want you to go into Pinchbrook all taut and trim, with your colors flying. "

"We haven't time now; the train leaves in a few moments. "

"There will be another in an hour. The folks are all well, and don't know you're coming; so they can afford to wait. "

Tom consented, and Captain Barney conducted him to several stores before he could find a ready-made uniform that would fit him; but at last they found one which had been made to order for an officer who was too sick to use it at present. It was an excellent fit, and the young lieutenant was soon arrayed in the garments, with the symbolic straps on his shoulder.

"Bravo, Tom! You look like a new man. There isn't a better looking officer in the service."

Very likely the subject of this remark thought so too, as he surveyed himself in the full-length mirror. The old uniform, with two bullet-holes in the breast of the coat, was done up in a bundle and sent to the express office, to be forwarded to Pinchbrook. Captain Barney then walked with him to a military furnishing store, where a cap, sword, belt, and sash, were purchased. For some reason which he did not explain, the captain retained the sword himself, but Tom was duly invested with the other accoutrements.

Our hero felt "pretty good," as he walked down to the station with his friend; but he looked splendidly in his new outfit, and we are willing to excuse certain impressible young ladies, who cast an admiring glance at him as he passed down the street. It was not Tom's fault that he was a handsome young man; and he was not responsible for the conduct of those who chose to look at him.

With a heart beating with wild emotion, Tom stepped out of the cars at Pinchbrook. Here he was compelled to undergo the penalty of greatness. His friends cheered him, and shook his hand till his arm ached.

Captain Barney's wagon was at the station, and before going to his own home, he drove Tom to the little cottage of his father. I cannot describe the emotions of the returned soldier when the horse stopped at the garden gate. Leaping from the vehicle, he rushed into the house, and bolted into the kitchen, even before the family had seen the horse at the front gate.

"How d'ye do, mother?" cried Tom, as he threw himself pell-mell into the arms of Mrs. Somers.

"Why, Tom!" almost screamed she, as she returned his embrace. "How *do* you do?"

"Pretty well, mother. How do you do, father?"

"Glad to see you," replied Captain Somers, as he seized his son's hand.

"Bless my soul, Tom!" squeaked gran'ther Greene, shaking in every fibre of his frame from the combined influence of rhapsody and rheumatism.

Tom threw both arms around Jenny's neck, and kissed her half a dozen times with a concussion like that of a battery of light artillery.

"Why, Tom! I never thought nothin' of seein' you!" exclaimed Mrs. Somers. "I thought you was sick in the hospital."

"I am better now, and home for thirty days."

"And got your new rig on," added his father.

"Captain Barney wouldn't let me come home without my shoulder-straps. I met him in the city. He paid the bills."

"I'll make it all right with him."

"I'll pay for it by and by. You know I have over a hundred dollars a month now."

"Gracious me!" ejaculated Mrs. Somers, as she gazed with admiration upon the new and elegant uniform which covered the fine form of her darling boy.

Presently Captain Barney came into the house, and for two hours Tom fought his battles over again, to the great satisfaction of his partial auditors. The day passed off amid the mutual rejoicings of the parties; and the pleasure of the occasion was only marred by the thought, on the mother's part, that her son must soon return to the scene of strife.

The soldier boy—we beg his pardon; Lieutenant Somers—hardly went out of the house until after dinner on the following day, when he took a walk down to the harbor, where he was warmly greeted by all his friends. Even Squire Pemberton seemed kindly disposed towards him, and asked him many questions in regard to Fred.

Before he went home, he was not a little startled to receive an invitation to meet some of his friends in the town hall in the evening, which it was impossible for him to decline.

At the appointed hour, he appeared at the hall, which was filled with people. The lieutenant did not know what to make of it, and trembled before his friends as he had never done before the enemies of his country. He was cheered lustily by the men, and the women waved their handkerchiefs, as though he had been a general of division. But his confusion reached the climax when Captain Barney led him upon the platform, and Mr. Boltwood, a young lawyer resident in Pinchbrook, proceeded to address him in highly complimentary terms, reviewing his career at Bull Run, on the Shenandoah, on the Potomac, to its culmination at Williamsburg, and concluded by presenting him the sword which the captain had purchased, in behalf of his friends and admirers in his native town.

Fortunately for Tom, the speech was long, as he was enabled in some measure to recover his self-possession. In trembling tones he thanked the donors for their gift, and promised to use it in defence of his country as long as a drop of blood was left in his veins—highly poetical, but it required strong terms to express our hero's enthusiasm—whereat the men and boys applauded most vehemently, and the ladies flourished their cambrics with the most commendable zeal. Tom bowed—bowed again—and kept bowing, just as he had seen General McClellan bow when he was cheered by the troops. As the people would not stop applauding, Tom, his face all aglow with joy and confusion, descended from the platform, and took his seat by the side of his mother.

The magnates of Pinchbrook then made speeches—except Squire Pemberton—about the war, patriotism, gunpowder, and eleven-inch shot and shells. Every body thought it was "a big thing," and went home to talk about it for the next week. Tom's father, and mother, and sister, and gran'ther Greene, said ever so many pretty things, and every body was as happy as happy could be, except that John was not at home to share in the festivities. Letters occasionally came from the sailor boy, and they went to him from the soldier boy.

Mrs. Somers was not a little surprised, the next day, to hear her son announce his intention to take the first train for the city; but Tom could not postpone his visit to No —— Rutland Street any longer, for he was afraid his uniform would lose its gloss, and the shoulder-straps their dazzling brilliancy.

Tom's courage had nearly forsaken him when he desperately rang the bell at the home of Lilian Ashford; and he almost hoped the servant would inform him that she was not at home. Lilian was at home, and quaking like a condemned criminal before the gallows, he was ushered into the presence of the author of his socks.

Stammering out his name he drew from his pocket the battered photograph and the shattered letter, and proceeded at once to business. Lilian Ashford blushed, and Tom blushed—that is to say, they both blushed. When he had presented his relics, he ventured to look in her face. The living Lilian was even more beautiful than the Lilian of the photograph.

"Dear me! So you are the soldier that wore the socks I knit, " said Lilian; and our hero thought it was the sweetest voice he ever heard.

"I am, Miss Ashford, and I did not run away in them either. "

"I'm glad you did not, " added she, with a musical laugh, which made Tom think of the melody of the spheres, or some such nonsense.

"I have to thank you for my promotion, " said Tom, boldly.

"Thank me! " exclaimed she, her fair blue eyes dilating with astonishment.

"The socks inspired me with courage and fortitude, " replied Tom, in exact accordance with the programme he had laid down for the occasion. "I am sure the thought of her who knit them, the beautiful letter, and the more beautiful photograph, enabled me to do that which won my promotion. "

"Well, I declare! " shouted Lilian, in a kind of silvery scream.

Bravo, Tom! you are getting along swimmingly. And he said sundry other smart things which we have not room to record. He stayed half an hour, and Lilian begged him to call again, and see her grandmother, who was out of town that day. Of course he promised to come, promised to bring his photograph, promised to write to her when he returned to the army—and I don't know what he did not promise, and I hardly think he knew himself.

But the brief dream ended, and Tom went home to Pinchbrook, after he had sat for his picture. The careless fellow left Lilian's photograph on the table in his chamber a few days after, and his mother wanted to know whose it was; and the whole story came out, and Tom was laughed at, and Jenny made fun of him, and Captain Barney told him he was a match for the finest girl in the country. The lieutenant blushed like a boy, but rather enjoyed the whole thing.

A sad day came at last, and Tom went back to the army. He went full of hope, and the blessing of the loved ones went with him. He was received with enthusiasm by his old companions in arms, and Hapgood—then a sergeant—still declared that he would be a brigadier in due time, —or, if he was not, he ought to be. His subsequent career, if not always as fortunate as that portion which we have recorded, was unstained by cowardice or vice.

FINIS.

* * * * *

Copyright © 2021 Esprios Digital Publishing. All Rights Reserved.

Lightning Source UK Ltd.
Milton Keynes UK
UKHW010628170921
390736UK00001B/96